Double
Agents

DOUBLE AGENTS

Tony Freyer

Quid Pro Books

New Orleans, Louisiana

Published in 2019 by Quid Pro Books, in print and digital editions.

ISBN: 978-1-61027-396-1 (pbk.)
ISBN: 978-1-61027-397-8 (cloth)
ISBN: 978-1-61027-395-4 (ePUB)

QUID PRO BOOKS
Quid Pro, LLC
5860 Citrus Blvd.
Suite D-101
New Orleans, Louisiana 70123
www.quidprobooks.com

Publisher's Cataloging-in-Publication

Freyer, Tony.
    Double agents / Tony Freyer.
        p. cm.
        1. Espionage, U.S.—Fiction. 2. Missing persons—Fiction. 3. Australia—Fiction. I. Title.
PS3563 .E527 F36 2019   2019858187
                                                                              CIP

*To my mother, Ida Marie Riggins,
and my wife, ZuZu.*

Double Agents

ONE

———————————

Beagle Island, 1988

The sea breeze carries Isabella's scream. Tom answers her on the cliff.

First out the cottage door fly Isabella's parents, Alex and Esperanza Quinn. Close behind races Tom's family: his older sister Ann, his father Jim, and I, his mother, Diana Berneray.

We sprint the sand path under giant cedars. The breeze becomes a whistling wind. Below the cliff ledge the breakers submerge volcanic island rock. With each stride closer, we hear Isabella's cry, *"Tom help me . . . ."*

The sand path and the cedars open out to a black cliff. The Pacific Ocean rolls and shimmers in the vast distance. The naked, dead, tree limbs point sharply at Tom's back.

Twelve-year old Tom knows there is an unseen gap in the cliff too wide to jump. Waves churn the seaweed in the rocks below. We've repeatedly told Isabella to avoid the cliff gap. She doesn't listen. Beloved children feel immortal until harm strikes.

Like Tom before her, the hypnotic wild, deadly beauty irresistibly pulls the running ten-year-old girl. In the same place Tom once saved himself. He's never explained how, instinctively keeping secrets from an early age.

We witness Tom going after his cousin Isabella. We face into the wind, silently trusting Tom. He doesn't look back. Tom knows the perils. He hears only Isabella.

Tom steps around the cracked rocks. Huge tree roots entangle rope-like vines across and over the cliff. Below, a massive thorn-shrub bramble thrusts out into space, filled with Isabella's sobs.

The brambles' bright black-red berries enhance the illusion that a leap over the cliff gap is child's play. Tom's boy-mind isn't fooled again. He carefully climbs over the cliff edge.

We rush to see. Twisted, crying Isabella lays atop a dense thorn shrub. Her long black hair tangled, white cotton dress torn, light brown skin bleeding.

Under the cover of thorn shrub, Tom descends the root-embedded cliff face. Rain and wind have eroded rocks, worn thorns, and carved tunnels within the bramble. Tom's strong boy hands, knees, and sandaled feet search and find safe spaces.

Inside the bramble limbs and branches are twisting tunnels. Through them Tom moves with care. Despite the wind all of us hear Tom repeating, "Nuestro corazón, uno. Nuestro corazón, uno." Our heart is one. Tom's words quiet Isabella.

Inside a bramble tunnel, Tom reaches Isabella, entangled atop the scrub-bush cover. "Stay still. Hold me when I say," he exclaims. Isabella's tears, trembling, nearly cease. Her bleeding somehow staunches. Tom's brave, sensitive persuasion awes us.

On a bramble limb, Tom balances. He holds onto a branch. His free hand draws the combat knife his father, Jim, gave him on his fifth birthday. He cuts, hacks, slashes away the thorn shrubs supporting Isabella. Tom then sheaths the knife.

Isabella's child weight shifts downward from the bramble cover. Tom yells, "Now!" Isabella lurches, grabs Tom piggyback.

Tom waits, gathering strength. His boy-body and mind are conditioned to maneuver his own weight and more. His father and his uncle, Alex, have trained Tom like a Marine.

Tom and Isabella entered the bramble separately. Now our families must help them escape together.

My daughter, Ann, and brother Alex, run to the cottage for a rope ladder. They're back quickly. With Isabella on his back, Tom balances on a limb. His two hands grip a thick branch.

At his father's call, Tom moves hand-to-hand, knees bent, side step, side step, side step. Slow. Slow. Tom carries Isabella.

Tom's foot and one hand slip. Isabella holds him tighter. Tom sways barely enough to regain balance with hands and feet. His body rests. He gasps for breath. He's shaking.

Over the cliff the two fathers, Alex and Jim, unroll the rope ladder. Gripping it, with help from my daughter Ann, they enable me to climb down the cliff face. I'm strong and small enough to barely fit into the bramble-tunnel entrance.

In the wind, everyone's silence bears down on Tom. He studies each hand and foot. Move. Stop. Move. Stop. Move. Stop. He trembles uncontrollably. The wind carries Isabella's repetition: *"Mi corazón."* My heart. Her words, his action entwine, releasing strength and courage.

They inch towards my outstretched arms. Tom slips, balances, slips, slips again. I lunge. Isabella's and my hands meet. Yanking my niece to me, I yell triumphantly: "Diana has brave Isabella!"

Tom falls. He grasps a bramble limb. His legs dangle. He gulps for air. Thorns cut, but his bloodied grip holds.

Isabella clings to my back now. We climb rung-by-rung up the rope ladder. Atop the cliff, Jim and I embrace as my brother Alex seizes Isabella and hands their daughter into his wife Esperanza's waiting arms.

My daughter, Ann, is left holding the rope ladder. She cries out, "Tom is just barely clinging to the bramble limb! Move faster, everyone!"

We rush to join Ann. As Jim, Alex, and Ann concentrate their strength on the ladder, I descend to my son.

Tom's arms around the bramble limb loosen and tighten, while his legs sway. Isabella can't stop watching Tom from the top of the cliff, even as her mother Esperanza cleans her wounds.

The wind whistles. I reach the bramble tunnel entrance. Mother to son is no true distance. Tom trembles as I speak to him: "We know you're special. You can do this. All of us together."

That's our family motto. Only we Berneray family members know the extraordinary thing Tom did when he was five years old when he alerted us to immediate danger. He bound us in family solidarity.

Hand-to-hand Tom moves the inches between us. His grip loosens, tightens, and suddenly gives way. Not too late—I have my son. I hold him, both of us recovering on the rope ladder.

Tom and I climb together to the waiting arms of the Berneray and Quinn families on the cliff. Tom and Isabella won't release each other.

We return together through the trees to the cottage. The wind rises. Raindrops become a downpour. Tenderly, Esperanza and I salve Isabella and Tom's wounds. Ann rests quietly, writing in her journal.

My brother Alex dons weather gear and goes down to the Quinn family's sailing schooner *Isabella,* at anchor in the cove. He'll watch to see if *Isabella* suffers storm damage. It could inhibit sailing from Beagle Island to San Francisco, and then on to San Diego, down to Santa Maria, Mexico, and half way around the world to North Australia—Arnhem Land.

Jim's sudden moans shatter our peace. We look at my husband's trembling. Jim stumbles from the room. He is gripped with paralyzing fear triggered by the heightened emotional events of the day. Post-Traumatic Stress Disorder (P.T.S.D.): caused by events years before in Vietnam, Jim has never been able to articulate exactly what happened. The silent horror haunts and imprisons Jim. It shakes and disturbs us, as we worry for him. But the panic attacks have become less frequent. Family therapy in the form of journal writing has helped Jim, as father and husband. He needs and receives our family's aid.

Ann immediately circulates her journal so we will write notes aiming to remedy Jim's pain. We write to convey our faith in Jim, our respect for him and our love for each other.

Ann's and Tom's written and spoken words are gradually growing into echoes of Jim's and my own language. Our family's minds and actions gain wholeness together.

I leave Tom and Isabella in Esperanza's care. I go to Jim in the study. Jim crouches, palms pressed together. His whole body shakes. He stares out the window facing west into the windy raining Pacific. Jim rocks like the storm-tossed *Isabella*, red signal-light flashing.

Jim's gaze jerks, fastening on the northern tip of Vancouver Island and the British Columbia coast. From there, my dearest friend Sarah Donaldson and I had aided anti-Vietnam War veterans who had left the United States illegally, rowing them across the many miles of open water to safety on Beagle Island.

Thirteen years ago in 1975 the Vietnam War finally ended in American defeat. Sarah Donaldson and I say nothing about our dangerous antiwar operations. As a Marine and a Vietnam War vet, Jim had sometimes assisted us. He, too, over the years has remained silent.

We've told no one, not even our children, for good reason. During the war, U.S. officials threatened to arrest and prosecute antiwar activists caught transporting American resisters into Canada.

As time has passed, our antiwar work has been buried. Sarah and I risk complacency.

Jim never feels safe. In his mind any present or past danger can unleash the nightmare.

The trauma lurks within Jim's consciousness, always right beneath the surface. His high draft number could have kept him from being called up. Yet Jim volunteered for the Marine Corps because of the festering pain of knowing that his beloved Marine brother died in battle in Vietnam. He had wanted to prove that his death was not in vain.

I see my husband now stare into the storm. Jim's conflicted consciousness feels our son Tom's brave yet risky rescue of Isabella through the lens of never-ending Vietnam trauma.

In the hours since Isabella's rescue the storm has abated enough to reveal intermittent moonlight. I embrace Jim. He whispers, "It got me again."

I hold my husband closer. "Listen to me, Jim. The children need you. They needed all of us today. You, with the rest of the family, helped Tom rescue Isabella. It took all of you to hold the ladder, Alex, Ann, and you. I couldn't have made it through the bramble and up the ladder with the kids without all three of you there."

Soft rain touches the windows. Moonlight flits and then grows within the room. I whisper to Jim, "You have to know after all these years, Jim, the family and I love you, broken or whole."

The years of experience have taught us how we as a family, fight Jim's anguish with healing words of faith in ourselves, together.

I touch Jim's lips with my finger and say softly, "Jim, listen to what the family's written for you. Ann, Alex and Esperanza, and even Isabella and Tom, despite their injuries, have messages for you. You've always grown stronger after receiving our words for you. You'll respond in kind."

Gently holding my face close, Jim's trembling hands steady. I whisper, "Listen to the messages Ann collected for you. She wrote first:

'Dad: You, Mom, Uncle Alex, Aunt Esperanza, and I all rescued Isabella and Tom today on the cliff. I love you.'"

I read the note in Spanish from Esperanza and Alex: "We couldn't have done it without you, Jim."

And Isabella writes, "You helped save Tom and me. We all love you, Uncle Jim."

More slowly, I pronounce Tom's message: "Dad, today we did what you taught us. Our family love is voluntary. Courage is earned."

Jim holds me tight. I feel his tears on my face. Like holy script, Jim rereads the pages from Ann's notebook. He whispers, "The family writes to support me, and I will write to them in return. We are whole . . . until the next time."

TWO

·————————————————·

To Arnhem Land, January 2009

My father, Jim Berneray, told me, "Tom, whenever you're tested, remember how you saved Isabella at the cliff on Beagle Island when you were twelve. You have the courage, intelligence, instincts, and strength to get you through whatever is thrown at you."

I'm still following my father's advice in January 2009, writing about my mission to Arnhem Land. I feel, express, and echo the words and actions I've learned from my family.

I'm reporting on this mission to my boss, Congresswoman Sarah Donaldson, who expects I'll keep things secret from C.I.A. agent Albert Jennings.

But I am also keeping a personal journal. This account should help my mother, sister, and me pursue the mystery of my father. He vanished in Arnhem Land a year ago.

Like the healing messages we gave him on Beagle Island in 1988, my Arnhem Land account might alleviate any new trauma that has befallen my father. We can't know until my family and I discover what's happened to him in Arnhem Land.

I

I am senior-staff attorney for U.S. Congresswoman Sarah Donaldson. Her district centers on greater downtown San Diego, including the U.S. Navy and Marine Corps installations. She is a committee Chairperson responsible for military intelligence and surveillance, especially satellites and drones. Her district blends war and peacemaking.

My responsibilities include intelligence operations at the Naval Electronics Laboratory in Point Loma and the Marine Corps units on Silver Strand. For the Navy and the Marine Corps I survey private contractors developing satellite-drone technology.

For my boss's military intelligence committee, I'm also an undercover special investigator.

From 2006 to the present, during the Iraq War, I've investigated many private contractors. By 2008, at the end of the Bush II Administration, some of these private contractors had violated U.S. satellite-drone surveillance agreements with Australia, Canada, and Mexico.

These are evils that the newly elected Obama Administration must address. My fellow staffers and I expect the new Administration will use our military intelligence expertise in Congresswoman Donaldson's Washington and San Diego offices.

Before the new Administration officially begins in late January 2009, Congresswoman Donaldson has asked to see me. Meeting her, I'm always conflicted.

She's my boss. Of course I carry out her orders. These include top-secret matters regarding satellite-drone technology, which her military intelligence committee funds.

Even more, Sarah Donaldson and my mother are intimate friends. She's known my mother and father since the Vietnam War, well before my sister, Ann, and I were born.

These personal ties entangle my professional duties. Committing errors would jeopardize not only my professional obligation, but could also hurt the deep personal trust Congresswoman Donaldson shares with Berneray family members.

These thoughts fill my thinking. As I go to meet my boss, I'm confident I'll do my duty. Yet I'm anxious about what happens if I don't.

At her district office in downtown San Diego, the panoramic view includes parts of Balboa Park, the 32nd Street Naval Base, the border with Mexico, and, across San Diego Bay, the Silver Strand, Coronado, North Island Naval Air Station, and the harbor entrance at Point Loma.

When I meet Donaldson in her San Diego office, she always tells me, "Tom, give Diana my love." My mother expects me to reciprocate her same feeling.

In a black and white photo on Sarah Donaldson's desk, undergraduates Sarah and Diana hold up a trophy for the U.C. Berkeley women's crew team marked "1972."

Nothing in Rep. Donaldson's office suggests that the two vigorous young U.C. Berkeley undergraduates, Sarah and Diana, were anti-Vietnam War activists.

Donaldson has never fully explained the connection between the two friends' antiwar activism and her husband to me. He was a Marine Major who authorized the family therapy that enabled my father to fight P.T.S.D. Combat veterans suffering from such trauma required authorization from a commanding officer for treatment. Major Donaldson provided that authorization.

These memories, personal issues, and unknowns press upon me whenever I meet Donaldson. She comes out from behind her desk and shakes my hand. We sit facing the San Diego view of big Navy aircraft carriers and luxurious pleasure yachts.

No small talk. Donaldson goes straight to several significant points: "Tom, our two families have been close over many years. We can talk in absolute confidence. Diana tells me that you and your father know about Arnhem Land."

I must learn what she's driving at. I reply, "Even for Australians, Arnhem Land is remote. After the Vietnam War, my father's Berkeley doctoral dissertation explored Aboriginal art forms as expressions of indigenous life and real events in Arnhem Land."

She nods. I continue: "Linguistic groups that Americans lump together as Aboriginals use Dreamtime images to explain their individual and clan life and ancestry. They don't all tell exactly the same stories. For example, in Arnhem Land, unlike elsewhere in Australia, the ubiquitous Rainbow Serpent isn't male, but female."

Donaldson clearly expects something from me. I stick with my father's story. "He regularly visited Arnhem Land in his global consulting business. Tribal elders authorized him to represent Aboriginal artists by exhibiting and marketing bark paintings embodying clan myths."

"And your father disappeared there last year, before the 2008 election. Diana told me. She knows I'm heartsick." Donaldson's sympathy is genuine. At the same time, she's still leading me.

So I say: "Australian and American officials claimed to be mystified. Preliminary investigation reports merely described my father's sudden absence. Investigators asserted he simply disappeared from an exhibition of Arnhem Land artists' bark paintings in Darwin, north Australia. He didn't return."

Donaldson's silence keeps me talking: "It happened amid Iraq War bad press. Mom told Ann and me, just like in Vietnam, distrust of the U.S. is repeating in Iraq.'"

I didn't have to reiterate my mother's ingrained suspicion of the U.S. ever since the Vietnam War. In protest, my mother gave up U.S. citizenship to become Canadian.

My boss's fixed stare drives me on. I continue, "Australian officials notified Mom about my father's disappearance. Mom flew from Beagle Island to Darwin on the north Australia coast. Government agents from Canberra investigated. Not local Darwin police. Too soon, the Canberra agents closed the investigation with little explanation. Mother said the Australian and American governments are 'equally untrustworthy.'"

Donaldson speaks like my mother, with confidence in me. "I'll confide in you Tom, Diana returned from Darwin believing that whatever has happened to Jim is being covered up. Before returning to Beagle Island, she stopped here in San Diego. We discussed her suspicion, hinted at by Australian investigators, that Jim vanished amidst a serious diplomatic violation known as the 'Darwin Incident.'"

I'm feeling Congresswoman Sarah Donaldson's commanding presence. My mother or father's involvement recedes as I see that my boss is preparing me for a mission.

"About the Darwin Incident," Donaldson explains, "In its final year, 2008, the second Bush Administration authorized a covert C.I.A. operation against our close Iraq War ally, Australia. Australian military intelligence's discovery of this illegal operation caused formal diplomatic protest from Australia and another ally, Canada."

Donaldson's steady gaze presses me. "Understandably, the Australians waited for the Obama transition team to begin before pursuing possible violation remedies related to the Darwin Incident. The new Administration's transition team has turned the matter over to my military intelligence committee and Australian military intelligence welcomes full cooperation."

Donaldson is now strictly all business. She leans forward and puts her hand over a stack of papers on the desk to her left. She removes her glasses and folds them. Her full attention weighs upon me.

"Tom, the following is strictly classified," Donaldson continues. "I've pursued long-standing covert channels with Australia military intelligence. They want you, Tom Berneray."

I'm speechless and confused. Surely, I didn't hear my boss correctly. Why would the Australians want me, an obscure Donaldson Committee staffer?

Donaldson's voice sounds like an order: "Tom, my Australian intelligence contacts have disclosed that shortly before the 2008 U.S. election, an American private security contractor targeted an Australian secret operation using a weather station in Arnhem Land as cover. Obviously, such American espionage is illegal against our Iraq-coalition ally, and a gross violation of Australia's sovereignty."

Her hand jerks dismissively and she explains: "Initially, the Bush Administration denied U.S. involvement in this Darwin Incident, describing it as private industrial espionage. But Australian military intelligence revealed the perpetrator was a C.I.A. private contractor, A.C.M.E. Security. That led to Australia and other allies' diplomatic protests, which suspended allied military intelligence-sharing agreements.

"Ironically, all parties agree, despite significant international law and global security violations, the espionage operation itself failed badly. A.C.M.E. aborted it for unknown reasons.

"The new Obama Administration must rebuild the trust that the Darwin Incident disrupted. And Australia military intelligence wants to talk in Canberra with *you*, Tom Berneray."

I sputter, "Why me?"

Donaldson's answer is about her, too. "I honestly don't know. Tom, you can easily be identified as my staffer. And it is my committee that will appropriate money supporting U.S. and Australia military intelligence-sharing. There will be no such sharing unless mutual trust and diplomatic agreements are renewed."

"We're tangling with the C.I.A.," I assert, recalling her claim that the C.I.A. was behind the Darwin Incident.

"Yes," Donaldson agrees, "and C.I.A. involvement is always complicated." I nod.

"I know you understand," my boss asserts, "to be credible, the new Obama Administration must renew inter-allied military intelligence-sharing. To be exact: the Australians need more satellite surveillance using drones. Classified U.S. data requires shared inter-allied military intelligence. The Darwin Incident stopped that data flow."

Donaldson pauses. In her mind, she's clearly smoothing out deep complexities. She then adds, "The Obama Administration is also committed to winning the respect of the C.I.A. It demands a role in my committee's work with Australian military intelligence. I decide what the C.I.A. role is. That's difficult since the Australians discovered the C.I.A.'s clandestine support of the private contractor, A.C.M.E. Security, in the Darwin Incident."

Donaldson's words hang in the air. "Understand," she says, "I don't know why or how the Australians identified you. Perhaps there is a connection with your father's disappearance. Honestly, I simply don't know. My point is: you're furthering our renewal of inter-allied military intelligence-sharing. I'm relying on you."

Donaldson's not finished, "One more thing: you'll work with a C.I.A. agent named Albert Jennings. I expect you'll handle the relationship with great care."

The mention of Albert Jennings is another shock to me. We were roommates at Harvard, class of '98.

Albert is from a prosperous Cayman Islands banking family, loyal British subjects in offshore finance. He and I disliked each other from the start. His self-centered egotism viewed the world solely in terms of himself. Albert saw me as motivated by the same narrow self-interest. He never understood that my close family ensured that unlike him, I'd be committed to fighting for others, as well as myself. I didn't trust Albert Jennings.

Donaldson stands, looks down at me, and says flatly, "Your Arnhem Land mission is difficult. Tom, you must proceed one step at a time. You'll have to trust me. During anti-Vietnam War activism Diana and I trusted each other. You can do the same."

As I absorb the surprises from Donaldson, there's a knock at the door. In walks Albert Jennings.

Albert shakes hands with Congresswoman Donaldson and me. Albert's smooth, natural greeting blends BBC and West Indian English. A six-three frame, tailored pinstriped black suit, Italian shoes, and college tie contrast with his albino, ghost-white, freckled skin, close-cropped reddish hair, and penetrating hazel eyes.

Albert takes the chair next to me. He shows no recognition of us having had an earlier personal connection. He presents himself as a complete stranger to me. I do the same in return. If Donaldson knows Albert and I share a past, she doesn't show it either.

I listen as Donaldson gives Albert Jennings a sanitized version of why he and I are sitting before her. Curiously, my boss is silent about Arnhem Land.

Donaldson is selective about the reasons the President's transition team and the Donaldson military intelligence committee require cooperation between C.I.A. agent Albert Jennings and her committee's special investigator, Tom Berneray.

Donaldson doesn't mention the diplomatic protests resulting from the Darwin Incident. She's also silent regarding Australian or Canadian distrust of the C.I.A.

All I'm hearing is Donaldson's clear, straightforward message. Our present meeting pursues a return to cooperation among Donaldson's military intelligence committee, our allies' military intelligence organizations, and the C.I.A.

Specifically, Donaldson emphasizes the President's need to provide public and private assurances. His Administration is reinstituting cooperation among American military intelligence, Australian and other allied counterpart organizations, and the C.I.A.

The previous Administration's recklessness in Iraq and elsewhere has destroyed cooperation, especially sharing allied intelligence to promote satellite-drone technology. Now cooperation must be reinstated.

Albert sits passively. I remember that tactic from our roommate debates. He'd try to lull me into thinking he wasn't listening. He'd then attempt to undercut my argument by recalling some obscure comment I'd made. He'd be angry if it didn't work with me. Yet he kept probing for a mistake, confident he was smarter than I.

Donaldson continues to remain silent about Arnhem Land. Generally, she emphasizes our allies' need for the U.S. to provide new satellite-drone technology in order to counter a mounting national security threat from non-nation powers. These include a new kind of terrorist: global cocaine cartels.

Coincidentally, my boss's reference to cocaine cartels recalls another memory of my college roommate experience with Albert Jennings.

Shortly before we graduated, Albert admitted to me: "Tom, we both know how much I owe you. When the Cambridge and Harvard police considered arresting me regarding my association with another student charged with cocaine possession, you lied for me, you gave me an alibi so I could graduate and take a job with the C.I.A."

As Donaldson talks on, my memory returns to the roommate experience that prepared me for Albert's dissembling. His apparent admission was really his attempt to suggest I might trust him because he was beholden to me.

My memory grows stronger. Albert had been trying to manipulate my potential trust. I rejected his effort, asserting, "Albert, you know I didn't lie. I just shifted the angle of facts about when you studied for finals in our room." My statement was objectively true and Albert knew it. Albert simply replied, "Tom, you're marvelous at keeping secrets."

That happened over ten years ago. Albert and I now present ourselves as strangers sitting before Donaldson. If I read her right, my boss doesn't want Albert to know just yet that I'm going to Arnhem Land. For now, it's her and my secret.

II

My thoughts rush back to our meeting in Donaldson's office. She's turning to my mission and Albert's role in it. She still doesn't mention Arnhem Land.

Finally, Donaldson introduces Albert and me to each other as if it's our first meeting. I'm confident she's delayed introducing us in order to see Albert's response.

Regarding Albert, Donaldson explains, "In the last Presidential Administration, Albert Jennings was the C.I.A. expert on legal and illegal uses of offshore financial centers. The cocaine cartel exploits legal uses for criminal purposes."

She acknowledges Albert Jennings' expertise: "Through those offshore financial centers, the cartels launder billions of cocaine dollars using shadowy corporate conglomerates. They implement new cocaine distribution techniques such as engineering tunnels across national borders, combining operations of sea vessels and land vehicles in remote geographic areas as a 'back door' to huge urban markets, and adapting lawful commercial drones to criminal purposes. The conglomerates pay mercenary private security firms to protect the growing cocaine cartel operations."

Donaldson points to me. "Tom is my military intelligence committee's chief investigator into private security companies. The previous Presidential Administration shifted many vital operations from the U.S. military to mercenary private contractors. This includes in the Iraq War, C.I.A. contracts with private security companies to use satellite-drone technology."

Donaldson emphasizes that her committee has been exploited: "Appropriations from my congressional committee have gone—with minimal C.I.A. oversight—to some private contractors' illegal practices like money laundering."

She exclaims, "The previous Presidential Administration enabled private security firms to take over some satellite-drone technology, which disrupted shared military-intelligence cooperation with close American allies like Australia. The new Administration has ordered my committee to renew the military's shared cooperation."

Silence prevails. Neither Albert nor I move. For the first time since entering Sarah Donaldson's office, I hear a clock ticking somewhere.

From a black box on her desk, my boss withdraws and hands me an ordinary-looking credit card and an iPhone. She explains, "As long as these two devices remain within a few yards of you, Tom, my Chief-of-Staff and I usually will know your location. The iPhone records and transmits most, though not all, of your conversations. Our Naval Electronics Laboratory has incorporated these and other modifications into the iPhone."

Donaldson adds, "In secured places like my Mansfield building office in D.C., we know you're there, Tom, but hear nothing. Also, certain locations in the world distort iPhone transmissions. If you encounter such a place, let us know, Tom."

I already know all this. She's showing Albert what he's being excluded from.

Still, my boss's meeting has moved too fast from routine to immediate action.

Blindly, I take in her orders: "Travel, contact and meeting info will appear on the iPhone. In a week I expect your complete report. Hurry

Tom, your plane leaves in a few hours."

I quickly leave her office and take a taxi home. My mind is reeling. I must think fast. At home, I prepare easily. I always travel light. My mind soon is focused.

Donaldson had said that she, my mother, and the rest of our two families have trusted one another for many years. She assured me that in this Arnhem Land mission I could trust her to show me the way, "step-by-step."

But in her office meeting, Donaldson demanded my trust on the run. First, I'm blindsided. The Australians want to confront me personally, a mere staffer. This somehow promotes the new U.S. Presidential Administration's return to inter-allied military intelligence-sharing of top-secret satellite-drone technology. Meanwhile, my boss left the possible involvement of my disappeared father unexplained.

Next, my boss shocked me, bringing in C.I.A. agent Albert Jennings. Then, without providing guidance as to Albert's or my exact operational roles, she ordered me away to Australia. She did this in Albert's presence, with no explanation. I know what my mission is. Albert doesn't know what my mission is. Probably she wants Albert to educate me with his technical expertise in offshore finance.

Regarding my Arnhem Land mission itself, Donaldson has also prepared me for the moment when the Australians will assuredly interrogate me.

The Australians will seek possible direct C.I.A. links because of the Darwin Incident. When they raise that failed C.I.A. operation, I'll say truly the information I'd received came from Donaldson herself. I'm no C.I.A. agent. I've not communicated with any of their C.I.A. agents. I have plausible denial.

Finally, I must admit: Donaldson ensured the meeting between Albert and I would enable us to measure each other without actually acknowledging each other. Our old distrust of remains valid despite the passage of years. My boss has impressed upon me that she and I shouldn't trust Albert too far.

Then I recall: Donaldson came with my family to my Harvard graduation. She saw that Albert and I were unfriendly to one another as college roommates.

Now ten years later, the 2008 election has given the C.I.A. an opportunity to order its agent Albert Jennings to work for the Donaldson

military intelligence committee. Donaldson is using me to outmaneu-
ver C.I.A. infiltration. I face yet another test.

Donaldson has rather cleverly prepared me for dealing with the
C.I.A., and the American side of my mission. I next must deal with the
Australians.

I leave San Diego, change in Los Angeles, and fly directly to Sydney. My iPhone's secret four-number code opens Fun Games, my mission information. It directs me to meet the Australia military intelligence Chief in Canberra. He'll send me to a field officer in Arnhem
Land.

During the twelve-hour direct flight, my mission acquires focus.
Years ago my family and I visited Darwin, Australia, and the Arnhem
Land visitors' museum. I learned the most about Arnhem Land from
my mother and her brother, Alex Quinn. Growing up, they visited Arnhem Land with their parents on Quinn Shipping vessels or a family
yacht.

After the Vietnam War, Alex Quinn sometimes sailed to Arnhem
Land from Mexico with his wife, Esperanza, and daughter Isabella. Esperanza is the granddaughter, and Isabella the great granddaughter of
Mexican Revolutionary hero, Juan Bermudez. My father first met
members of the Quinn and Bermudez families in Mexico in 1970.

After the Vietnam War, my mother's family connections to Quinn
Shipping and the Mexican Bermudez family helped my father. Berkeley
Ph.D. in hand, he developed a consulting business, partly in Sonora
Mexico and primarily in Arnhem Land, Australia.

These happy family connections shattered in 2001. Our beloved Isabella was murdered under strange circumstances in Santa Maria,
Mexico. Her parents Alex and Esperanza Quinn escaped, sailing away
in their schooner across the Pacific into hiding.

My suffering from Isabella's death has become still more unbearable now that my father has vanished in Arnhem Land. Mexico and Arnhem Land bind me in pain.

I must confess my Arnhem Land mission for Sarah Donaldson
helps me to bear the pain. My father once told me: "Tom, action is con-
solatory."

As Donaldson committee investigator I analyze satellite GPS data.
It locates Arnhem Land east of Darwin, Northern Australia, across the
Alligator River, to the Gulf of Carpentaria, touching Torres Straits,

south of the Arafura Sea and Papua New Guinea.

Arnhem Land is not only geographically remote. Arnhem Land also possesses extraordinary, even unique, sea and wind currents.

Australia military intelligence reports that the unusual land-sea combinations in Arnhem Land "can disrupt" satellite-drone surveillance.

Yet my iPhone Fun Games data includes secret Australian communiqués.

Donaldson undoubtedly convinced her contacts in Australian military intelligence to give me these communiqués. They probe the implications of the U.S. 2008 election for reestablishing allied military intelligence-sharing with Australia.

Other iPhone Fun Games data selectively reveals the illegal Darwin Operation. It was C.I.A. authorized, implemented by the private contractor, A.C.M.E. Security. Sentence-paragraph fragments run together due to censorship deletions throughout the Fun Games data transmitted on my iPhone.

Australian intelligence analysts combined pieces of damaged A.C.M.E. documents. Readable phrases reveal the C.I.A. covert operation targeted a hidden "weather station."

These damaged documents present disconnected data passages. They together suggest Australia military intelligence uses the so-called "weather station" as a cover for operating computer spy technology.

Clearly, the Fun Games iPhone data is fragmentary. Still, it suggests Arnhem Land Weather Station computers can intercept intermittent signals from C.I.A. spy satellites.

The Fun Games data also suggests that the Australians experiment with new satellite-drone technology.

Taken together, the piecemeal data signals growing Australian independence from U.S. intelligence influence preceding the Darwin Incident.

The Arnhem Land Weather Station is located amongst rugged coastal terrain and remote, broken bush country, somewhere between Darwin and the Gulf of Carpentaria.

Fragmentary Fun Games data also partially records the Darwin Incident. The partial data seems to be intercepted transmissions from a C.I.A. drone.

The incomplete Darwin Incident transmissions report drone surveillance of an unnamed "subject." The ACME agents aborted surveillance during a struggle pitting them against unidentified "others." Exposure by unnamed "officials," isn't explained.

After studying the Fun Games data, I eventually fall asleep. I'm awakened by the arrival in Sydney. I change planes for Canberra. I imagine I'm prepared to address Australian demands. In my imagination, I can be overconfident.

In Canberra, I meet Australia military intelligence Chief Gilbert Glick. "Call me 'Chief G,'" he orders me.

We meet in a modest-sized, old colonial government building near the Australian National University (A.N.U.). Chief G's English is Oxbridge, with a slight Aussie accent. Chief G looks like a middle-age academic wearing wire-rim glasses and tweeds.

The dark-haired younger woman with Chief G is tall, slender, and deeply tanned. She conveys easy, confident swagger just shaking my hand: "Gidday, Gwen Tone from Queensland." This, her strong voice suggests, is all I need to know about her.

Chief G speaks kindly, "Tom, we've asked you to come all this way just to have a chat. Why do you think?"

My answer is straightforward, "My boss, Sarah Donaldson, emphasized the need to reestablish the trust allied military intelligence shared before the Iraq War disrupted it."

My reply to the Chief decidedly doesn't impress Gwen Tone. She exclaims: "Mate, tell us what you know about this."

Before my eyes Tone shifts an oddly configured stick. She grips it so tightly her tanned knuckles have turned white. The stick is the size of a baton rely runners pass. Colorful figures and shapes cover its surface.

My hands fold to stop them trembling.

Tone asserts, "Recently, an Aboriginal Law Man delivered this message stick to our Arnhem Land Weather Station. The Law Man's message stick gave us quite a start. You can you imagine why, can't you?"

"Not really," I lie.

Chief G interjects, "Tom, given the circumstances Gwen has imparted, we know too much and not enough about your situation. Only the truth will do, actually."

I study both interrogators. My father once told me amidst painful

P.T.S.D. family therapy: "When they question you, Tom, use delay to turn the tables."

Finally, I plead: "Please believe me. I've never seen this message stick before. Gwen Tone seems to suggest it somehow triggers my involvement in this whole chain of events. Truthfully, I have no idea how or why. I know nothing about a Law Man."

Tone's gaze is even more relentlessly suspicious. I realize I've indicated that I know what a "message stick" is. She now assumes I can be pressured. We'll see.

"Not a bad story, Tom." Chief G's reply is warm, practical. He almost smiles. "We're making progress. We must understand one point so we can be informed in reports to our respective superiors: You're a double agent."

"I don't know what you mean," I hope my words convey genuine surprise. My father once said, "Before you avoid telling a truth, learn exactly what they want."

Standing back, Chief G conveys the impression that separation provides clarity.

Chief G speaks softly, but his words hit home. "Tom, the art of lying, like all espionage, demands staying as close as possible to, without actually divulging, a truth. Alas, time flies. You conveniently ignore, the Darwin Incident, that shocking American assault on Australian sovereignty that also coincides with your father's disappearance."

I answer back too quickly, "That's a coincidence, surely. I don't understand what else it might be."

Chief G's apparent faith in my perceptiveness dissolves into disappointment. Shaking his head, he turns to Tone for help.

Tone speaks behind, over me. "You dance around evidence we all see." On my shoulder, her clinched fist waits.

Tone's logical evidence slashes at me. "In the so-called Darwin Incident, C.I.A.-A.C.M.E. agents for some unknown purpose pursued an unnamed 'person,' who we believe to be your father, Jim Berneray, a noted indigenous art consultant in Arnhem Land. A.C.M.E. agents didn't explain who exposed their illegal operation against Australian sovereignty."

Tone's fist presses firmly yet painlessly against my throat. The feeling leaves more to my imagination.

Chief G speaks calmly. "You're a bright boy, Tom. Let's reconsider what you've suggested is mere 'coincidence.' Your father was present, and then disappeared during the unlawful Darwin Incident. Surely, you've considered that the A.C.M.E. agents' surveillance of the unnamed 'subject' actually targeted your father. He and unidentified 'others' beat back A.C.M.E. so badly that those agents aborted their own espionage operation. My perfectly reasonable question to you, Tom is: 'why' did A.C.M.E. agents care enough about your father to abort their own espionage operation for the C.I.A.?"

Chief G concludes: "The agents failed to locate the Arnhem Land Weather Station. The failure ended allied military intelligence-sharing. This espionage disaster occurred because A.C.M.E. agents for some reason went after Jim Berneray, who then vanished. My scenario recognizes, of course, that you are Sarah Donaldson's special agent. I'm sure you're also your father's secret agent. Could you also work for the C.I.A.?"

The events since the meeting with my boss in San Diego acquire focus; staying close enough to the truth may enable me to avoid revealing it.

Tone's clenched fist still rests near my throat. My father told me, "Tom, having people believe you are afraid can be useful. Even better: they underestimate you."

I use my natural sincerity: "Threaten me all you like. You suggest I know enough about this case to be manipulative. But I'm here solely because you've commanded my presence. You imply that I know about the message stick and an Arnhem Land Law Man. Truthfully, to me they're both new revelations. I admit they're both consistent with the obvious trust between my father and Aboriginal artists. I see no evidence that indicates I'm lying about anything, including the C.I.A. Show me the evidence, if it exists."

Chief G and Tone's silence conveys creeping doubt. I push my luck.

I can also use logic's razor. "You tell me: the message stick and the Law Man arrive at the Arnhem Land weather station months after the Darwin Incident. I assume the time lag bothers you. It bothers me. Explain it."

I swat Tone's fist away. She lets it drop. Maybe I make my own progress. "Truly, I hope the message stick and the Law Man concern my father. My mother, sister, and I share painful unknowns since father disappeared. We hope you feel our pain."

I study them both before insisting; "You can help my family and me if you wish."

Intently, they look at me. I feel their certainty slipping.

Weighing uncertain consequences, Chief G answers, "An anonymous Arnhem Land individual informed us about your father's presence in the Darwin Incident. We believe without clear proof that this individual aided your father's escape. Your father's present whereabouts is unknown."

Now, they listen to me. "What evidence connects the message stick, the Law Man, my father, and me?"

Chief G's words seem like confession: "Frankly, Tom, you are here because a certain Law Man in Arnhem Land apparently believes it is time that you understand those connections."

Tone admits, "My Deputy Director at the Arnhem Land Weather Station is Tony Malangi. He is an Arnhem Land clan leader. Malangi gave me the message stick. In Arnhem Land we depend on Malangi. You were unknown to us until Malangi identified you. Chief G has known Sarah Donaldson for years. He easily determined that Tom Berneray is Sarah Donaldson's staffer."

Chief G explains, "Malangi revealed that your father's presence coincided with the Darwin incident. Malangi and I decided to test whether the 2008 U.S. presidential election would enable us to renew allied military intelligence-sharing. Tom, you present us with an opportunity to pursue that goal through Sarah Donaldson. She revealed an unavoidable C.I.A. presence to us. Despite her assurances, we had to be certain that through you we'd not somehow be confronting the C.I.A., which was behind the Darwin Incident."

Chief G now instructs me. "Malangi urges you, Tom, to follow the message stick. Meet and learn from the Law Man in Arnhem Land. He'll return you to Malangi. He'll bring you back to us."

Chief G assumes my report will be satisfactory to all. The mysteries connecting the Darwin Incident, my father's disappearance, and the Law Man's message stick naming me will be solved. Inter-allied military intelligence-sharing will be restored. I'll then return to San Diego. Everyone satisfied.

"The contrary results are unpleasant to contemplate," Chief G exclaims. "Tom bungles the Donaldson committee initiative seeking renewed allied military intelligence-sharing, and Tom thereby also fails the Berneray family hopes."

Tone takes over matter-of-factly: "In order to meet the Law Man in Arnhem Land, for the rugged bush country, you need tough clothing." That requirement is easily met. We're soon airborne in Tone's small airplane, flying west towards Arnhem Land.

III

Gwen Tone's opinion about me becomes clearer. She says, "Why an Arnhem Land Law Man would trust you in the first place is suspicious. Chief G thinks it's simply pragmatic to trust you. But I don't trust you, Tom Berneray. My brother was wounded serving the Americans in your political Iraq War. He needs two canes to walk now."

Tone finishes. "In Arnhem Land Malangi, our Deputy Director, knows what he's doing. We depend on him. Whatever the Law Man's message is, it had better be good for me to believe an American like you who serves more than one master."

I wish I knew why an Arnhem Land Law Man I've never even heard of wants me.

From Canberra, Tone flies us to Darwin to refuel. Darwin is a small city beside a blue-green sea, amongst jungle punctuated by wild terrain. Darwin borders Arnhem Land, the Aboriginal Homeland, where my father disappeared.

Tone pilots us into Arnhem Land. She flies low over expansive tangled green bush, immense boulders strewn like marbles across brown-red earth, interspersed amidst various sizes of open spaces. At tree-level, she follows along a twisting river that disappears into dense natural growth. Her little plane feels even smaller.

She lifts us above jungle, while staying below the overhanging rim of a towering dark escarpment. Far into the distance it merges with blue sky slashed by wispy clouds. Hard shapes and vaporous spaces shimmer together. I feel I'm flying into an illusion.

"Somewhere in here you'll meet the Law Man," Tone says with an unfriendly smile.

The escarpment ends in translucent green-blue water lapping sand so white my eyes hurt looking at it. Tone loops the plane over open sea, coming back low along an empty, rugged coastline.

Towers of a small weather station appear. Amidst engine noise I shout, "Big towers for a small station. They look like something used for spy satellites, not just weather."

"Given your intelligence analysis, you should know. Just remember the comment came from you, not me, if someone asks." Tone isn't joking. I remember Fun Games data fragments suggesting that Australians are developing satellite technology less vulnerable to Arnhem Land distortions. Perhaps that is what A.C.M.E. was after.

Tone lands the plane near the coast on an airstrip cut into the bush. Several large white wood-frame buildings border the field. The white structures coexist with thick undergrowth and broken ground. I hear but can't see the nearby ocean.

Beside a four-wheel drive Land Rover stands a short, dark man dressed in rugged bush gear similar to what Tone and I wear. Tone introduces us. Tony Malangi's broad smile and firm handshake suggests familiarity.

"My father told me that a David Malangi bark painting appears on the Australia dollar bill. Is he any relation to you, Tony Malangi?" I hope he likes the question.

Becoming quite serious, he replies, "David Malangi is part of the Manharrngu tribe. I am Tony Malangi, from a different tribe, the Gunwinggu. I have permission from Gunwinggu Elders to take you to a Law Man. Are you ready, Tom Berneray?"

At the station door we leave Tone holding my bag. Malangi guides the Land Rover through thick bush interspersed with rugged open spaces. The weather station dissolves into memory.

After intermittent hours of talking about the bush-country followed by silence, we stop. Malangi passes me a tin cup filled with coffee, and a "tucker" or food bag. "Kangaroo meat," Malangi says, "in a nearby site lives the spirit kangaroo, Kalkberb. He permits the Gunwinggu people to kill kangaroo so we can eat. As a poor student at A.N.U., I often remembered that."

I see and feel that rock clusters, tangled bush, and sandy open spaces all have life.

Malangi is quiet. I sense he guides me to the rocky escarpment. The sand is covered with imprints of bare feet. He explains, "Gunwinggu people walk here in harmony with 'Mimi spirits.'" He studies me to see if I understand.

I reply, "My father taught me that 'Mimi spirits' are tall, thin fairylike beings that live in rocky escarpments. They once had human forms. 'Mimi spirits' can be mischievous. Usually they're harmless. They exist in different space and time dimensions."

Malangi says nothing as we depart. His consciousness perceives the path we follow. He knows the spirit sites scattered across shifting terrain. These sites embody remembered stories or "song lines." Law Men's "singing" these "lines" keeps the Gunwinggu people in touch with food and spiritual nourishment they need to survive.

When I was a boy, my father showed me the painted images in his Ph.D. dissertation, which embodied "song lines" he had recorded in interviews with Arnhem-Land artists. Later, I understood how my father's ability to translate these images into words enabled his consulting business in Arnhem Land. Artists trusted his skill, an ability that other whites lacked.

My father's dissertation introduced these "image sites" using a sign posted somewhere in Arnhem Land: "CEREMONY COUNTRY - Beyond this point lies sites of traditional significance to Aboriginal People - PLEASE RESPECT THE SANCTITY OF THIS AREA - Special permission must be obtained from traditional custodians before proceeding further - Penalty for unlawful entry up to $20,000."

In the country we're passing through, Tony Malangi gives permission. Declining sunlight deepen shadows over red-brown earth. Darkening vibrant colors spark faith in invisible life.

Beginning with dissertation fieldwork, my father traversed this ageless ground. Learning from my father, and now Malangi, I'm attempting to discover their path.

Finally, Malangi asks, "What do you know?"

I feel pressure to speak truthfully. "Days ago American government bosses told me an Australia military intelligence chief called me to Canberra. He has enabled me to search for my father."

Words have driven my faith in strange doings. "From Chief G and Gwen I learned you delivered a message stick naming me, Tom Berneray, and calling me to meet a Law Man in Arnhem Land. I'd be unknown here, unless somehow my father was involved."

I plead: "During the Darwin Incident, after fighting side-by-side with Arnhem Land artists against C.I.A. agents, my father disappeared. Have you seen him?"

Malangi answers in a command: "Learn, Tom Berneray. Gunwinggu artists have respected your father. He's brought the artists' bark paintings to *Balanda* [white people] in Sydney, New York, London."

Malangi explains my father's disappearance in a new light. "In Darwin, *Balanda* attacked Jim Berneray and Gunwinggu artists. Law Man's sacred paintings have shown that Ngalyod [Rainbow Serpent] needs Jim's son to bring justice."

Malangi has reminded me that my father's dissertation specifically examined barks and cave paintings. My father followed George Chaloupka's identification of cave painting as an art and research field.

I say to Malangi: "My father taught me how important the Rainbow Serpent is throughout Australia. Don't the Gunwinggu also call Ngalyod the Snake Woman?" Malangi nods affirmately.

I admit, "I don't understand why my father's disappearance, bark and cave paintings, an Arnhem Land Law Man, and my presence here are vital to Ngalyod."

"You will understand," Malangi promises quietly. He lets me think in silence about that promise, as we travel a few more hours.

At twilight we stop in a bush clearing. Black escarpment towers overhead. Its broken rim is sharp against receding, glowing light.

"We walk." Malangi's speech suddenly sounds like Gunwinggu people of this "Ceremony Country." His clothes are still like mine, but Malangi's self seems to be shifting.

Malangi moves to where black rock parts at a trail opening. He disappears and then reappears somewhat above me, now a shadow. The trail twists upward into gloom. At first I keep close to his shape and footsteps. Starlight partially illuminates the trail.

After a long climb, I've lost him. Darkness weighs me down. I call his name again and again. No reply, only emptiness.

Above me, light flickers. My hands and body press rock. Slowly I move up the trial. The light becomes steady.

At last I stumble into a cave filled with firelight and shadows. The flickering light comes from smoldering fire rings located around the cave.

Extraordinary images acquire focus. Strange shapes discernible as kangaroo ears, eyes, legs, tails attach to distorted grey-brown bodies. Vaguely similar features are distinguishable as small hares. Thin, elongated bodies are surely Mimi spirits. From other shapes protrude the spear-like teeth of an evil spirit, Flying Fox.

My father's dissertation paintings are like those surrounding me now. These cave paintings aren't the ones examined in my father's dissertation. His cave was elsewhere in Arnhem Land. But Malangi has led me to cave paintings that make me feel closer to my father than at any time since he disappeared.

Smoldering light from fire rings give the painted images shimmering life. I can't shake the illusion that my father's presence is real.

I try to reason logically. Caves shelter painted images presenting Aboriginal life—stretching back thousands of years. Cave images record the Dreamtime, when great spirits like Rainbow Serpent created land, animals, and Aboriginal clan ancestors.

Images record Dream "lines" clan members "sing" in ceremonies and rituals so that they remain connected to spirits and ancestors. Cave paintings can reveal the good Rainbow Serpent and bad Flying Fox. The unpredictable Mimi spirits are always present.

Fire-ring light accentuates colors: separate, mixed, blended red, brown, blue, green, orange, white, and black. They convey timeless life and death.

Cave paintings can inspire bark paintings. Through sales aided by my father, bark paintings support spiritual and economic life in Arnhem Land. This ensures the artists' continuing trust in my father.

Cave and bark paintings influence rituals that "Law men" of one generation pass on to the youth of the next generation.

I hope the Law Man has sent the message stick to Malangi in order for my father to communicate with me. This thought suddenly dawns on me; I think it through slowly. This is a connection I hadn't even imagined I needed to hide from Chief G.

Shadow light illuminates high walls covered with the many curious images. From my father's dissertation, I recall learning that the painter creates individualized images of Dreamtime spirits and ancestors.

Faithful to customary law rooted in Dreamtime, a painter records and explains each group's life and environment. On the walls surrounding me, generations of clan artists over millennia have always refreshed their paintings. Throughout time, they've shown shifting images of Dreamtime spirits such as Rainbow Serpent or Flying Fox.

I easily grasp some paintings that record events vital to clan life. In one painting, images of hunters search for water aided by Kangaroo Spirit. A bright, long-tailed comet is clearly visible overhead.

Another painter captures a square-rigged ship that Makasans from the Celebes Islands sailed to trade with tribes in Arnhem Land. The trade occurred centuries ago. Yet the painter's presentation is vivid enough to suggest the ship sails today.

I'm surprised. A detailed cave painting shows a Japanese plane bombing Darwin. My father wrote he'd heard of cave paintings that recorded the enemy attack during World War II, but he said he'd never seen a painting of it. I yearn to tell him I've found that cave painting. Other more ambiguous images scatter across cave walls.

From the shadows a white figure emerges. Without our rugged bush garb, Malangi appears in his secret calling: a Law Man empowered to grant or withhold permission to be on a sacred site in Ceremony Country.

Ceremonial white paint used in cave and bark painting covers Malangi's body. A beaded cord fits close around his neck, held at the throat by a white bone. In customary law "pointing the bone" is deadly. Withholding a bone connotes delivering justice.

At a cave wall, barely within nearby fire-ring light, Malangi, the Law Man, sits. Dimly visible stones form a fire ring beside his crossed legs. He lights a fire. He begins working on the large, flat surface spread before him.

Malangi's upright body shimmers. Hands and forearms move steadily. "Click, click, click," interrupts strange words which seem very old yet timeless. The hypnotic, recurring rhythm pulls me to a place across from the ring beside the wall.

Shifting light, shadow, flames suck away breath, fracture vision. I'm lifted into darkness. I look down on the painted surface Malangi fills with colors, figures, shapes.

From what feels like great height, I fall to my knees. In fire-ring light Malangi's painting and the wall images blend.

Malangi's painting comes into focus. I recognize Kangaroo Spirit, Lightning Spirit, and Rainbow Serpent. Malangi also disperses thin, frail figures throughout his painting, Mimi spirits who help or harass people.

A few images feel familiar. A red van travels from seaside cave in rugged terrain to city storefront gallery. A figure wears glasses, khakis shorts and shirt, battered bush hat. It is my father, Jim Berneray.

I remember that my father meets Gunwinggu artists in Darwin at

Mary's Gallery. They prepare bark paintings for sale there. I watch as Malangi captures this human scene set amid Dreamtime spirits and landscape. All's well.

Malangi's bark painting shifts the scene away from Mary's Gallery. Gunwinggu artists and my father struggle with faceless *Balanda* figures.

The artists and my father recover bark paintings that the faceless *Balanda* have stolen. The largest *Balanda* strikes my father, and flees into the air as Flying Fox spirit, ready to do more evil. Other *Balanda* pursue the red van into Kangaroo Spirit country. Lightning Spirit kills the *Balanda* pursuers.

Malangi's bark painting shows Gunwinggu artists carrying my wounded father into a cave by the sea. On the moonlit coast, a big sailboat waits.

Rainbow Serpent rises over the water, promising her law will punish Flying Fox. Far away, the evil spirit laughs. Wounded Jim departs the cave in the big sailboat.

Malangi's bark painting depicts my father's presence, struggle, arrival, departure. I weep. Malangi's chanting ceases, the ring-fire dies. Malangi is gone.

Slowly, I regain steadiness. In fire-ring light I see Malangi has taken the bark painting he just made. My memory fixes on the scene he created: my father and the artists struggling with the *Balanda*; the sailboat carrying away wounded Jim from the cave; Flying Fox laughing; Rainbow Serpent rising.

Mimi spirits encompass my father and the big sailboat. They restore my fragile composure. Time swirls away. I don't know day or night, if I'm awake or dreaming.

Changed back into his rugged-bush garb, Malangi returns. He motions for me to follow. From cave darkness, through a short tunnel, we emerge into moonlight.

On a ledge we overlook the expansive white beach washed with low-rolling waves. Across dispersing foam and smooth, shifting water a shining path reaches right up to a full moon. I've seen moonscapes like this before from Sunset Cliffs in San Diego.

But in Arnhem Land even a seemingly familiar scene is strange. Small figures appear one by one from lapping waves, stroll across white sand, and disappear below us.

"Penguins far from home," Malangi says. "Just so, months ago in the moonlight your father escaped in the big sail boat. He said to me only: 'Tell my son, he knows what he must do so that Ngalyod brings justice to the evil spirit, Flying Fox.'"

Dumbfounded, I yell into his face, "My father was here. Where did he go?"

Watching, testing, helping me, Malangi speaks: "The Gunwinggu artists, Chief G, and I, Tony Malangi, none of us know where Jim Berneray is now. I'll find him when you follow Ngalyod and defeat Flying Fox." Malangi disappears back into cave shadows.

Trembling, I can't move. Curiously, I have a memory of seeing penguins come from surf to shore. Years ago, Father took Mother, Ann, and me to Dunedin on New Zealand's south island where the phenomena is a tourist attraction. But Dunedin is thousands of miles from Arnhem Land.

"Malangi," I plead, "I don't understand. What does it all mean?" He's gone. I run back through dimly lit cave images, and stumble down the escarpment trail. We meet at the Land Rover.

Malangi drives from night to dawn. He says nothing, giving me his bark painting to hold. I unroll and study it using my iPhone light.

Exhausted, my head throbs. All that's happened to me finally coalesces around the bark painting. At last, I rollup and return the painting to Malangi.

At early morning light, we meet in Gwen Tone's small Weather Station office. Malangi initially stands beside me.

Tone doesn't find my condition satisfactory. "Looks like you've had bit of a bad trip. Your bag is down the hall to the right. Shower and shave, make yourself respectable. Malangi and I'll have a wag."

I soon return. Sitting at her desk, Tone says, "Test time. You better be good." Malangi stands behind her, obscured by window light. My words transmit to Chief G in Canberra. He wants to know what I've learned. I want the same thing.

IV

I need to find my way to acceptable truths. I don't know what Malangi has told Tone or Chief G about my trip into Arnhem Land. I don't know if they know her Deputy Director, Malangi, and the Law

Man are one and the same. I'll think and talk my way to understanding.

As a boy twenty years ago, I carried Isabella from inside the thorn bramble. I earned courage, true to my family. Their faith is with me here and now.

Facing doubts, I state what I know. "Deputy Director Malangi and a Law Man have called me here. I'm known to them because my father, Jim Berneray, has aided Arnhem Land artists. Somehow his relationship with these artists became entangled in the 'Darwin Incident' and the current renewal of shared allied military intelligence regarding satellite-drone technology."

I continue, "The 2008 U.S. presidential election enabled American Congresswoman Sarah Donaldson and Australian intelligence Chief G to begin redressing the fallout from the previous Administration's disastrous Darwin Incident. I received the fragmentary Fun Games data that had been given to Congresswoman Donaldson by the Australian government. It provided partial evidence indicating facts, causes, and consequences of the Darwin Incident."

"Fun Games," I said, "showed that the previous U.S. Administration had authorized the C.I.A. and private contractor A.C.M.E.'s illegal operation targeting the Arnhem Land Weather Station. C.I.A.-A.C.M.E. violated international law by attacking Australia's sovereignty; it was a reaction to the Australians using the Arnhem Land Weather Station to intercept C.I.A. satellite transmissions.

"Even if fragmentary, the Fun Games data provided by the Australian government reveals legal ambivalence. On the one hand, the Arnhem Land Weather Station intercepts of C.I.A.-A.C.M.E. drone transmissions in an Iraq War zone were illegal. On the other hand, in Australia's self-defense, the Weather Station's intercepts of drone transmissions of cocaine cartel operations in Arnhem Land were lawful."

I pause and make a judgment. "In terms of legal technicalities, the Australian espionage was moderately culpable. The C.I.A.'s attempted retribution, however, was extreme, illegal, an overreaction."

"The C.I.A.'s blatant violation of Australia sovereignty ended ironically," I conclude. "In Darwin, agents bungled the operation and then aborted it. These agents never got close to locating the Arnhem Land weather station. Whether agents actually entered Arnhem Land from Darwin was unclear from the Fun Games data.

"Initially, neither Sarah Donaldson nor I knew why I was wanted in Arnhem Land. I've admitted that, along with obeying my boss's orders, I am also seeking my father. Chief G and Tone have made it forcefully clear that they assumed the latter was my motive.

"When I arrived here, I learned from Chief G and Tone that an Arnhem Land Law Man and the Deputy Director of the Weather Station there, Tony Malangi sought me. They handed me a message stick that was addressed to me personally. It told me to go to Arnhem Land. Following the Law Man's message stick led me to new evidence about the Darwin Incident. The new evidence is unusual.

"Weather Station Deputy Director Malangi took me into Arnhem Land. The new evidence we found is embodied in cave and bark paintings. They reflect factual and causal experience as well as spiritual inspiration.

"Years ago," I continue, "my father researched cave and bark paintings for his Ph.D. dissertation. Since then, his ongoing consulting business with Arnhem Land artists has shown Gunwinggu bark and cave paintings of actual and imaged action to be marketable art. The cave and bark paintings I was shown cast new light on the Darwin Incident.

"Malangi confirmed that Gunwinggu Elders authorized a Law Man to meet me in the sacred 'Ceremony Country' cave site. Implicitly, the Elders have authorized me to interpret sacred cave and bark paintings. Their permission enables me to interpret my father's role in the Darwin incident and its bearing on his disappearance."

I pause again, aware of the dilemma of not revealing Malangi's dual role as both tribal Law Man and Deputy Director. I will have to refer to the bark painting, which has been taken from the sacred cave site in Arnhem Land by Malangi while not explaining that Malangi himself painted it in his Law Man persona.

"The Law Man's bark painting," I say, "begins with a scene showing Gunwinggu artists in a red van transporting the artists' own bark paintings from the Arnhem Land sacred cave. The following scene shows a Darwin art gallery, in which the artists meet my father.

"The bark painting then changes from the scene in Darwin to portray faceless *Balandas*, white people. They're attempting to steal the Gunwinggu artists' paintings.

"The next scene shows a struggle against the *Balanda* in Arnhem Land. Spirits help the artists and my father win the struggle and recover the artists' own bark paintings. Flying Fox, the evil bat, escapes skyward after wounding my father. The artists, carrying my wounded father with them, return their bark paintings to the sacred cave.

"In the last bark painting scene, Kangaroo Spirit and Lighting Spirit have destroyed the *Balanda*. My wounded father has recovered sufficiently to depart the sacred cave in moonlight on a big sailboat."

Malangi has remained silent standing behind Tone. She's admitted to not having seen the bark painting. Until she has examined the painting herself, she refuses to acknowledge that my interpretation might be plausible.

Dramatically, Malang moves from the sunlight behind Tone. Across her desk, he unfolds the bark painting he'd painted in his Law Man persona in the sacred cave.

To my listeners Chief G, Tone, and now my boss, Sarah Donaldson, Malangi exclaimes: "Tom Berneray satisfied the Law Man. This bark painting records Arnhem Land artists and Jim Berneray struggling against *Balanda* and Flying Fox. I agree with Tom's reinterpretation of the C.I.A.-A.C.M.E. failure in the Darwin Incident. He has used the Fun Games data and the bark painting to interpret what happened."

Malangi's declaration substantiates my conclusions.

"First," I say, "C.I.A.-A.C.M.E. agents didn't understand that because of unique local conditions, standard satellite GPS couldn't locate the Weather Station in Arnhem Land.

"Consequently, agents started out isolated in Darwin. In the Law Man's bark painting, the faceless *Balanda* are surely C.I.A.-A.C.M.E. agents. They encounter the Gunwinggu bark painting exhibit at Mary's Gallery, located in Central Darwin.

"Stymied while using GPS to find the Arnhem Land Weather Station, *Balanda* agents assumed Gunwinggu artists were local people who could sell information and be hired as guides. But the agents couldn't communicate with Gunwinggu artists.

"Understandably, the agents approached the consultant working with the artists, my father, Jim Berneray. According to the Fun Games data, the agents didn't actually identify their subject by name. I believe, given the circumstances, that it was my father.

"Fun Games data showed the *Balanda* agents pursuing their subject using drone surveillance," I add.

"The C.I.A.-A.C.M.E. agents' conduct was undoubtedly suspicions to my father and the Gunwinggu artists. These *Balanda* agents became even more isolated.

"The bark painting scenes show the agents becoming desperate. The local artists and their consultant colleague weren't responding to the *Balandas'* 'good faith efforts.' An alternative was intimidation.

"The bark-painting scenes suggest the agents possessed limited imagination. They stole Gunwinggu bark paintings from Mary's Gallery.

"According to the bark painting images, this theft of Gunwinggu artists' own bark paintings reflected the *Balandas'* twisted logic. They incorrectly assumed local artists and their consultant colleague would trade the stolen Gunwinggu paintings in return for directing agents to the Arnhem Land Weather Station.

"This logic perhaps seemed less problematic, given the agents' desperate motivation: their espionage targeted Australians using the Weather Station as cover to intercept illegal C.I.A. drone transmissions. But the agents lacked local knowledge.

"The agents also bungled using a drone to stalk the 'subject,' who was in fact my father. Local Darwin and Arnhem Land people perceived the unusual mechanical device—not yet identified as a C.I.A. drone—to be an alien force.

"Gunwinggu artists and my father, by contrast, embodied local knowledge. Using it, they thwarted the *Balanda* agents' theft of Gunwinggu bark paintings. The agents never located Arnhem Land Weather Station, failing to halt Australian intercept of C.I.A. satellite-drone transmissions," I finish.

For my listeners Chief G, Donaldson, and Tone, I emphasize: "Gunwinggu artists and my father defeated the C.I.A.-A.C.M.E. agents. But I believe they *badly* wounded my father. In terms of customary law in the 'Ceremony Country,' the agents lost because they lacked the Elder permission required in Arnhem Land.

"In practical legal terms, this *Balanda* failure means Australian intercept of C.I.A. drone transmissions continued. And the fiasco disrupted shared military intelligence between America and close allies, particularly Australia.

"The bark painting has directed us, specifically *me*, to apply the customary law of the 'Ceremony Country,' in Arnhem Land, where Rainbow Serpent's Law demands justice.

"Thus, pursuing the Gunwinggu's red van, the faceless *Balanda* are the C.I.A.-A.C.M.E. agents. Having entered Arnhem Land without permission, they're destroyed for violating Kangaroo and Lighting Spirit's sacred sites. The van's driver led these uniformed evildoers into the spirits' destructive places.

"In the bark painting the evil Flying Fox image probably represents the stalking C.I.A. drone. Flying Fox could also reflect more general organizational evils, such as a cocaine cartel, and even the C.I.A. itself.

"The painting also possesses broader meaning reflecting symbolical logic. This interpretation is that the Darwin Incident justifies using counter force."

I explain, "The reasoning from symbolic to real power basically means: foreign mechanical (drone) and organizational (cocaine cartel/C.I.A.) evil demand action in Arnhem Land. This action requires Australians deploying satellite-drone technology.

"But deploying this technology should recognize customary law in Arnhem Land reflected by the Law Man's bark painting. The path to it began with his message stick calling me, Tom Berneray, to Arnhem Land.

"So, Malangi received the message stick and got the attention of his boss, Chief G, and Congresswoman Sarah Donaldson. And then, the focus for the American and Australia renewal of military intelligence-sharing became Arnhem Land.

"Like my father, I received permission to enter the sacred cave. The result is that I was given the Law Man's bark painting." I stop, let this sink in, and begin again.

"The bark painting reveals that after the Darwin Incident my wounded father escaped on a sailboat. One credible view is that the spirit images constitute evidence that technology will miss." I stop, instinctively looking at Malangi.

Malangi removes the bark painting from the desk and rolls it up.

I continue, "I've explained the message stick calling me to Arnhem Land. I've used cave and bark painting images in conjunction with Fun Games data. This enables the three leaders, my boss, Congresswoman Donaldson, Intelligence Chief G, and Deputy Director Malangi, to rebuild cooperation using new evidence that values local knowledge." I briefly pause and then add, "Chief G and Gwen Tone also seek significance in my father's disappearance. I believe my father is warning his family that we're threatened." I think, but don't say: like Alex and

Esperanza Quinn since Isabella's murder.

Tone takes over. "Chief G has recorded this report. He and I'll talk."

"Well done, Tom," says my boss from half a world away.

Malangi and I walk outside the station. Wild bush and broken ground surround us, encroaching on the airstrip. I can't see the ocean just yards away. A.C.M.E. agents had no chance of finding the Weather Station.

Parked behind one building is a battered red van. Malangi takes a cardboard tube from it. He tells me, "Keep the bark painting nearby at home. Study it. You'll learn more about why your father is important to Rainbow Serpent's justice." A cord around the tube holds the bone worn at the Law Man's throat. Malangi gives me the white bone to point for death or to withhold for justice.

I meet Tone at her plane. She flies me to Canberra. Briefly, I talk with Chief G. He praises my report, saying, "Malangi's leadership is central as Congresswoman Donaldson and I move ahead with reestablishing military intelligence-sharing. Also, Tom, please believe me, we did nothing to involve your father in the Darwin Incident."

Chief G grips me by my shoulders, "You should take the message of the bark painting to be valid. Regarding your father, events were entirely beyond our control until Malangi and Jim Berneray met in the spirit cave."

Chief G studies me, appealing: "Tom, I know all these happenings leave you and your family in a terrible position. Trust us. We'll work with Donaldson to keep harm at bay. Not only because she demands it. We owe it to you and your family."

I insist I don't follow what Chief G means about my family. He echoes Malangi, "You will understand." He assures me, "Sarah Donaldson waits for you. Until the next time, Tom," and Chief G salutes farewell.

V

The flight seems less long returning, via Los Angeles, to San Diego. Awakening from restless sleep, I wonder why C.I.A.-A.C.M.E. agents targeted my father. But Malangi's message from my father to me predominates: Ngaloyd needs me to defeat Flying Fox.

Finally, certain I'm fully conscious, I choke, remembering Isabella's murder.

"Sir, you seem to be having a nightmare." A flight attendant startles me fully awake. Recovering from grogginess, I see her face become a ghostly Isabella. I'm trembling.

My feeble assurances are unpersuasive. Flight attendants watch me until I leave the plane in L.A. It's an easy walk with my carryon bag through customs to my flight home.

Through a clear, star-filled, moonlit night I fly, approach, land in San Diego. City lights radiate peace, hiding war powers. First off the plane, I lead the dispersing passengers through the nearly empty international terminal. I'm almost home.

From the wide terminal, passengers leave security, narrowing into a down escalator. At the top, I halt briefly, so quickly that the man behind bumps into me before hurrying around.

Before she sees me, I see her. My mother wears worn brown hiking boots, baggy kaki overalls, a faded lumberjack shirt. I know her bright blue silk scarf is from Paris.

Cropped grey hair, tanned smooth face, piercing stare. I've seen her intensity like this since my childhood. I'm sure my mother came recently from Beagle Island.

Smiling, she strides towards me. Her small, compact body exudes energy. People instinctively let her pass. Clearly middle-aged, she still radiates an athlete's force.

One hand grips a large manila envelope. Mother's other hand caresses my face. She hugs me so tightly. I remember her strength pulling me toward her after we saved Isabella from the bramble in my childhood.

Before I speak, Mother presses the large manila envelope hard onto my chest. "It was left two days ago in your musician neighbor's box at Puck Place—he realized it was for the Berneray address. He called me. I came from Beagle Island immediately."

Suddenly, I feel far from home. I draw out a handwritten manuscript from the envelope. I don't read beyond the initial words: "*Old Mexico*, by Jim Berneray."

THREE

Old Mexico Manuscript

This manuscript appeared one night at my home in San Diego months after my father, Jim Berneray, disappeared. My father appeals to our family unity, formed in Old Mexico, in order to help us defy the cocaine cartel now, in January 2009. My family and I do not know how the manuscript was delivered or where it came from.

Tom Berneray

Jim Berneray's Narrative

This narrative will be sent to my family without revealing my location. My wife's brother, Alex Quinn with his wife Esperanza, also remain in hiding. Cocaine cartel operatives are pursuing us. I hope these memories will help reunite us soon.

The first three parts are rooted memories. Like the memory of my wife, Diana, delivering our first child, Ann, after forty-eight hours of labor. Like a Marine's memory of first combat. My memories explain the love that bonds the Bermudez, Quinn, and Berneray families. The same love our Revolution hero, Juan Bermudez, embodied in Old Mexico.

The fourth section exposes the violence Alex and Esperanza Quinn told me about. It reveals the cartel leaders, the Diaz family's criminal cocaine trade. This criminal business endangers the Bermudez, Quinn, and Berneray families.

I hope this narrative helps our families fight the cocaine cartel.

How I Met the Quinn and Bermudez Families

In 1970 the American border crossing at Calexico ended at the U.S. Immigration and Naturalization Service (I.N.S.) building. Carrying a battered leather suit case, I followed the other San Diego passengers leaving the Greyhound bus.

We stopped at the I.N.S. building entrance. Nearby was a grey United States Navy bus. Marine Military Police herded aboard civilian-dressed young men with very short hair.

More or less drunk, most of the youths followed the M.P.'s orders meekly. But the tallest young man reacted to a shove. He lowered his fist, club-like, onto the M.P.'s white helmet. M.P.s converged, swinging billy clubs. They forced the young man's face into the side of the bus, leaving a bloody smear.

"Coming back from their last night on the town before they go to Vietnam," a man before me said to no one in particular. "The military cops should be considerate." No one else in line spoke.

I nearly stumbled as the others in line pushed me through the I.N.S. building entrance. I joined the roped-off aisles, which stopped behind a yellow line.

Across the yellow line, a blank-faced I.N.S. official waited. Hands shaking, I presented my tourist visa. The official glanced at the folded white paper form, saying nothing. He motioned me through the open glass door at the back of the building.

Outside, the asphalt burned through my shoes. Sweat soaked my shirt. A short, slow walk brought me to a barbed wire-topped chain-link fence. On the other side was Mexico.

Through a gate another line formed heading into a small concrete building. Through wooden doors, a weary, clean-shaven officer sat at a battered, black wooden desk. His khaki uniform was pressed. Armed guards at loose attention flanked the table. Their uniforms were rumpled.

Before me was a young American with shoulder-length hair. "Seize him," the officer ordered. The guards gripped the youth's arms, holding him at involuntary attention.

The officer walked around the table. Eye-to-eye, he yanked the American's hair. Softly in English he said, "We do not want hippie draft dodgers coming to Mexico."

The American clutched a visa. He would not have a visa from the U.S. government if the draft was a problem. "I have a good lottery number," he protested. Without comment, the officer let go of the American's hair. The guards returned the American to the U.S. gate.

I handed over my visa. The officer's expression remained unchanged. "Mr. James Berneray, why do you wish to enter Mexico?" I said, "I have an invitation to visit the Bermudez family in Santa Maria. I have a letter here . . . ." The officer said, "I know the name Bermudez. The letter is unnecessary."

A guard took me to a gate that opened onto a fenced parking lot. I walked across it to the Mexican border-town's main street.

I was surprised that the officer knew the Bermudez name. I'd only learned it myself a week ago.

The rough treatment the longhaired American received also perplexed me. What he said about the draft was true. This year the American government, for the first time, used a lottery to choose draftees. The higher the number, the increased likelihood that a draftee would escape going to Vietnam.

Before the lottery, young men 18 to 26 were draft-able, unless you had a deferment. The Selective Service drafted every eligible person and many who were marginally ineligible. A TV commentator said the lottery ensured the Americans fighting the war now were twice unlucky.

Two years earlier, my older brother had volunteered for the Marine Corps rather than be drafted into the Army. On patrol in the Vietnam Central Highlands thirteen months later, he'd died.

My number was 777, so high it was virtually impossible that I'd be drafted. Because of my brother, I didn't feel lucky.

I walked across the parking lot to the traffic-jammed street. Taxi drivers yelled, waving me toward their cars. Ragged children, some bare foot, others wearing scuffed shoes without laces, pressed around me. Palms raised they yelled, "Money! Money! Money!"

Clutching the suitcase, I struggled into a taxi—green, white, and red stripped. "Take me to the bus station," I said breathlessly in English.

The driver said nothing, pushing into the traffic swarm. In the rear-view mirror, he grinned. Horns blared. Drivers shouted and tires screeched. Engines revved. Collisions were narrowly missed. The driver touched a St. Christopher's medal dangling by a red cord from the mirror. I clung to the door handle.

The brief ride seemed endless. We finally reached the bus station. Following directions in the letter, I bought a First-Class ticket on the Three-Star bus. I departed in twilight becoming blackness.

I had a seat to myself in the half-full bus. Most passengers ignored the "No Smoking" sign. Soon my head ached. Passengers around me spoke little, in whispers.

In the bus hard facts confronted anxious quiet. My brother, Doug, was dead. He died on patrol a few days before he was set to return home from Vietnam.

Our Mom and Dad died seven years before in a car wreck. Our father sold insurance. He protected his family with insurance covering the worst that might happen.

The worst did happen. My brother and I held title to a house, a car, and a modest income for the rest of our lives. "You are fortunate," Dad's partner said. We did not feel fortunate.

The way I learned about my brother's death was strange. I had come home after my last class at the junior college. I heard a hard rap on the door and I opened it. A Marine in full dress uniform, like a re-cruiting poster, stood at attention. Under his left arm was a folded American flag. He saluted crisply.

"Do I have the honor of addressing a near or distant relative of Cor-poral Douglas R. Berneray, United States Marine Corps, serial number 633-41-9506, operational designation, rifleman?"

"He is my brother." My mouth was dry.

"It is my sad duty to inform you that on Tuesday, the 6th of Febru-ary, 1969, at approximately 2300 hours, Corporal Berneray died in the line of duty, in the Ia Drang Valley, Central Highlands, Republic of Vi-etnam. Although a tragic loss to his family, the U.S. Marine Corps, and his country, he died honorably in the best tradition of the Corps."

The Marine thrust the flag toward me. "God bless the United States of America," he exclaimed.

He faced my vacant stare, confused. Silence between us. He saluted sharply, turned on his heel, marched robot-like down the walk. He climbed into a white Navy car. It pulled away, tires screeching.

Standing in the doorway I said, "What about me?"

In the bus window I saw my face. The darkness slowly receded before silver light. A spreading luminous desert landscape emerged. Shadow rocks, ridges, cactus.

A moonrise, first the rim, then a bright white disk.

Hard, the bus lurched. Again, again, and again, each time more smoothly. Shifting down the gears, the driver finally stopped the bus. The passengers were silent. No one moved.

The two-lane highway was white. In the road stood a man, western hat, saddle bags hung over left shoulder. One hand held a rifle. The other rested easy on a holstered pistol.

The driver left the bus. In the headlights' glow both men talked. Money passed. They entered the bus. Boots clomped down the aisle. The driver said something. I understood only "*gringo*" and "Bermudez." The man stopped. Hand on the pistol, he said, "At your service." The driver laughed.

The young stranger stopped at my seat. He placed the hat, saddle bags, and rifle in the overhead shelf. He sat beside me. Grinning, he said, "*Buenos noches.*" He then slept, gently snoring.

The bus moved into the night. I saw a pickup truck parked across the highway, hood up. A man leaned against the closed door, arms folded, waiting.

Bus passengers slept. Memory kept me awake, head no longer aching. The moon descended. Desert shadows shifted in starlight.

Doug's former platoon commander called me after the robot Marine delivered the flag. The phone voice was strong but unsure. "This is Alexander Quinn. I'm passing through San Diego, demobilization completed at M.C.R.D. Can I see you before I go home to Mexico?"

The robot Marine's mechanical notice of Doug's death had left me pained and angry. But Quinn's call made me remember. My brother's letters from Vietnam said his Lieutenant Quinn was trustworthy. "Sure, Lt. Quinn, we can meet." I gave him directions to our house at the end of 32nd Street in San Diego.

In twilight, a taxi left Quinn at our house. He wore a plaid shirt, blue jeans, and worn, well-polished cowboy boots. Quinn sat across from me in the small, sparsely-furnished living room. His brown hair was short. Quinn's face was deeply-tanned. His sad dark eyes held me.

Head titled forward, he gazed intently around the room and at me, searching. "That photograph on the mantel—is that you and your brother with your parents? You are young," he said.

Quinn's gaze embraced me. In the photo, Mom and Dad stand behind Doug and me, hands resting on our shoulders. It was our summer vacation on the north rim of the Grand Canyon. That same summer our parents died. California family services said my older brother could take care of me.

Gripping his knees, Quinn asked, "What are you going to do in the future?" I replied I didn't know what I would do.

My older brother had known what he wanted. He volunteered for the Marine Corps. Our father served in the Navy during World War II. In San Diego he met and married our mother. The G.I. Bill paid for his education. Our parents said we should give something back, too. Doug agreed.

I told Quinn how the robot Marine had delivered the flag. Quinn explained that Marines tried to visit the families of the dead. The growing number of Vietnam casualties required many, many visits. The practice became routine, unfeeling. "This happened to you. I'm sorry," Quinn said.

Quinn did not stop with apology. Voice controlled, he said, "In Vietnam I lost only one man under my command, your brother. Everyone liked and trusted him. I'm obligated to you, his surviving family. My duty to the Marine Corps has ended, I am returning to my wife's family in Mexico. I'm originally from San Francisco. My wife, Esperanza, is the granddaughter of Mexican Revolution hero, Juan Bermudez. Visit me and my family, and I'll explain more."

I told Quinn I could feel his guilt about Doug. But his professed obligation to me was alien.

I confessed surprise that an American from San Francisco who was also a Vietnam War veteran made his home in Mexico.

"Still," I said, "I understand what marriage does. My father stayed in San Diego after World War II because my mother wanted to be with her family here. My father was originally from Iowa."

Quinn said, "I'm happy you're opened-minded about Mexico. You'll understand even better if you meet my family there."

I accepted Alex Quinn's offer without thinking. My motivation clarified after Quinn's letter arrived. He explained the tourist visa procedure. He provided bus directions to Santa Maria. Regarding memory of my brother, action fended off sadness.

As the bus rolled through desert night, finally I slept. White morning light blurred my returning sight. The young man beside me grinned, pointing out the window.

The highway curved along the Sonora Desert coast and the blue-grey Gulf of California. A town clustered around a small harbor. My companion said, "Santa Maria."

The bus arrived at the station on the harbor boardwalk. The driver explained to a stationmaster why the bus was late. The young man collected his saddle bags and rifle. I followed him to the street.

Outside the bus station, Alex Quinn waited. Passengers dispersed. They stared at the woman standing beside him. She was tall, slender, with aristocratic bearing. I'd never seen a woman so hauntingly beautiful. Undoubtedly, this was Quinn's wife, Esperanza.

Walking away, passengers looked back at the woman. She drew the natural desires of others into herself. Yearning to be caressed, craving the thrill of Tango dancers' entwined bodies in the street during Mardi Gras. She knew herself completely. She seemed both young and in her prime.

Absolutely undistracted, she embraced my companion from the bus. "Sister, I bring him," he said to her in poor English. He then spoke rapidly in Spanish. I did not understand.

Grasping my hand, Quinn said, "Miguel didn't introduce himself, I see. He's my brother-in-law." I tried but failed not to be confused.

Awkwardly, we four stood in the street. The bus pulled away. Still desert and harbor air held us.

Quinn introduced, "Esperanza, my wife." She weighed me in a balance. "Welcome," she said.

From the bus station walked a short, slender, grey-haired man. Piercing hazel eyes like Esperanza's. Weathered brown face and hands. "Juan Bermudez, my grandfather-in-law," Quinn said.

The old-young brown face came close to mine. He had a rich scent of Spanish cologne. A firm grip. "Welcome, Quinn's friend." He turned to Esperanza, Quinn, and Miguel. They stood at attention.

In English, for my benefit, I felt, Juan Bermudez explained. "Miguel's truck broke down half way to Calexico. He figured out the right time to meet the bus carrying Quinn's friend. Miguel stopped it and paid the full fair back to Santa Maria, the stationmaster says. I've sent my man, Hernandez, to get the truck going."

I soon learned the obligation Quinn felt towards Esperanza, Juan, me, and Old Mexico.

Three Families Become Important to Me

I came to Mexico because Quinn cared about my brother's death in the Vietnam War. Quinn was in Mexico because he and Esperanza loved each other. Esperanza's grandfather, Juan Bermudez, bound us together.

For some months I lived with the Bermudez family in Santa Maria. Quinn, Esperanza, and Juan spoke English rarely, immersing me in Spanish. Thinking in Spanish enabled me to learn family stories.

My border crossing at Calexico and bus ride to Santa Maria added modestly to these stories. The Mexican officer acknowledged the status of the Bermudez name based only on my word. Miguel's stopping of the bus provided memorable melodrama. I learned bigger and more significant family stories.

During the Mexican Revolution, Juan Bermudez captained a steamer on the Gulf of California. He ran guns and supplies to General Alvaro Obregón fighting in Sonora. During a battle with government troops, Juan saved the life of his first mate, Li Sung.

After the Revolution Li went to San Francisco and worked for the Quinn family's shipping firm, run by Alex's father. He formed trade connections between Quinn Shipping and Chinese merchants in re-mote places like Torres Straits and Arnhem Land, North Australia. Many small Chinese traders combined into a high-volume business for Quinn Shipping.

Using these contacts, Li built an import-export business in San Francisco's Chinatown. Li became wealthy. He let young Alex Quinn sail the Quinn family to Santa Maria to meet Juan. Beholden to Juan for saving his life, and the Quinn family for business success, bringing them together fulfilled Li's soul.

Quinn met Esperanza during that first visit. Li's sloop yacht was anchored among Juan's fishing boats in the harbor. On the pier, teen-ager Quinn stood apart from his father, mother, and younger sister. They listened to Juan's stories. Esperanza walked onto the pier and joined the adults. Juan stopped talking.

Esperanza announced to all, "I've been selected for Mexico's Volleyball Team in the Pan American Games this summer!" All congratulated her. Quinn reckoned they were about the same age. He was a Berkeley undergraduate. He had sailed Li's sloop to Santa Maria. He doubted either would impress Esperanza.

Quinn multiplied reasons to visit Santa Maria. His undergraduate honors thesis was titled: "General Obregón and the Revolution in Sonora." His Spanish honors paper examined "Discourse on Revolution in Obregón's Sonora." Quinn's sources included interviews with Captain Juan Bermudez.

Juan told Esperanza that Quinn's motive for the research and interviews was to court her. Juan went along for Esperanza's sake until Juan's affection gradually embraced Quinn. The old hero proudly read his own name in Quinn's work. It was the next best thing to writing a book himself, Juan said.

The Bermudez family marveled at Quinn's fluent Spanish. Unlike most Americans, Quinn felt Spanish like a Mexican. His sensitivity for the language showed his love for Esperanza.

Hoping to impress Juan, Quinn sailed his own boat alone from San Francisco to Santa Maria. The young Juan had served on windjammers that worked the western coasts of North and South America before the Mexican Revolution.

Juan noticed Quinn's lone sailing. The sea was unforgiving of human error, Juan told Esperanza. Yet Quinn understood that the sea rewarded skillful maneuver, despite endless change.

Quinn entered a Graduate program at Berkeley. For two years he did further research on the Revolution in Sonora, including Juan and his compatriots. He usually stayed with the Bermudez family.

Slowly Quinn learned Mexican humor. Sailing alone from San Francisco through storms, he arrived late in Santa Maria. Knowing he was expected, Quinn went straight from his boat to the Bermudez home.

At the door he greeted Esperanza's mother, Alicia, courteously before asking for her daughter. Alicia looked at Quinn blankly. As if recollecting someone quite unfamiliar, she said, "Oh, her, she just left for Mexico City, I think." Red-faced and wide-eyed, Quinn said, "Oh, I did not know."

Quinn's helplessness made Alicia smile. Sympathetically, she said, "*Pobrecito*. Perhaps I am wrong. She might be here after all." As if she was his own mother, Alicia hugged Quinn. His bewilderment ceased only after Esperanza appeared. Alicia explained the friendly joke. Esperanza laughed and so did Quinn.

Juan understood that Esperanza's love for Quinn equaled her love for her family. As a seaman, ship captain, and revolutionary leader, Juan gained loyalty, and learned how to show others mutual respect. From Juan, Esperanza learned her own absolute self-worth grew stronger by winning the respect of others, including Quinn.

Juan's shared life experiences shaped Esperanza's faith in her self-worth. As a boy working on sailing ships, Juan began acquiring an instinct for right action. That instinct grew during Juan's bloody combat in the Revolution. He won deserved status as a hero in Sonora and beyond.

Love between Juan and Carmen, his betrothed, involved the danger of the Revolution. Carmen's family, like Juan, supported Obregón's leadership in Sonora. An opposition general occupied Santa Maria. Carmen's father was shot. The family was placed under house arrest.

Juan's rescue of Carmen was a family story that became legend in Santa Maria. Juan prepared an escape plan. An old Seri Indian woman smuggled the plan to Carmen. With the tide running high at night, Juan brought his boat into an isolated estuary where a Seri ally waited with horses.

Juan knew the enemy commander placed guards along the roads running north, south, and east from Santa Maria. Boats patrolled the harbor entrance to the Gulf.

The rugged country bordering the estuary ran along the unguarded Seri reservation. The enemy saw an impassible broken coast. The Seri knew the estuary as familiar home territory. On the Seri horse, Juan rode into Santa Maria. As the guards slept outside Carmen's house, Juan stole her away.

The rising sun found the lovers far out into the Gulf of California, heading hard for an isolated Baja cove. In a Seri chapel a Catholic priest married the couple.

Each time Esperanza heard Juan tell the rescue-and-escape story, Carmen was braver and more beautiful. Others might see only dangerous drama. In young Esperanza, Juan's story inspired emulation.

Once aboard Quinn's boat, her grandparents took Esperanza to visit the ruined Baja chapel. Amidst the rubble, Carmen told Juan, "Old man, it was a rough ride that night." Ever since Esperanza could remember, Carmen called her husband "old man." Carman died in her sleep, next to Juan.

Bermudez family stories taught that loyalty to others increased and rewarded self-respect. Against heavy odds, Obregón won victories in the Revolution that led to his election as President of Mexico. Obregón rewarded allies like Juan whose loyal struggle in Sonora enabled victory.

Juan's service in the Revolution brought the Bermudez family small rental properties along the estuary and a trading franchise on the Seri reservation. In Santa Maria, the family received other property, including ice houses that serviced both the community and Juan's fishing boats.

"The Revolution was just," Juan told Esperanza solemnly with a hint of a smile, "and profitable—a little."

Esperanza and Quinn knew that with gains from the Revolution Juan aided others. On properties in Santa Maria and the estuary, Juan allowed his renters to pay late. Widows of the veterans who served under Juan's command paid nothing. On the reservation, the Seri trusted Juan as a fair trader.

The men working on his fishing boats and women laboring in the ice houses received the best wages from Juan. Juan paid families compensation if either parent was injured or died in Juan's employ.

Courageous war service in the Revolution earned Juan profitable *public* respect. Paternalism conferred upon fellow veterans, seamen, renters, and workers fortified Juan's *self*-respect.

Juan possessed the serene and absolute confidence that some beneficent power had bestowed upon his imperfect self a condition of grace. It was a condition of obligation, demanding conduct consistent with that which was freely given.

Juan impressed upon Esperanza the obligations she inherited. Winners in the Revolution celebrated heroic women who as fighters and mothers aided victory. In town squares throughout northern Mexico stood statues commemorating the *Mujeres de Guerra* (women of war). These were the Sonora Revolution's heroes. Other South American nations celebrated such women.

In Santa Maria, the statue of the woman warrior held a child. Slung over the warrior-mother's shoulder was a rifle. The mixed-race Indian and white *mestiza* woman possessed fierce dignity. She reminded fellow citizens of their duty to keep the Revolution alive through brave, strong families.

The child Esperanza often walked with her grandfather Juan through Santa Maria's town square. Usually they stopped before the *Mujeres de Guerra* statue. Juan looked down into the glistening hazel eyes of his granddaughter's beautiful, upturned face.

"A man's name lives on if he has a son or writes a book," Juan told Esperanza. "But from the mother the child learns what the name is worth."

The Santa Maria community identified the Bermudez family name with Juan's courage, humility, and fine accomplishments. Esperanza's father, Juan's son, detracted from the family's good name.

Esperanza's father owned the only Cadillac in Santa Maria. He hired a man to keep the big blue car clean, waxed, shiny. He drove the car too fast around the town's streets and harbor. Esperanza's brother, Miguel, warned her, "People say Juan's son is not respectful of others like Juan is."

Esperanza understood why her father had lost respect. Her mother, Alicia, washed, starched, and ironed her husband's seven white dress shirts. The husband denounced some perceived irregularity in the ironing of the shirts. Taking the children, Miguel and Esperanza, he confronted Alicia.

The husband pulled each folded shirt from the drawer. His large hands shook and crumpled each shirt before his wife's face. He threw each shirt on the floor. He hissed, "Woman, must I pay to have it done right?" He stormed out of the room. Alicia, trembling, held back tears. Esperanza and Miguel cried.

Juan knew the shirt incident was consistent with his son's weakness. Unlike Juan, his son was tall and handsome, quick to laugh and easy to anger. He was too proud to strike anyone first, especially if they were weaker. Yet at the merest hint of perceived insult, he became combative.

Juan's son collected the rents from the Bermudez family properties in Santa Maria. He rolled the peso payments into a wad that bulged in his jean pocket. He usually wore a large revolver. Long into the night, he and his compatriots drank at a cantina. Inevitably, random gun fire resulted.

Neighbors resented such conduct. Juan's life and exploits elevated self-respect within the whole Santa Maria community. The son's bad conduct reminded the community of its human weaknesses.

Until one day. While haranguing Alicia about some perceived affront, Juan's son gripped the left side of his chest with both hands. "I . . . you . . . ," he gasped, collapsed, and died.

The body of Juan's son lay on one side, knees together, slightly bent. Big fingers crumpled the starched white shirt pocket over his heart. Alicia trembled in silence. The teenage Esperanza said, "He looks like a bad child who went to sleep praying for forgiveness."

The whole Santa Maria community attended the funeral of Juan's son. The priest administered the final sacrament, conferring God's grace. God's grace saved the soul of the son, husband, and father. God's grace protected the Bermudez family from evil. Juan's life confirmed that the priest spoke the truth.

Juan's son died not long before the Quinn family appeared in the harbor aboard Li's yacht schooner. During the next few years, young Quinn courted Esperanza. Instinctively, Quinn did the right things to earn Juan's admiration and the affection of Esperanza's mother, grandmother, and brother.

In Santa Maria of Old Mexico the custom was that the grandmother decided whether Esperanza would accept a marriage proposal. The family knew Quinn had convinced Carmen he was worthy of being Esperanza's husband.

All agreed, Quinn wanted to marry Esperanza. The only uncertainty was when he would ask her. Carmen died shortly after Quinn sailed her, Juan, and Esperanza to the Seri chapel in Baja. Esperanza's mother said Juan should decide whether her daughter could accept Quinn's expected proposal.

Juan's life showed decisions and actions that balanced good among the one and the many. After Carmen's death, the one he loved most was Esperanza. The Bermudez family liked and respected Quinn.

Juan said, "When Quinn proposes marriage, whether or not to accept is Esperanza's decision."

The Bermudez family welcomed Quinn. He accepted Juan's life lessons in Old Mexico. Quinn assuaged guilt over my brother's death in Vietnam by enabling me to learn those same lessons.

Esperanza accepted Quinn's marriage proposal. He joined the Bermudez family. I, Jim Berneray, also became part of Quinn and Bermudez family stories. How that happened involved certain events.

Diana and the Storm

My relationship to the Quinn and Bermudez families grew because of three events. First, I met Quinn's younger sister, Diana. The second was a storm. The third was our mysterious departure from Santa Maria. Juan shaped the meaning of all three.

After I'd lived some months with the Bermudez family in Santa Maria, Diana arrived. She was on a short break during her freshman year at U.C. Berkeley. "Jim Berneray," I introduced myself. "Diana Quinn," she smiled a smile I wouldn't forget, a forceful presence more memorable than youthful attractiveness.

Two days later we went sailing in the Gulf. Quinn, Esperanza, Diana, Juan, and I were aboard Quinn's boat. We anchored off an empty Baja beach.

The Gulf was windless, still. The sailboat's taut rigging silent. Esperanza and Diana plunged again and again into clear blue-green sea. Afterwards, on deck, they sunned themselves bikini-clad.

"We have been married nearly two years," Esperanza said to Quinn. Quinn replied, "I missed too much time because I served in Vietnam." He did not mention my brother Doug's death.

Diana exclaimed, "I demonstrate against the Vietnam War. As do my teammates on Berkeley's women's crew team. Marrying Esperanza and the acceptance of Revolutionary hero Juan Bermudez changed my brother's life for the better."

"Stop," Quinn told his sister. Behind dark glasses facing the sun, Diana ignored Quinn.

Juan leaned against the mast, scanning the Gulf. Esperanza lay quiet. Wet auburn hair pulled back, face absorbing sunlight. She watched Quinn. I looked at Juan for guidance.

"I'm not saying someone is necessarily bad because they go to Vietnam. Look at the draft lottery. Those people are twice unlucky. And sure, Quinn volunteered. He didn't have to. But he was under the worst personal pressure," Diana said.

"No more, Diana," Quinn hissed. Now he stood over his sister.

"What personal pressure?" Esperanza asked evenly, body still. Esperanza's question hung over the quiet sea. Juan turned away from the Gulf. He waited for an answer. I did the same. Standing between sister and wife, Quinn did not move.

Diana sat up. Removing the dark glasses, she spoke up into Quinn's face. "You, dear brother, brought Esperanza home to meet Dad and Mom to explain wedding plans in Santa Maria. You arrived on your boat at the San Francisco Marina. Dad met you both with open arms."

"What is your point Diana?" To Quinn's question Juan, Esperanza, and I nodded.

"Remember where you introduced Esperanza to Mother." Diana was not asking a question. Quinn was silent.

"Our family home is in Hillsborough. Esperanza first met our mother in Mom's study. One wall is glass. Alex and I often faced Mother at her desk, framed in the view." Diana's voice was flat. Esperanza said, "I remember the breathtaking view of San Francisco Bay."

Diana said, "Alex and I hardly ever noticed the view. Mother's desk was filled with photos. She was Santa Clara County Equestrian Champion. Years later, I won the same honor. At ten-years-old, Alex was San Francisco Bay Area All-Around Sailing champion."

For a moment Diana seemed happy. "Mother had a worn photo of Alex as a teenager and Father standing arm-in-arm, haggard, smiling aboard my brother's sailboat. It was a high school graduation present. Father and son have sailed from San Francisco to Honolulu in record time."

Diana looked towards the Baja beach, serious. "Middle-aged mother Susana Quinn graduated Magnum cum laude from Stanford University. Son Alexander Quinn graduated from Berkeley, receiving same and more honors."

Diana's voice went low. We almost did not hear her. "In a recent color photo, Mrs. Susana Quinn is solemn in a trim blue dress just reaching the knees. She holds a plaque. It reads: 'California Republican Woman of the Year.' She's shaking hands with grinning Governor Ronald Reagan."

Diana said finally, "Mom had photos taken at Alex and Esperanza's wedding in Santa Maria. Everyone is happy. But in no picture were

Mother and Esperanza alone together. She also didn't have a picture Dad took of me. Our Berkeley boat had won the freshman rowing title against Washington."

Esperanza was not satisfied. "I still don't understand, Diana. How does all you say answer my question? What 'special pressure' do you mean? Can you help your sister explain, Alex?"

Alex Quinn had not moved. He could speak only truth to Esperanza. His voice was hard. "Mother's room routine never changed. Child or adult, Diana or Alexander stood facing her behind that desk, those photos. She stared into her son's or daughter's face, imploring."

He stopped. No wind. Sea lapped boat and shore. The wordless emptiness was unbearable.

Surprise jolted us when Alex Quinn spoke again. "She always began, 'Alexander.' Dad said 'Alex' or 'Big Alex.' Finally, I told people, 'call me Quinn.' I didn't want to hear Mom's shaming voice in my name. Her next line was, 'You know we, your father and I, are so proud of you.' Then she'd get to the point."

Quinn spoke faster. "Mom did her room routine when I had to decide about volunteering for Vietnam. A year after the wedding, I was in Berkeley to defend my thesis. Mom called. Asked me to see her 'at home in Hillsborough.' I said 'Santa Maria is home, with Esperanza.' But I went to Hillsborough."

"Ling, the butler, showed me to Mother's study. I walked to her desk. Before I opened my mouth, she started in the usual way. Her point was, 'Alexander, you have a moral obligation to do your duty, to serve your country. Your father did that in World War II. You should do the same now in Vietnam.'"

Quinn's words rushed on. "Anger choked me. I walked out. I drove to my boat. Dad was waiting. He'd come from Quinn Shipping headquarters on Union Square. Black suit and tie, like a Scottish undertaker. Ling had called him. They both knew I felt safe running away on my boat."

Quinn came to an end. "We could never resist Dad's Scottish accent. He came to the U.S. as a youth, but never lost his burr. He said, 'Alex, I love you and your Mother. The decision to volunteer for war is yours alone. You'll probably ask Esperanza, though.' That was all. He said nothing about his Pacific service in the Navy with the Marines during World War II."

Red-faced, Diana stood, screaming at Quinn, "If it wasn't Mother, *why did you volunteer*? The war is so *wrong*! You had a student deferment! You were married to a Mexican and living in Mexico!"

His sister's rage left Alex Quinn speechless. The boat was still, the sea quiet. There was no wind. Juan observed the scene in silence.

Finally, Juan spoke. "Before he talked with his wife about leaving for war, Quinn asked me," Juan said. "Quinn's father told his son to decide for himself. But he recognized Quinn was not alone. I agreed. Quinn came to me because of Esperanza."

Juan's formal English words poured over us. "For leaders war is politics. Maybe some, like Obregón, mixed politics with a belief the cause is right. Take property from the rich. Give it to people like the Bermudez family. Surely that was right, ha, ha, ha."

Juan looked at the deck. "Some think it is good to fight and die for glory. This was not good for me and most of my comrades. There was a kind of love and fear."

Esperanza exclaimed, "Afraid! Everyone says you were never afraid Grandfather!"

"Yes," Juan said. "But those fighting with us knew courage or fear worked together. Finally, you fight for each other. Truly, love mixed with a fear you'll let down comrades. Remember saving Mr. Li, Esperanza? I did what I did for him. He would have done the same for me. It is true."

Quinn told his sister, "Politics didn't control me. Whether communist or not, most Vietnamese oppose the U.S. But think how you and I were raised. Always, *we must do right*. Where is 'right' in Vietnam, Diana? Not in politics. I see right among Marines fighting for each other. I believe in that."

I interrupted Quinn. "What about my brother, Doug? Among men under your command, he alone died."

Quinn answered me slowly. "A Marine platoon is individuals making a whole. Each Marine learns what to expect from the others. Doug was the rare individual platoons pray for. He sensed impending danger. Because of that he always volunteered to walk point. I was not far behind him."

Juan exclaimed, "Dark clouds!"

But Quinn held our attention. "Doug saved the platoon many times. He felt danger before it happened. We always reacted in time, until Doug's last patrol. He was set to rotate back to the States. The attack surprised him like the rest of us. He died. Three others were wounded, including me."

Sudden forceful wind silenced Quinn. Rolling blackness blotted out sun. Splat-splat-splat on deck, turned into hard, pounding rain. Running to the boat's helm, Juan yelled, "*Chubasco!*"

Quinn scrambled up mast to raise sail. From the deck Esperanza pulled on a shirt. "Cover your body best you can," she exclaimed, pushing a sweatshirt towards Diana. Esperanza followed Quinn.

Juan guided the helm with skill. "Too near shore, gain open water." Uproar muffled his cry.

Diana and I slammed onto the deck. Shrieking, Diana swept towards helm. I gripped a life preserver.

Waves ascended, smashed over me. Terrified, my scream choked. Quinn's and Esperanza's grasp on sail slipped, lost again, again, again.

Atop the mast, lightning flamed into a blue-violet ball. The mast-top glowed lantern-like, shaken wildly in the wind. Caught in the rigging, Quinn and Esperanza were stunned.

Light sparks filled the waves washing over me. My scream escaped. I gulped, gulped, and gulped air. I crawled toward the mast. Hand-over-hand, I gripped the latch, hatchway, rigging. I hugged the mast.

Wind-whipped, a free sail-line slashed my head. Blood blinded me. My back pressed the mast. My hands searched for, lost, found the darting line. Rain restored blurred vision. I twisted the line into a cleat.

Hand and foot, one at a time up the rope ladder twisting in wind I climbed. I reached Quinn tangled in yardarm lines. "Esperanza," Quinn gasped.

The mast rolled sharply. I thrust into it. On the opposite yardarm Esperanza's body lay limp in the wind-ripped rigging. My chest burned for breadth. My strength drained, I couldn't reach her. I clung to the mast.

Weakness consumed me. Thoughts of Doug flashed. Fingers, hands, legs slipped.

Quiet engulfed me. The storm roar became distant. Above me rain sheets parted around whiteness. Whiteness formed into arched wings. An enormous white bird hovered.

Quinn shook me. "Follow," he bellowed. Quinn shimmied along the yardarm towards Esperanza.

Wind and rain dissolved the quiet. The bird's wings straightened from its huge body into a white cross. It disappeared in the torrent.

My arms and legs loosened around the mast. I shifted my weight on to the yardarm. The storm didn't stop me. I reached Quinn. His legs gripped the rigging, his arms embracing Esperanza.

"Hold her," Quinn commanded. His hands slide untangling lines from her legs and arms.

In starts and stops, we moved her to the mast. "Hold her," Quinn screamed again. Fumbling, he removed his shirt. He tied it around Esperanza and the mast. Through wind and rain he held on to her.

I twisted my arms and legs into the ropes. Amid the storm, I glimpsed the rocking deck. Juan and now Diana guided the helm. Juan looked up at Quinn, Esperanza, and me. Juan crossed himself.

I'm unsure how long the *chubasco* battered us. Later Juan said it arose suddenly, but soon fiercely blew out. The Gulf of California's distinctive wind-sea pressure currents periodically unleashed it. Locally, it was quite destructive. From miles away it looked like any thunderstorm.

The *chubasco* ending left an eerie sunset. Broken, flaming orange clouds turned into dark spider legs. In the dwindling light Quinn, Esperanza and I slowly climbed down. Esperanza revived in the storm.

In the twilight we assembled on deck. Only Juan was without rope burns, cuts, and bruises on head, arms, and legs. "Next time I face *chubasco* I won't wear a bikini. Too much bare skin to hurt," Diana sighed. She thanked Esperanza for the sweatshirt.

Juan said, "Miss Quinn learned well at the helm." Diana replied, "It was kind of like rowing."

The night sea was smooth. Clouds hid stars. Near shore the boat rested at anchor. In the cabin Quinn found first aid, food, water, a lantern. In flickering light, we assessed ourselves.

Juan spoke quietly. "Quinn, Esperanza, and Jim got the sail working in time. The crashing wind, rain, and sea did not stop you. Storm wind blew us into deeper water off shore."

We addressed our struggles.

Juan and Quinn called the glowing masthead light "St. Elmo's fire." It arouses sailors' superstitions. Usually, it is a good rather than a bad omen. Juan and Quinn had seen it before. For them, the "fire boded well." I knew the light sparked my escape from fear.

Juan and Quinn agreed the white bird was an albatross. Quinn recalled seeing one. "Sailing with my Dad from San Francisco to Honolulu, the bird appeared. It stayed with us night and day. Dad saluted it each morning. The trip was hard, invigorating. The bird left when we sighted Diamond Head."

Juan first saw the white bird in a storm off Terra del Fuego. He was a very young sailor ordered into the highest rigging. Terror had seized him. From the sleeting rain the bird had emerged untroubled over him. Juan found his strength. He did his job. The bird disappeared into the storm.

Diana saw it ghostly through the rain. "I remembered the *Rime of the Ancient Mariner* from English class. This was real life. When the bird appeared my brother and Jim were finally able to help Esperanza."

Quinn and I agreed Diana was right. The bird lifted the daze from Alex Quinn and returned my strength.

Esperanza spoke with deliberation. "After St. Elmo's fire struck, I was barely conscious. Each of you saw this white bird. For me it was hardly an aberration. Quinn and Jim moved me. I didn't feel them doing it. I regained consciousness, Quinn's arms around me. I felt safe in the storm."

Juan said he'd never before seen an albatross in the Gulf. An old Seri shaman woman told him her mother's mother did see one. The Seri people knew it was a spirit. The Spaniards tried to kill it, but the bird escaped. It returned to the distant Pacific. The Seri killed the Spaniards. Ravens then ate the Spaniards' flesh.

Juan's curious words left us content with our conduct in the storm. Like the Seri we believed in each other. We fell asleep on deck.

A shout in the cloudless dawn and steady breeze awakened us. Juan's man, Hernandez, aboard a fishing boat. He had found us. He'd been unable to raise Juan on the radio, so he'd begun searching the Gulf. He stayed far from the *chubasco*. In the distance he saw St. Elmo's fire. He hoped it was a good omen.

Hernandez had fixed the location of St. Elmo's fire. From it, he set course along the Baja coast. He watched the storm die by sunset. Running at night, he sighted the lantern. He anchored and waited.

When he met Juan in the morning, Hernandez delivered a message. A foreign vessel had arrived in Santa Maria. The owner wanted to see Juan.

Juan said to prepare the boat to sail home. Esperanza guided Diana and me. We three worked steadily. Beyond our hearing at the stern Juan, Quinn, and Hernandez talked. Finally Hernandez returned to the fishing boat. We three joined Quinn and Juan.

Quinn said, "The stranger waiting in Santa Maria could cause problems for us. Juan says the strangers are members of the Diaz family who are identified with the cocaine cartel. They like to attack Americans. This could be a problem for Diana and you, Jim. They know I'm Juan's grandson-in-law. That qualifies me to be Mexican now. So I'm okay."

Quinn then ordered his sister and me: "When we reach Santa Maria, collect your things, get some food. Juan's man, Hernandez, will run you to Guaymas. There you can choose to bus or fly home. I'll explain later."

Without speaking, Esperanza followed Quinn to set the sail. Juan took the helm. "If the storm wasn't enough, we'll know each other even better now," Diana said to me. Again, she was right.

The breeze took us into the Gulf. At first Hernandez stayed with the sailboat. Soon he dropped behind. Quinn took over the helm, heading true north. His boat cut a smooth wake to Santa Maria.

No one spoke. With the common instinct of sailors, Juan, Quinn, and Esperanza kept the boat flying. Diana and I watched the Baja recede. The Sonora coast grew nearer.

In the cloudless late afternoon, we swept into Santa Maria harbor. Among Juan's fishing boats and other vessels towered a big motor yacht. Juan, Quinn, and Esperanza ignored it. Diana and I did too.

We left Quinn's boat at the dock. Walking fast, Juan led us to the Bermudez home. Diana easily collected the things she'd brought for a short stay. I had fewer belongings. Still, departure was harder for me. Over the months, my room had become a home where I comprehended all I was learning about life, love, strength, courage.

Esperanza and Quinn hugged Diana. "I'll explain later. Give Mom and Dad my love," Quinn said.

"I have a huge story to tell Mom and Dad, and another one still forming, awaiting telling," Diana told her brother, Alex Quinn. Quinn and Esperanza embraced me. Juan shook my hand. He said, "Well done Jim Berneray."

Hernandez appeared with a bag of food. We all hurried back to the harbor. Diana and I boarded Hernandez's fishing boat. No one waved farewell. Hernandez wheeled away from the dock toward the harbor mouth. We passed and again ignored the motor yacht. I learned its story much later.

Hernandez took us to Guaymas. From there we went by bus to San Diego. Diana then flew to San Francisco. I soon followed her. We grew close at Berkeley. I, like Alex, made the hard decision to go to Vietnam with the Marines. Later we learned what the appearance of the motor yacht meant to our families. I now record it in the following section.

Esperanza and Isabella

Quinn and Esperanza told me about the following violent incidents long afterwards. The first incidents involved the motor yacht's arrival in Santa Maria. Other events concerned Isabella's murder decades later. The violence ended Juan's Old Mexico. It endangered the Berneray and Quinn-Bermudez families.

The story of the motor yacht started simply. The yacht's owner was Manuel Diaz. His father was a Santa Maria merchant. On the winning side in the Revolution, the father was wealthy. With his father's blessing, Manuel Diaz became a successful businessman far away in Mazatlan.

Manuel Diaz returned to Santa Maria with a new business plan. His father's wealth could not buy community support for it. The one man with sufficient local trust was Juan Bermudez.

Manuel came to Santa Maria seeking the support of Captain Bermudez. Manuel brought with him his three sons. The Diaz family was making an appeal to the Bermudez family.

Manuel met Juan in the church, a neutral site. Manuel's two older sons remained at his father's house while the youngest son wandered about Santa Maria. Esperanza was at home. Quinn and Miguel worked on storm damage done to Quinn's boat. Neither family was prepared for what happened.

One church entrance was on a side wall. During the Revolution, people were shot at this "wall of shame." Juan used that door. Juan did not know Manuel Diaz's full purpose. Quiet in the old church encouraged Juan to listen to Manuel.

Manuel Diaz explained: Manuel and his sons observed the sailboat's passage into Santa Maria's harbor. They hoped the boat's storm damage was small. The yacht had arrived from Mazatlan two days before without incident.

Manuel then stated what he wanted from Juan. The Bermudez and Diaz families triumphed in the Revolution. Manuel now pursued business opportunities that would aid each family's next generation.

But Manuel Diaz's business plan was sensitive. The Vietnam War increased American demand for illegal drugs, such as cocaine. Some U.S. drug pushers justified illegal consumption by employing anti-government rhetoric. Some returning American troops used drugs to hide from public condemnation of their wartime service.

Remarkably, U.S. intelligence agencies secretly funded the marketing of illegal drugs like cocaine in America. The clandestine U.S. operations served powerful people in anti-communist regimes, including Mexico. These regimes, in turn, supported the U.S.'s Vietnam War efforts despite aggressive anti-Americanism.

Manuel Diaz's business plan facilitated transit of illegal drugs. From secure Mexican land and seaports, drugs such as cocaine reached the border and crossed into the U.S. Manuel identified Santa Maria as an ideal transit point. It had a good but underused harbor. His family's bank could provide safe financial services.

Juan did not reply. Manuel said more. He had learned some of the business from his two older sons. One son earned a business degree, the other a law degree, both from American universities. An unidentified "big man" in the Mazatlan business community explained U.S. intelligence agencies' clandestine drug operations.

Juan finally spoke. "What about your third son?" Manuel turned cautious. "In my business, sometimes 'persuasion' is necessary. He is a strong boy. He can be very persuasive."

Juan asked where such "persuasion" stopped. Did it reach everyone in Santa Maria, including the Bermudez family? Juan insinuated Manuel's motives were nefarious. The illegal drug economy undermined the community's shared self-sufficiency, which Juan's paternalism supported in Santa Maria.

Manuel professed to be hurt. He said ordinary Mexicans had simple wants. His business plan satisfied those needs with good-wage jobs transporting high-value products that earned American dollars.

He continued. "Mexicans are hardworking and honorable. But they lack forward-looking leaders. The Bermudez and Diaz families could provide such leadership. Captain Bermudez's American grandson-in-law is connected to U.S. shipping. Manuel's two sons know American law and business."

Manuel concluded, "Americans use power and wealth to satisfy their appetites. My business plan turns Americans' bad habits to Mexicans' advantage."

Juan said, "Americans attack any legal or illegal competition they cannot dominate. They are a dangerous enemy—wealthy, powerful, and self-righteous. Some, like my grandson-in-law, believe united effort might achieve America's high ideals, despite corruption in the Vietnam War."

Neither Juan nor Manuel finished speaking. The priest's rapid steps and Hernandez's cry filled the church, "Esperanza has been attacked at home!" Hernandez then sprinted to Miguel, Quinn, and the police.

Juan led the running men. They found Juan's wife, Alicia, seated at the kitchen table crying. Esperanza embraced her mother. On the table lay her father's revolver. From the kitchen, out the backdoor, went a line of blood. Breathing hard, Quinn, Miguel, and the Police Captain arrived. They avoided the blood.

Juan comforted Alicia. Esperanza stepped apart from them all, even Quinn.

"I was pounding beef for dinner with the mallet," Esperanza said flatly. "Then dung entered the backdoor. I smelled it. I turned. It filled the door way: drunk—broken yellow teeth—twisted lip."

"Twisted lip? It was my son," Manuel exclaimed on his knees, beseeching the priest. "He blasphemed Captain Bermudez's married granddaughter. He saw her from our yacht when the Captain entered the harbor yesterday. His brothers and I condemned his evil. I slapped his face, hard."

Manuel's trembling words and self did not exist for Esperanza. She stood steady.

Esperanza's mother sobbed. "In my room, I heard the vile words. '*Woman, is there bread of any kind?*' A sharp crack and a weight dropped onto the floor. Esperanza ran into my room. She took my husband's gun from the drawer. She ran out. I went after her into the kitchen. There was only blood."

The Police Captain spoke solemnly. "It is invasion of a married woman at home. The coarse use of 'bread,' means women's genitalia. Under the circumstances it is attempted rape of Captain Bermudez's granddaughter. In Mexico of the Revolution, the penalty is death."

"I missed with the mallet," Esperanza said. "I aimed for the mouth, but I hit between the eyes. I was slow getting the gun. When Mother and I got here, blood was on the floor. We smelled dung and drink."

We understood that Manuel's son of the twisted lip had attempted to rape Esperanza. Badly wounded, he left behind a trail of blood, escaping in his grandfather's truck. The Police Captain organized pursuit. With Juan's man, Hernandez, Miguel stayed behind with his mother and sister.

The Police Captain sent Quinn and Juan, as the federal agent, to the Seri Reservation. The Reservation was federal territory, which meant it was under the leadership of the Seri's federal agent, Juan. Even the police were subordinate to Juan on the Reservation. Two highways leaving Santa Maria paralleled the Reservation. The broken dirt road into the Reservation was deceptive; from the highways, entering the Reservation was easy. The problem was getting out.

Inside the Reservation, Juan and Quinn met a Seri rider. He said a wildly driven truck had entered the labyrinth of canyons. The bleeding driver abandoned the truck. He was hysterical and quickly lost.

Quinn asked the Seri, "Will it take long to find the driver?"

The Seri's reply was curious. He studied the furrowed canyon walls and ravines. His hand raised, palm upward. Juan and Quinn looked into the white-blue sky. In the middle distance, a raven appeared. Others joined it, circling. Finally, the Seri answered, "Long enough."

They searched the canyons many hours, finding nothing. The ravens remained in the distance. At sunset, Juan and Quinn returned to Santa Maria. The Seri promised their search would bear fruit.

Two mornings later a Bermudez cousin living near the Seri reservation phoned Juan. An old Seri woman was seen walking through the dessert toward Santa Maria, a mule following obediently with an unusual load.

On horseback near town Quinn and Miguel identified the odd couple. The woman's bare feet and shins were almost black. Bright orange, red, green, and blue squares covered her thick cotton dress. Grey hair hung loosely around her weathered brown face. The white mule carried a strange contraption.

The Seri and her mule ignored Quinn and Miguel. The four went along the harbor toward the police station. Miguel left to tell Juan. Hernandez informed others. Quinn stayed behind.

Step-by-step the strangers and Quinn reached the police station. From it rushed Juan, Esperanza, Miguel, the Police Captain, the priest, Manuel Diaz, his two sons. A crowd gathered. Some said the Seri was a witch. Others called her a medicine woman. Juan greeted her as a friend.

Boats floated gently in the windless harbor. Everyone heard the Seri speak in her own language to Juan. He translated. "An evil presence polluted our ancestor spirits' resting place. I serve these spirits. Like my mother's mother, I called ravens to cleanse the evil. I return it to your people."

A wooden frame like a saddle was strapped to mule. It held a large basket. When the mule stopped, pulling on the straps laced into the basket would move what was inside it.

The Seri pulled the straps, shifting the basket contents to one side. She removed a cover over a hole in the same place. From the hole a hemp bag fell to the ground. The lumpy bag did not move.

She rearranged the basket within the frame the mule carried. Juan signaled to let them pass. The crowd parted. The old Seri woman and her mule returned the way they had come.

Policemen cut open the hemp bag. The ravens the Seri women had called had left a mutilated, bloated body. The stench was strong. On swollen fingers, Manuel identified his son's rings. The two brothers recognized a gold chain around the thickened neck. No longer were there eyes to see.

The ravens left the broken bone and bloodied flesh between the eye sockets untouched. The Police Captain asked Esperanza if her mallet had struck that place. It did, she acknowledged.

"The ravens' inattention to that open wound was passing strange," the Police Captain said. The priest observed, "We know God's ways often are subtle." Manuel believed it was "a sign. God had turned against the Diaz family." People in the crowd declared it showed that "God protected Juan's family."

The crowd dispersed. The Priest and Police Captain went about their business. Manuel ordered crew members to take his son's body aboard the yacht. "We leave for Mazatlan within the hour."

The Diaz son, trained as a businessman, told Juan, "Our brother made a costly mistake. People in Santa Maria will be slow in forgetting. Implementation of our plan will be delayed. But our business plan is inevitable given the Americans' drug appetites. We will meet another day, Captain Bermudez."

The brutal death of the Diaz son occurred in 1970. Twenty years later, the other Diaz son's prediction partly came true. During the 1980s, mechanization squeezed older fishing practices. Juan Bermudez sold his fishing boats. The icehouses closed. His former employees found work in warehouses and docks the Diaz bank built. Juan saw but did not speak with Diaz family members.

The Diaz bank used lawful transportation and financial contracts to hide illegal drug transshipments. The illegal cocaine business was very profitable. Illegal earnings funded high wages in *legal* businesses. Higher wages than Juan had paid in Santa Maria. But unlike Juan, the illegal Diaz enterprise addressed problems with violence.

The Diaz illegal operations belonged to the drug cartel. It was the primary supplier for American drug addiction by the end of the 1980s. The cartel diversified from marijuana into heroin and cocaine. It developed new markets in Europe and the Pacific Rim. And the cartel often used deadly violence.

The Diaz business success left the Bermudez family dependent on elderly renters. Quinn and Esperanza had a child, Isabella. The Quinns did not want to burden the Bermudez family, so Alex and Esperanza took Isabella to live in San Francisco. Alex Quinn became his family's manager of the Quinn Shipping trade among Chinese traders in Arnhem Land, northern Australia, where they had traded for many years.

Diana and I, Jim Berneray, married in 1974. Our children, Ann and Tom, were born after the end of the Vietnam War. I finished my Ph.D. at Berkeley and ran a consulting business that worked with Alex Quinn and Quinn Shipping in remote Arnhem Land.

Diana had aided anti-Vietnam War Marine Corps veterans like me. When we saved Tom and Isabella on Beagle Island in 1988, Diana was continuing to help me with P.T.S.D. therapy. She still does.

The Berneray family moved to San Diego. The Quinns generously gave us our home at Puck Place. Our children Ann and Tom grew up knowing the Quinn family in San Francisco and Bermudez family in

Santa Maria. After graduating from Harvard in 1998, Tom became engaged to Isabella.

The Quinn and Berneray children knew their great grandfather, Juan Bermudez. Juan died in his sleep in 1991. At his funeral in Santa Maria both families bid Juan farewell.

At the funeral, the President of Mexico commemorated a "hero of the Revolution." He said Juan's passing signaled an "end to Old Mexico."

The Diaz brothers attended the funeral. A newspaper quoted the lawyer Diaz: "Captain Bermudez lived to see a new prosperous business order in Santa Maria and Mexico." Manuel Diaz had died years earlier in Mazatlan. After his son's shameful death, Manuel never returned to Santa Maria.

The new business order included attacks targeting critics of the illegal cocaine trade. In Santa Maria, an effective critic was Miguel Bermudez. Older residents listened to Miguel because he was Juan's grandson. Miguel demanded a public investigation of the Diaz bank's business.

Miguel hoped to expose drug traders' involvement with the Diaz bank's warehouses and wharfs. Sometimes Esperanza, Alex Quinn, and Isabella joined Miguel's protests. Alex Quinn would sail the family from San Francisco to Santa Maria. Berneray family members, especially Tom, sometimes participated too.

Miguel's agitation partially succeeded, but at a tragic cost: the murder of Miguel and his niece, Isabella. Mexico's federal government had begun investigating the Diaz bank. Isabella and her parents had arrived in Santa Maria to support Miguel.

After visiting Bermudez cousins living near the Seri Reservation, Miguel and Isabella were attacked and killed on their return through the desert to Santa Maria. Corrupt police reported the perpetrators were unidentified "bandits." They were never found.

Following Isabella and Miguel's murder Quinn and Esperanza fled Santa Maria. They sailed into the night, destination unknown.

At the time of the murders, I was in Australia. Diana was on Beagle Island off Vancouver Island, British Columbia. Our daughter, Ann, was in Boston running a consultancy after graduating from law school.

Tom, shocked and bereft, left San Diego immediately and arrived in Santa Maria alone to face Isabella's death. No one in our families predicted how much her murder would bring Tom's love and courage to the front.

Tom learned how dangerous Santa Maria was, and continues to be, for the Bermudez, Quinn, and Berneray families. The priest had said if "Mr. Thomas Berneray" had been with Isabella he, too, "would have died." The priest did not explain Quinn and Esperanza's escape. He said the Diaz bank investigation ended without result after Miguel's murder.

Last month, in December 2008, Alex Quinn gave me the information to write this narrative with the revelation that the attempted rape of Esperanza, her assailant's death, Miguel and Isabella's murders, and afterwards, her parents' disappearance at sea, are all linked. The common factor is the Diaz family and its role in the illegal drug trade.

Quinn gave me direct proof of Diaz family involvement in Isabella and Miguel's murders. Shortly before Quinn and Esperanza escaped at sea, an old Seri woman visited them. Her mother was Juan's shaman friend. Hidden in the desert, she saw that the killers wore the security guard uniforms of Diaz Security.

Conclusion

Once the Berneray family understands these revelations, we can better fight the cocaine cartel endangering the Quinn-Bermudez families. Writing this also helps me confront personal demons, unleashed again because of recurring P.T.S.D.

We know when Juan Bermudez died and Isabella was murdered. I disappeared in Arnhem Land, North Australia, in late 2008, amidst another deadly peril.

Jim Berneray, narrative written in hiding,
on the run, New Year's Day 2009

FOUR

———————————•———————————

San Diego

I'm Ann Berneray. After my brother Tom returned from Arnhem Land, Sarah Donaldson hired me for my expertise with satellite-drone technology. I'm testing this combined technology so that it can be transferred to Australian military intelligence.

Tom and I serve Representative Donaldson's intelligence committee. Since Tom's Arnhem Land mission, the Donaldson committee expects that military intelligence-sharing should reflect local knowledge. My consulting firm adapts satellite-drone technology to environments as divergent as San Diego and Arnhem Land.

Sarah Donaldson trusts Tom and me. Sarah and our mother, Diana, share deep friendship and an obscure past. Sarah thus promotes Tom's and my welfare. Yet Rep. Donaldson's intelligence committee work triggers danger.

Father expands on these family bonds in his "Old Mexico" manuscript. It mysteriously appeared at our Puck Place home when Tom returned from Arnhem Land. Father is still absent. Yet his words have filled a void, inspiring our family's solidarity. I am writing my own account to help my father's P.T.S.D. therapy—whenever he returns.

Isabella's murder, reported in Father's manuscript, only reinforced Tom's natural fearlessness. Tom wants justice. We're uncertain how to deal with Albert Jennings.

I

Once Tom came home from Arnhem Land, I left for San Diego from Boston. Earlier, Mother already had come to San Diego from Beagle Island. Family and professional obligations converged around Tom.

Our old family home is in San Diego, near Balboa Park, Puck Place. I've not been there for some years. But Tom, working at Rep. Donaldson's main district office, lives here now.

Alone, I enter our small living room. The bark painting Tom brought from Arnhem Land dominates. I agree with Tom's assessment: the bark painting is beautiful.

Otherwise, the bungalow has changed little. The bookcases and the desk seem as used as they did during my brother's and my earliest school days. The kitchen is neat from small use.

Tom shaves each morning beside a family photo taken at a San Diego marina just after his Harvard graduation in 1998. He begins every day in that picture, arm-in-arm with Isabella. Other photos have frozen the happy couple together. Or Isabella alone, teasing Tom to follow. My mind struggles with knowing that Isabella was murdered in 2003.

When he got back from Arnhem Land, Tom had asked me about using satellite-drone technology to track Mexican cocaine cartels. His questions were unusual. Tom has avoided mentioning Mexico ever since Isabella's death.

Our reddish cedar bungalow is one of several residences located on a cul-de-sac overlooking Balboa Park's Marston Canyon. The small neighborhood is away from busy streets. Mom and Dad received the bungalow as a wedding present from Mom's parents.

Tom startled me by coming through the backdoor. In coat and tie, he's bicycled from Congresswoman Donaldson's office. Cross-training enhances his long distance-running. Tom's body is strong. But Isabella's murder haunts his mind.

"So good to see you, Ann," I love my brother's smile as he embraces me. "Sarah Donaldson said you'd been experimenting in San Diego with satellite-drone technology. Mother has joined us for moral support. Three of us are together again."

Tom's excitement becomes more animated, pointing. "Look at the bark painting, Ann. It can guide us to Father. He must be somewhere in Arnhem Land. I know you remember our trip there together as a family when we were kids."

I agree, "It's an amazing painting. Yes, let's talk about it. But what's the connection to Mexican cocaine cartels you've asked me about?"

"Please Ann, I know what needs doing. The bark painting helps us understand why Dad disappeared in Darwin. He briefly reappeared on the Arnhem Land coast less than a year ago, leaving a strange message for me. If I translate certain Dreamtime images, I believe we can find him. Coincidentally, a cocaine cartel may be involved."

Tom's single-mindedness had always heightened our family's love for him after childhood incidents on Beagle Island like Isabella's rescue from the bramble. Other incidents we rarely mentioned.

Captured by memories, I try indirect-caring: "Tom, take it easy with your tired sister after her long trip. I assume Mom will be here soon. You can take us to dinner."

"Sure Ann. You're right about Mom. We'll eat at my favorite Hillcrest café." Tom's mind usually runs ahead.

I ready myself. Tom works on a laptop. Since childhood, Tom has combined action with unusual prescience. His leadership in rescuing Isabella is our happy family memory. Other incidents were family mysteries.

Mother opens the front door. About a month ago, Mother met Tom at the San Diego airport when he returned from Arnhem Land. She had given Tom Father's "Old Mexico" manuscript. She visited Sarah Donaldson, and then went back to Beagle Island.

After being away for a short time, she's back in San Diego again. I envy her ease of travel.

As if she's read my mind, Mother says, "Ann, remember the Commander at Beagle Island Rescue Station, my old friend? He introduced you to Kara. He let me ride on the Vancouver mail plane! Then I caught a direct commercial flight to San Diego."

Not yet speaking to Tom, Mother barely kisses my lips. She says, "Kara keeps you in shape, Ann."

Age mid-fifties, grey hair cropped, our mother maintains her rower's body from her student days at Berkeley with Sarah Donaldson. Less than five-feet tall, Mother exudes life energy. She's always exercised a powerful influence over me.

When we helped Tom save Isabella from the thorn bramble, I was thirteen. Mother was in her mid-thirties. Twelve-year-old Tom embodied unusually sensitive action.

Our father's manhood-bravery was still entrapped in Vietnam War trauma. Mother remained a woman in action, without trauma.

Mother and Father showed me that the courage and violence of piloting deadly drones was little different for men or women. Mother particularly taught me that women can think more about consequences for families.

My father led Tom and me, throughout our lives, to respect the naturalness of Mother's very close relationship with Sarah Donaldson. Sarah's married to a retired Marine Corps General. He also has been totally fine with the two women's long relationship.

I met Kara Conrad, a United States Air Force drone pilot, at the Beagle Island Canadian Rescue Station five years ago. I'd already long embraced my gay self-identity.

Reunited in our old family home, Mother has me thinking about myself within the family. Our parents always have told Tom and I: "Only you yourself can really know your true self."

While Mother and I briefly converse, Tom waits, silently. I've watched Tom since we were children. He believes in his own actions or self-restraint. He lets family or strangers respond. To outright passion, Tom's always reacted carefully.

Mother holds Tom's face in both hands. "Something happened to you in Arnhem Land, son. Mission success isn't enough for you. Sarah says an Australian leader needs you. Sarah's worried about you continuing. Think, think about what you're doing." Hands drop. She looks up into Tom's blank stare.

Tom says nothing. Puck Place is quiet. I know my brother. Feeling true to himself, he's true to us. Our reunion, father's disappearance, a bark painting, Isabella's murder, her parents Alex and Esperanza's escape: we're all Tom's obligation. His duty to Sarah Donaldson and the Australians follows naturally.

"Mother, you must be hungry. I know Ann is. Let's eat before we talk anymore." Tom speaks through indirection, finding directions out.

I follow up, "Mother, Tom is taking us to dinner at his favorite Hillcrest café." I don't have to tell them that Hillcrest is now recognized as a prominent gay neighborhood.

I drove. Years away haven't dimmed the route from Puck Place to Hillcrest in my mind. The San Diego map is indelible. Admittedly, not like Tom's understanding, which is rooted in running and biking. But close enough.

Mother and Tom exchange anecdotes from Arnhem Land and Beagle Island. My mind is with Kara, who is in our Harvard Square control center three thousand miles away. Kara pilots the drone that follows Tom, my mother, and me through Rep. Donaldson's San Diego district. It's part of our test preparation for transfer of American satellite-drone technology to the Australians.

We soon enter Café Cayman, its floor-to-ceiling windows fronting a busy street. Passersby once saw inside a bank. Now, visible in the renovated building, couples talk and individuals face laptops.

At the counter Tom hails, "Julio, meet my mother and sister, Ann. Julio is an active Sarah Donaldson supporter. In Julio's fine café, I meet loyal constituents."

"Very good to meet you my dear ladies," Julio salutes. "Tom speaks of you both with deepest affection."

Julio appraisingly studies Mother and me. His hand slaps his face. Julio whispers conspiratorially, "I tremble to confess. Tom has failed to do your graciousness the justice both of you deserve, dear ladies." Mother and I are beaming.

Julio gallantly draws himself to his full, yet short height. "Cayman Café is the meeting place for Congresswoman Donaldson's Rainbow coalition constituents in Hillcrest. Tom is her very able spokesperson. Mrs. and Ann Berneray are most welcome here."

Taking hold of Tom's arm, Julio's voice lowers. "Tom, my fellow Caymanian seeks you."

Tom's immediate gloom is palpable. In a corner away from the windows sits Albert Jennings. Tom recovers smoothly. He maneuvers Mother and I across the floor, around tables. Tom insists, "Albert, this must stop."

The tall man in a tailored, light Italian suit rises. Albert's ghost-white, freckled face and hazel eyes expresses apparently genuine astonishment. He says, "This time, my friend, you surprise *me*. You're accompanied, if memory of our Harvard graduation serves, by your charming mother and sister."

"Albert, you're not too surprised. Julio says you're looking for me." Angry, Tom ignores the mention of us.

"I'm unprepared for your mother and sister's delightful presence.

Otherwise, yes, my countryman is correct. We must talk business, Tom." Albert seems miserable.

"Of course, Albert Jennings, Tom's roommate at Harvard," my mother intervenes calmly. "Ann and I remember you well, though it's been over ten years."

I take Mother's cue: "Albert, you're unforgettable." Mother's naturalness, even for her, maybe seems a little too natural.

Caught in a corner, he looks left, right. The only escape is in broad daylight, over, under, or through two women. Without emotion, his body stiffens. C.I.A. agent Albert Jennings is trapped by feminine manners.

"Tom, perhaps Julio will oblige us with takeout meals. We can all have a restful time back at Puck Place." Mother's gracious smile is withering.

"Absolutely not . . . . Mother, you have no idea . . . . Not even Albert would . . . ." Tom sputters, gags in speechless rage.

"I have no wish to intrude, Mrs. Berneray." Albert seems relieved as much as confused.

"Alright, Albert, we'll do as my Mother says. Puck Place isn't far." Tom struggles to regain composure. Brother, like sister, is used to giving into Mother's overt kindness.

"Oh, I think I know the way, Tom. I don't recall who told me." Albert is ready before Tom is.

Back home at Puck Place, Mother eases Tom's anger. She encourages Albert to talk about his Cayman background. "Julio and I are two Caymanians who have succeeded far from home. We'll retire there," Albert concludes a long story wistfully.

Snared in Mother's seemingly honest fascination, Albert runs on about "unfair" media coverage of Cayman offshore finance. "Money laundering is easier in Delaware than Cayman," Albert exclaims.

Albert believes Mother really is hanging on his every word. I've seen her persuasive stare often. My feeling grows—Mother's "interest" is calculated. She could also be on Sarah Donaldson's payroll.

Amid another rendition of complex offshore tax manipulation, Albert suddenly stops. The spy's subconscious warning signals finally cut through Mother's smothering attentiveness.

Albert asks vaguely about the bark painting. We don't know what, if anything, the bark painting means to Albert. Tom's careful inquiry reveals that Albert is simply using it to change the subject.

Quiet engulfs our old living room. Mom then recalls times when Tom and I were children. How she and Dad would discuss family turning points and crises. Again, Albert is being lulled into complacency.

Tom's silence seems to embolden Mother. She says, "I would never interfere in your business, Tom. But it's not unreasonable for me to ask why you're angry about Albert's presence here. This is our home, too." She looks to Albert for an answer.

I'm confident now that Mother is manipulating Albert with an ulterior purpose. I don't grasp whether Tom perceives what Mother is doing. I know her. Mother is stealing into Albert's ego. He seems oblivious.

"Mrs. Berneray, I'd rather not discuss why Tom distrusts me," Albert says confidently. "Nevertheless, he should concede we were of use to each other during his successful mission in Arnhem Land."

If Tom now realizes Mother's covert end he's not showing it. Mother says, "Albert, our family learned of Tom's unusual perceptiveness when he was a little boy." I'm surprised. Our family rarely mentions the incidents on Beagle Island to strangers.

Tom blurts out: "Albert couldn't care about any of those incidents on Beagle Island, Mother. Ann and I were children."

If Tom is acting, he's fooling me. And I've watched him our whole life together, the older sister studying her little brother.

Albert's widening hazel eyes signal deep, compulsive attention.

Mom begins. "My family owns a cabin on Beagle Isle, off northwest Vancouver Island. In local Haida culture the locale is known as the 'end of the world.' Our parents took my brother and me there summers when we were children. My husband and I did the same with Tom and his sister, Ann."

"Tom was five," Mother asserts. "We're at the island's rock-covered beach near our house. Sand meets woods. Tom was crouching about ten yards from the lapping sea building stone and stick forts. Jim and I were treading water, watching Ann on the beach. Tom was beyond her at the edge of the trees."

Mother's memory flows as if in real time. "Windless warm day, cool, still sea, children happily self-absorbed, parents reveling in family love. Tom leaps up, arms waving. He sprints towards us, yelling, 'come in, come in . . . .'"

Mother expresses triumph: "Screaming Tom crosses the sand. Terror seizes Ann, staring at us. The sea swells. My husband and I struggle into the shallows. Spitting, gulping air, we emerge on our knees. Near where we had treaded water, a sleek, grey black shape rises, streaming sea flowing off its back. Towering, the killer whale falls away. Waves rush in and overturn us onto the beach."

"Our children cling to us. We four hold each other. 'All of us, all of us, all of us, together,' Tom cries."

The Berneray family prevails united.

Mother now shares a lesson: "In San Diego, visitors watch from a distance while killer whales perform within landlocked pools. Alone, our family closely encountered one of those whales at sea off a remote beach on Beagle Island."

Mother expresses wisdom: "The Haida believe seeing a killer whale is a good omen, a vision Tom confirmed. He yelled to my husband and me, *before* the rising creature's swell engulfed us. We began swimming to the beach. The swell carried us into the shallows. Tom *felt* the danger and warned us in time."

"His cry 'all of us together' is our family pledge. The family initially explained his premonition as something like sensitive coincidence. Incidents accumulated on Beagle Island and elsewhere. More recently, such incidents appear in his Arnhem Land story. His unusual facility no longer surprises us," Mom concludes.

Albert reacts, "Mrs. Berneray, I never understood Tom's kindness to me while we were college roommates, but now I see that his loving family rather than an inherited lineage shaped his character."

"Enough about me," Tom fumbles to change the subject, "tell us more about you, Albert."

Albert can't resist the opportunity: "Because of my albino appearance, I am usually alone. I recall handshake introductions to cosmopolitan Harvard men and women who self-consciously looked at their hands afterward to see if I had rubbed off. Not Tom, to him I was just me. He was the closest I ever felt to having a friend."

Conspicuously, Mother and I notice, Tom studies the bark painting, declining to speak.

"Perhaps the empathy goes back to his Dad," Mother says. "My husband Jim is an orphan. We know so little about his family origins. By contrast, we know my own father left Vancouver for San Francisco.

Coincidently, he was a Scottish émigré from Berneray, an ancient Irish name for a western Scottish Island."

Mother understandably ignores what we've learned about Father's past from his "Old Mexico" manuscript. She's carefully selective with our family facts, probing for Albert's self-identified weaknesses.

"I'm grateful you entrust me with family truths, Mrs. Berneray." Albert might well be sincere. He continues, "The assistance I hope Tom renders me requires certain confidences, but I can say that some facts he reports concerning your husband's disappearance coincide with the factors demanding my presence in San Diego."

"Please explain yourself, Albert. I've been open with you. You must understand a wife and mother's pain grappling with her husband's disappearance." Mother is more blatant than I expected.

Albert's covert self reappears. "I know you understand, Mrs. Berneray, that Tom and I must talk in confidence. If he discusses certain points with his mother privately, I am powerless to stop him."

At the door Mother, Tom, and I watch Albert go. He'd arrived at Puck Place in afternoon sunshine. Albert departs in darkness.

Mother's performance has apparently captured Albert's sincerity and sympathy for a while. My mother's persuasive skills are familiar. Though I wonder if Albert really has succumbed.

Puck Place is in starlight as Albert's shadow moves from the cul-de-sac to his car parked on a main street. Tom's neighbor plays *Blue Miles* softly on muted trumpet. Marston Canyon is blackness.

Tom sits pondering the bark painting. Mother and I stand behind, looking over his shoulders. Sarah Donaldson has more in store for us than I imagined. Manipulating Albert once was his fault. I doubt it happens twice.

II

Mother's and my presence seems to invigorate Tom. He refocuses on Donaldson's military and civilian constituent work, taking into account his Arnhem Land mission and Father's disappearance. Mother and I share Tom's pain over Isabella's murder. We support Tom for our family and Rep. Donaldson's purposes, which now include Albert.

Rep. Donaldson expects Tom and Albert to further the intelligence duties she'd assigned each one separately. An agent best preserves plausible denial about one's own espionage. Rep. Donaldson has ordered me to provide Tom and Albert different satellite-drone data. The sharing must be selective.

A few mornings after Albert was our guest at home, he picks up Tom and me at Puck Place. Albert says, "Ann Berneray accompanies brother to work, Tom clad in running garb. We're in informal San Diego."

Tom remains calm. "We'll talk near the Shelter Island Marina, Albert. Afterwards, I'll do my morning run before work, as usual. Coming back home, Laurel Street Hill will be a challenge. Ann has her own plans."

Yachts, small pleasure craft, government and police boats, and science vessels from all over the Pacific share the marina. Expensive condos and apartments cluster outside Fort Rosecrans Naval Base on Point Loma. Inside the Naval Base, hidden satellite-drone surveillance equipment enables tracking my own and Tom's work.

Tom, Albert, and I walk along a path beside the marina across San Diego Bay from North Island Naval Air Station. Planes and helicopters taking off and landing little disturb the early morning quiet.

Albert begins, "We have had President Obama's inauguration. It's now late February 2009. The C.I.A. has agreed: Rep. Donaldson's intelligence committee will shift my offshore money laundering inquiries to particular satellite-drone contractors here in San Diego."

Tom replies, "It sounds like that offshore criminal conduct is a long way from Arnhem Land."

Albert ignores Tom's comment, seeking closer cooperation. "Since your successful Arnhem Land mission, you've had a one-track mind, which facilitates the search for your father. Rep. Donaldson allows you flexibility, but I won't assist you unless you help me."

Albert explains, "Technically, I'm assigned to the Naval Criminal Investigative Service. The C.I.A. and Rep. Donaldson have ordered me to use the N.C.I.S. cover."

Straightforwardly, Tom replies, "Donaldson knows I distrust your primary loyalty to the C.I.A. Yet she expects us to find a basis for cooperation."

"You encourage me, Tom. In San Diego, the Navy and Marine Corps and their private contractors are among Donaldson's leading constituents," Albert says, asserting what we all know.

Albert has a revelation: "Donaldson wants my N.C.I.S. cover in order to investigate a major security breach in which certain private contractors in her district are laundering money offshore. Once the nature of the breach is clear to her, she'll bring in you and Ann—before she authorizes that, she wants a clear picture of how to use your expertise."

Albert states succinctly: "My investigation pursues evidence linking certain satellite-drone technology to the criminal offshore financial practices of private contractors. The cocaine cartel may be involved and the investigation could result in a big court case."

"Such complex legal factors should be vulnerable to a good defense lawyer," Tom asserts.

"Yes, Lawyer Tom," agrees Albert. "But the odds shift when judge and jury face security issues within the War on Terror. In San Diego, especially, judges and juries highly respect the U.S. armed forces."

Tom responds with caution, "All right, Albert. I'll think about how to approach Donaldson to discuss our cooperation while preserving plausible denial."

"Fair enough. Also, remember, if the cocaine cartel is connected to the Navy satellite-drone private contractors' money laundering, our investigation is even more dangerous." Albert lets us draw our own conclusions.

From Shelter Island Tom runs home, where he'll shower and then bicycle to Rep. Donaldson's district office. Albert drives away, his formal investigation underway.

I stay behind. Walking around the Marina, I reach Fort Rosecrans. Beachfront and apartment buildings obscure a small gate with a Marine guard. She checks my pass. I stroll to a nondescript three-story building. On its roof is amassed a satellite-drone communications apparatus.

I pass through the building security system, into a hallway maze. People enter and exit office spaces. I speak to no one. No one speaks to me.

In my designated room, I log on to my assigned computer. Despite the three-hour time difference with our Harvard Square office, Kara is waiting. We give each other progress reports.

In two hours I retrace my route. A different Marine guard opens the gate onto the public street. I follow satellite GPS instructions down empty alleyways. I'm under my drone cameras' surveillance. I drive off in my designated car.

Driving through half an hour of light traffic, I rendezvous with Tom at Donaldson's district office. We'll be meeting a "Veteran Affairs counselor" and a spokesperson for a San Diego bankers' group.

Meanwhile, my mother is having tea with Rep. Donaldson at her Mission Hills home. Later, Tom and I will learn yet again exactly what their profound friendship means for us.

At Cayman Café Tom introduces me to Veterans' counselor Father Brasher Davis. As a Chaplain, Father Davis served with the Marine Corps in Iraq and Afghanistan.

Father Davis's Episcopal Church and its neighborhood counseling center are near Balboa Park. Homeless veterans frequent all three places.

Tom's introduction is vague regarding my "work with drones." Father Davis is sorry about our father's disappearance. The priest insists to me: "Drones serve Marines well in a combat zone."

Despite white collar, horned-rim glasses, and average height, Father Davis looks like a wiry black Marine drill instructor. His body moves like he speaks, without waste. He says to Tom, "I need money for P.T.S.D. counseling, drug rehab, night classes, meds."

"Yes, Father Davis, here is new paperwork. The election put everything on hold," Tom replies.

Father Davis won't let up: "The election didn't stop American soldiers and Marines from suffering wounds, from dying. My people still face broken families, are homeless without jobs, have torn minds and bodies."

"Father Davis, Rep. Donaldson's record on Veteran affairs is among the best in Congress," Tom responds forcefully.

"The election has raised hopes to unreachable heights, and a failure to provide veterans with a humane life will dampen those hopes. Politicians must move now!" Father Brasher Davis: the Christian advocate.

"Father Davis if we could, we would move faster. I answer your calls immediately," Tom pleads.

"In your case, Tom, I don't blame the agent any more than I blame the victims. Your father is a Vietnam War veteran. God bless him, wherever he is. I trust him and trust his son." The priest has spoken truth.

Father Davis's decisiveness falters as he seeks the right words. "I have a message for you. One of our counselees receives unusual P.T.S.D. treatment. In Iraq he was Military Police in some of the worst places."

Father Davis looks into our souls. "From helping with your father's family therapy, you both know that cruel facts demand special treatment. Our medical and psych people agree that this veteran's treatment must address his delusion that public safety requires *his* patrols. He tells us, 'The police need me. They can count on me.'"

With care, Davis explains, "Some San Diego police are veterans, so I approached them with a plan to allow our counselee to 'patrol,' certain neighborhoods and canyons near my church at night. His phone has a direct police line. He's unarmed."

The priest smiles: "His late-night call stopped a burglary on Bankers Hill. It made the police look good and they trust our man now. His self-confidence is growing. He's 'one of us' again. Otherwise, he's anonymous."

"Maybe I see what you're driving at, Father Davis," Tom speaks slowly. "During early morning runs around home and the canyons, a man in civilian clothes returns my salute when I pass. No more."

"He's the one," Father Davis says. "His message to you is that very late at night a stranger intently eyes your house on Puck Place. One morning, he saw this stranger in Marston Canyon where you run."

Father Davis leaves us with a final thought. "For now his therapy requires anonymity. You will get his messages through me because he knows you assist our people. He has an indirect trust, you could say. If he has more for you, I'll be in touch. And tell Rep. Donaldson I said she needs to move faster." The priest goes, doesn't look back.

We have time before we meet the bankers' public affairs person. Most bank-finance people have posh offices outside downtown San Diego. Still, the actual banks are located in Rep. Donaldson's downtown district.

Tom guides me to an overlook point in Balboa Park. The view includes bank and condo buildings, the Naval Air station, Coronado, and Silver Stand connecting to Imperial Beach and the border with Mexico.

Tom thinks aloud: "I assume your drone surveillance is taking all this in, Ann. Kara and your associates are far away, yet right here with us. You're preparing to transfer combined satellite-drone technology from Donaldson's committee to Chief G, Australian military intelligence."

I have to dissuade Tom from his single-mindedness. "The transfer is our ultimate goal. But first, you must understand, Rep. Donaldson will have to resolve the security breach Albert mentioned. Australian military intelligence Chief G will expect it, too."

"Yes, Ann. Donaldson, Chief G, and, don't forget, Malangi, require resolution of the security breach. The satellite-drone technology transfer from the U.S. to Australia depends on it," admits Tom. "My problem is Albert's influence."

I hear myself preach, "You're right, Tom, except that Donaldson expects us to handle Albert. She requires his expertise in illegal offshore financial practices like money laundering. She needs Albert, like us, in order to address the security breach. This is now a precondition for transferring combined technology to Chief G."

Tom simply walks away alone. I know he's thinking. He seems oblivious about our scheduled banking meeting. I watch him go up the street.

An athletic, dark-haired young women in shorts and tank top uses crutches on the sidewalk. She has one leg. Tom salutes her. She could be an Iraq War veteran.

Tom passes a couple sitting on the grass in the shade of Eucalyptus trees. Their possessions fill a shopping basket. Tom may or may not know if either or both are veterans. He knows they're homeless.

Tom hurries back to me. Our family knows Tom can be prescient. He says, "Those people show the consequences of a military-civilian complex in San Diego. I feel their painful vulnerability. Albert hides something I should see. But I'm missing it."

On Bankers Hill, I park in a driveway beside a Porsche sports car. In the street with pay parking, I see no Porsches. The Bankers' Association uses the house as a customer center for downtown San Diego. "We reach our customers, wherever they are," the Bank Public Affairs officer tells Tom, making small talk.

"As you know, Rep. Donaldson firmly supports the banking community servicing her district's constituents. She publicly acknowledges your Association's generous support," Tom intones.

The bank officer replies: "We're pleased with Rep. Donaldson's solid voting record. Not perfect. Still, quite reasonable. In that spirit, we ask Donaldson to consider our position on a timely issue."

The officer is a handsome older woman in a tailored grey suit who sits at an antique desk. She may believe she has Tom's full attention. Recalling her last name, Tom affirms, "Ms. Anderson, we're here to serve."

"Please, I'm Carol. And you introduced yourself as Tom. First names are friendlier." Her smile is perfect white teeth. "We supported the President's election. After his predecessor, this country needs all the hope it can get. We *hope* to inform his administration on a major public issue."

Tom is certain: "Carol, Rep. Donaldson's District office can assist your Bankers' Association."

Carol is certain, too. "In the Senate and during his campaign, our new President was highly critical of offshore tax havens. It's a complex subject. We ask, after such an impressive election, that he listen with an open mind to those with a fuller understanding. We think Rep. Donaldson is such a person."

Tom sounds very serious: "Carol you must mean Rep. Donaldson possesses 'fuller understanding' because certain military and private contractors in her district have used your offshore financial entities."

"Exactly, Tom, that's why we hope she and her staff listens when the time comes. We must meet soon to discuss this difficult issue. Sadly, I have another appointment."

We leave the customer center together and watch Carol's Porsche drive away.

Tom's phone buzzes. Donaldson wants to see us at her family home. Checking the time, I notice that Mother's tea with her dear friend finished not long ago.

Driving from Bankers Hill to the Donaldson Mission Hills home takes only a short time. The house is late-nineteenth century, pretend-old California architecture. It's located on an out-of-the-way street.

Tom and I meet the butler at the door. Marine Corps General George Donaldson (Retired) is there too. He greets us, "Good to see you both again. Sarah is waiting in the sitting room. After you finish, she'd like us to chat." Smiling, the General takes us to Sarah Donaldson.

She stands, viewing the heart of the district she represents. Sitting room French windows overlook historic Old Town, the Marine Corps

Recruit Depot, downtown San Diego, the Harbor, the airport, Shelter Island, and Fort Rosecrans.

"Please sit down, both of you." She faces us. No preliminaries. "I've spoken with Albert Jennings. He understands he erred by discussing a N.C.I.S. investigation without my authorization."

"He said there's a security breach in the district." Tom sounds too confident.

"Do not interrupt me." Her middle-aged figure is silhouetted against window light. Her voice is steel cold. "Jennings knows security issues must be addressed strictly through military and civilian criminal process. As a lawyer, you knows that quite well. Our Chief-of-Staff Megan Wright's monitoring actually discovered the breach."

Donaldson moves directly before Tom. Her words drill into him. "These complex technology, finance, and security issues demand cooperative investigation, I agree. Our intelligence committee recognizes that Albert Jennings' offshore finance expertise warrants employing him. His C.I.A. connection raises the potential for divided loyalties."

"Perhaps the Berneray family's recent encounter with Jennings has been coincidental. Diana has given me a mixed report. I trust your mother's judgment as surely as I do Tom's, and yours, Ann." Rep. Donaldson doesn't sound reassuring.

She turns diplomatic. "Our office operates fully within the law. That applies to everyone in the office, from me, to Megan Wright, to you, Tom. I'm circulating my memo explaining my staffs' obligations in Washington and San Diego. I'll tolerate no action beyond what I authorize. Jennings talked with you without my authorization."

Stern mouth, fixed gaze, she stands over Tom. "You trouble me, Tom. If anything happens to you, even because of something I've authorized, what do I tell your mother? I don't want to find out."

Sarah Donaldson left Tom with formal instructions. I wonder if confronting General Donaldson will be easier.

Tom startles. General Donaldson speaks behind us. We rise to face him. "Sarah wants me to confide in you both. Before retirement, I charged a Gunnery Sergeant to report only to me. In the Vietnam War, Corporal James Berneray aided a Gunny doing the same duty. They informed me about units under my command."

General Donaldson's mention of our father catches me off guard. About Father, Tom is always more alert. "Frankly, General Donaldson

I don't see what I could be doing I'm not doing already."

General Donaldson shakes his head. "Tom Berneray combines his mother's natural reliability with his father's oversensitivity. My brother, the combat psychologist, told me that when he prepared the P.T.S.D. family therapy for Jim Berneray during the Vietnam War. No good deed goes unpunished."

Tom and I next experience General Donaldson, the diplomat. "Sarah is right. Jennings erred in mentioning the security breach to you without her authorization. The breached technology might implicate a cocaine cartel. These dangerous people might read a lack of legal authorization to mean that someone near Sarah could be bought. It increases the likelihood that such people become deadly when money doesn't work."

He points into the air. "Problem: These cocaine cartel people have their own rules, which can be unpredictably deadly. Their violence can be ordinary killing behavior or more bizarre actions. Moneymaking gives way to ego satisfaction, vendettas, revenge."

"I'm not afraid," Tom says.

General Donaldson sighs deeply, and exclaims, "A bigger problem is whether Albert Jennings just made a mistake. Or Jennings could be acting purposefully for someone other than the C.I.A., or even more simply, for himself."

The General's voice is flat. "Marines know fear is normal unless you're stupid or a believer in predestination. You're neither, Tom. Wound too tight, focused on finding your father, you're always moving. You're strong, smart, distracted, inefficient—raising risks for us. Instead of letting fear use you, use fear."

Standing face-to-face with General Donaldson, Tom remains cool. "You know better than I do how I can best serve you."

General Donaldson resumes authority: "Jennings has maneuvered to be chief N.C.I.S. investigator regarding top secret intelligence satellite-drone technology leaks. Chief-of-Staff Megan Wright's oversight budget accounting implicates two Navy private contractors in my wife Sarah's San Diego district."

The General elaborates, "The N.C.I.S. preliminary investigation indicates a money trail beginning with a satellite private contractor at Fort Rosecrans Naval Base on Point Loma. The trail goes to a drone private contractor at 32nd St. Naval Base in San Diego South Bay. The money trail includes a border private security firm and a cocaine cartel. Violence is likely."

Tom's assignment is: "You'll work with Jennings. Watch him. We're all addressing the security breach. We must understand what Jennings is after, and for whom. He may be perfectly legitimate. Though, frankly, I very much doubt it."

Sarah and General Donaldson clearly want to keep Tom and Albert's roles within narrow procedural limits when it comes to investigating the satellite-drone security breach. Tom wants the same as long as his mission contributes to finding our Father.

III

Tom hears from Father Davis. "Two mornings and evenings the same big man passed the Café Cayman windows. Each time, he appeared after Tom left. He seeks an opportunity, no doubt."

That evening Tom and I wait at Café Cayman. Tom admits to Julio that we really don't know what's happening.

Clack. Clack. Clack. A skateboard approaches. Tom and Julio face the windows. A cellphone holds the blond rider's stare.

The skateboard flies up. The boy collides into a dark figure emerging from the alley shadow. Tom sprints out of the door, onto the sidewalk, into the alley gloom. Julio reaches the writhing boy. In deepening darkness, the stranger is gone. Tom returns from the shadows.

Tom rejoins Julio, the boy, and I in the Café. "Thanks for bandaging my knee and elbow, man. My board and phone are ok," the boy says as he leaves.

Tom and I go back to Puck Place, ignoring Marston Canyon. Despite the Café incident and General Donaldson's orders, Tom studies the bark painting.

I'm reminded that our father's Ph.D. dissertation examined Arnhem Land Gunwinggu people. Their Rainbow Serpent, Ngalyod, is snake *woman*. She enforces justice for evil done to families, women, and children.

Tom explains to me: "From Malangi in the Arnhem Land cave, I, as the son, received Father's Rainbow Serpent Ngalyod message. I read it to mean Flying Fox threatens the Berneray family. I feel now, Father's Rainbow Serpent Ngalyod message also embraces the justice of remedying past evil."

Tom asks me to follow his evolving ideas. He explains, "One extended family member who demands justice for evil already done is murdered Isabella. If I'm reasoning correctly, this Rainbow Serpent Ngalyod message connects to Father's "Old Mexico" manuscript."

I'm skeptical. "Tom, a connection might be simply that Father hides in Arnhem Land. Recovering from wounds, he meets Malangi the Law Man in the cave. Soon after, sailing away, Father writes the "Old Mexico" manuscript. It's somehow delivered to us."

But Father's "Old Mexico" manuscript has new implications for Tom. In "Old Mexico," Isabella's murder warranted family revenge. Diaz family agents not only murdered Isabella, they forced her parents, Esperanza and Alex Quinn to flee.

Tom and I face painful facts. Isabella is Tom's fiancée, his "promised one." In "Old Mexico," family justice is Tom's duty. That was also Ngaloyd's charge to him in Arnhem Land.

Yes, Tom and Isabella are cousins. In certain parts of America and elsewhere first cousins can't marry. In most states and countries, however, cousins can and do marry. Einstein and Darwin were famous examples doing so. In traditional societies like Old Mexico or Arnhem Land cousins marrying is acceptable.

Our reasoning brings forth my brother's confession. After Isabella's funeral, Tom was alone with the Mexican priest. Tom repeats the priest's words to him: "'If you had been with your fiancé, they would've certainly killed you, the American.'"

Tom becomes silent. Only facts matter. Isabella's murder in 2003 left behind lost love, hard loneliness.

My brother has never returned to Mexico. The San Diego Red Trolley carries tourists to and from the Tijuana border free-trade zone. Drug cartels rob, but rarely kill tourists. Tom isn't a tourist. He's family.

Tom urges me to reconsider Dad's messages. At the Arnhem Land cave, Malangi transmitted Tom's obligations to pursue Ngaloyd's justice against Flying Fox. That image embodies various evils, from drones to cocaine cartels. Dad's "Old Mexico" manuscript obligates Tom to do justice against the Diaz family for the murder of Isabella. Through Tom's obligations, these images and the text link Arnhem Land to Mexico.

Tom's meeting with Carol from the Bankers' Association sparks further speculation. The Diaz Security firm and a cocaine cartel use offshore practices such as money laundering. This is Albert's area of expertise, embracing whatever he's hiding.

I see Tom's point. His bundled connections implicate the Diaz family. Their offshore criminal practices benefit a cocaine cartel in Arnhem Land and Mexico.

Tom's investigation must connect these bare facts with legal evidence and proofs that hold up in court.

Tom's speculations guide his next meeting with Albert. I rig Tom with a concealed listening device. Our satellite and drone visually track Tom's meeting with Albert. Our experiment is to record both men talking. Images and words combined.

Albert's highly-specialized offshore finance expertise enables him to selectively choose data he'll reveal. Tom hopes our satellite-drone experiment enables us to covertly check Albert's comments against other data sources without his knowledge.

Albert chooses a meeting-place seemingly removed from ordinary surveillance: the Veterans Cemetery, Fort Rosecrans, on Point Loma. In neat rows, white headstones march up to a fenced ridge overlooking San Diego Bay. Under low grey clouds, boundaries between military and civilian life become indistinct.

Tom bicycles from Puck Place to the cemetery. Albert confidently expects nothing less from Tom.

High above, our drone cameras record the meeting. Tom carries a concealed listening device. I'm monitoring it all on my computer at Fort Rosecrans.

Tom arrives. Albert studies head stones. The drone camera sharply defines both men. I'm observing, watching the drone transmissions and picking up an intermittent verbal exchange.

Tom's listening device picks up Albert's partial sentences. "[Garbled] .... Lawyer diplomat .... Tom maneuvers ... family, friends, and himself .... Always respected your skills, Tom ...." [Albert's voice turns clear] "Surely we can follow Donaldson's orders and still help each other."

Albert's and Tom's sentence fragments flow into a comprehensible whole: "Offshore data is complex .... We must isolate legal violations provable in court ... we have thousands of civilian contractors and military personnel .... Naval Bases cover thousands of acres within greater San Diego."

Albert, clearly, "Your analysis of security reports helps to narrow my investigation. Our focus will be two private contractors in Rep. Donaldson's district."

Albert or Tom speaking, indistinguishable: "... questions must stay within proper channels ... probable court case involves 'dangerous people' .... Cocaine cartel linked to security leak ... two Navy private contractors .... Your investigation .... Your analysis of reports .... We accept dangers."

Albert is evasive about "offshore finance data," except to say, "that's my job ... will unravel complex data .... Donaldson committee ... learns what it must learn ... anticipate court case. The focus of our investigation is crimes on the U.S.-Mexico border."

Each speaker's sentence fragments become comprehensively repetitive. They agree preliminary evidence identifies a security breach arising from two Navy private contractors in San Diego and that they should stay focused on the U.S.-Mexico border. The cocaine cartel and offshore data are dangerous. They promise one another full reports with Rep. Donaldson's authorization.

The meeting ends. Albert drives away. Tom bicycles through Fort Rosecrans. At a gate a Marine guard checks his pass, waves him on to me. At my assigned office computer we agree with Kara, our drone pilot in Cambridge: "We're a modest success!"

Tom and I further test the concealed listening device within the combined satellite-drone technology. Back in Puck Place I connect my PC to Kara's computer. I follow our drone, tracking Tom's morning run in Marston Canyon, Balboa Park.

Marston Canyon allows muscle-power recreation only. Our drone flies high above. I hear and see ravens caw, swarm from trails into trees, then go airborne. Quiet prevails over the low hum of Highway 163 traffic.

Tom leaves Puck Place and heads into Marston Canyon. Fences or stone walls separate houses and patrolling German Sheppard dogs from steep hillsides. Walking, biking, and running trails twist through the broken canyon ground and hillsides.

Tom runs by a red cedar kiosk. I recall a map behind glass. Canyon Friends, Scouts, Cabrillo School, City Parks and Recreation, Interns, and the Naval Base Petty Officer Association maintain park trails.

Tom passes open spaces, gullies, chaparral thickets clustered with cactus, dispersed single trees groves shedding palms, twisted cedars, bending cypress, gnarled pines, and peeling eucalyptus. In the cultivated wild, people-powered recreation coexists with coyotes, raccoons, and skunks.

In the bright dawn-light, the drone camera shows me Tom is alone, until . . . .

Steep hillside on Tom's right. The trail curves sharply left. From the brush, a quick dark shape and thrusting knife stabs Tom. One step ahead, Tom—bleeding—sprints up the hillside.

Sweat-soaked, shirt-back red-stained, wounded Tom runs with short, pumping strides. Tom gains fifty steps. Tom knows the steepness well. The dark figure's quickness dissolves. Gasping, the figure lumbers uphill, fixated on Tom's bloodstain.

Tom strides towards a broken stone and concrete wall. On the ground he seeks a weapon. He stops, crouches, wall at his back. Ravens caw in trees, guard dogs bark. Noise aggravates waiting, observing through the drone camera and listening device.

Tom shifts stone and concrete fragments. I'm sure my brother's left arm throbs with pain. Yet on my PC screen I see him handle a large, sharp-edged piece of concrete.

The dark figure plods uphill, falls, slowly rises. In his line of sight, I see Tom's head and shoulders above a ridge. Side-to-side moves the knife blade. The dark figure runs towards the ridge. He collapses, rises, trudges forward. Knife blade held too close, unsteady.

In plain sight Tom waits, crouching. The dark figure's swaying blade reaches ridge level. Tom springs. Into his attacker's surprised face he slams the mangled concrete block with its sharp stones.

The dark figure collapses, falls backward, twitching. His hands slowly fold, as if in prayer, over the cutting concrete edges. The knife has fallen to the ground.

"Sir, sir," I hear through Tom's listening device. On my PC screen, a young Latino man in civilian clothes talks into a cellphone.

I watch him join Tom. I hear him speak: "The police are coming. I'm Corporal Montoya, assigned to Father Davis for special police patrol. Your wound needs attention, sir. The church infirmary is not far."

I watch two police dirt bikes skid to a stop. In black shirts and shorts, S.D.P.D. patrol officers stride uphill. "I'm Carson," the black woman says, "This is Smith."

The blond male partner, Smith nods. He examines the dark figure's body; a broken object under ragged concrete weight.

Tom holds his injured arm, silent. Carson talks fast, "Montoya reports you're Mr. Berneray. You work for an elected official. You're running here in Marston Canyon. This man assaulted you and you defended yourself. Montoya is now taking you to a nearby church infirmary. You'll make a report there. Detective White will meet you."

Tom consents, cold body now shaking. Montoya phones Father Davis to expect them very soon. I know the priest's infirmary is a room in the church basement. I drive there in about five minutes.

I listen from the infirmary open door. Father Davis confirms Tom has a flesh wound. Bleeding has stopped. Father Davis treats the wound like a Medic administering essential minimum aid during combat. Warmed in a blanket, Tom thanks the priest and Montoya. My brother smiles at me.

The S.D.P.D. detective arrives. Plainclothes, trim, middle-age, graying brown hair. She says, "Well done Montoya. You gave us what we need. Father Davis, your work blesses the neighborhood."

"I'm Detective White," she tells Tom. "Mr. Berneray, given your wound, we'll only do preliminaries. I know what Montoya told officers Carson and Smith. I'll take your full report later."

Tom says sincerely hopeful, "I'm fortunate Corporal Montoya was there."

"I wish that were enough." Detective White wants more from Tom. "Unfortunately, the situation is complicated. The public has come to expect complete safety in Marston Canyon. Voters in surrounding neighborhoods are important."

"I live in Puck Place," Tom agrees. "I work for Congresswoman Donaldson. Federal grants help develop Marston Canyon. Grants also assist in funding the S.D.P.D. bike patrols. This morning I've benefitted."

"I remember you, Mr. Berneray," Detective White announces. "You did the follow-up briefing after Congresswoman Donaldson spoke about the S.D.P.D.'s role in Homeland Security. You present problems."

Tom uses his most sympathetic voice: "Detective White, you have my full cooperation." Tom's self-discipline prevails over the third time in as many days he's been called "a problem."

Detective White looks perplexed. "I appreciate your helpful attitude, Mr. Berneray. You understand this incident is suspicious. Montoya says the perpetrator has been stalking you. The Café Cayman proprietor has reported that the same person injured a boy quite recently. You were involved. Now the stranger has knifed you. One problem is the attacker's motivation."

Tom insists: "I have no idea. Father Davis gave me Corporal Montoya's warning. Someone has been watching me, and my home. Julio informed me that the man who collided with the skateboarder is same one I pursued into the alley. I only saw his back briefly. Whether he's the one in the canyon just now, I truly don't know."

Detective White reasons, "Father Davis vouches for you. I believe you're unaware the assailant is a Mexican Green Card holder from El Paso-Juarez. His employer is the border security firm, Global Security Solutions. We find him in San Diego, tracking Congresswoman Donaldson's staffer. It's another problem."

Detective White lets Tom absorb the problems hovering over him. She delivers her punch line: "A further problem is that within the last few days, your name has come up in a major N.C.I.S. investigation."

Tom's conceals surprise. I'm sure my brother thinks to himself: "Albert, again."

"N.C.I.S. and S.D.P.D. can cooperate in criminal investigations," Detective White admits. "Another problem is that your assailant's employer, G.S.S., is a security firm under N.C.I.S. investigation."

Detective White's problems with Tom finally stop: "The last issue is that Montoya arrived when you received the knife wound and began sprinting up hill. He said you moved fast enough to avoid the full thrust of the knife. Like maybe you half-expected it. If I'm missing something, I don't want surprises."

"I felt something was about to happen. If I'd moved as fast as I felt danger, he might not have blooded me at all." Tom speaks evenly.

Detective White's blank stare expresses incredulity.

Montoya reacts, "When a Marine feels like that, he takes the point."

"Montoya means that some trusted Marines can feel certain kinds of danger before it occurs," Father Davis explains. "If a squad is lucky enough to have such a person, he takes the risks of leading."

"As far as I know, Berneray isn't a Marine." Detective White is relentless.

Father Davis, the merciful, ever faithful priest: "His father is a Marine Corps Vietnam War veteran. He's missing in action, you might say."

Tom interjects. "My father and I ran together in Marston Canyon with seventy pound packs. I filled mine with rocks and concrete from broken walls on the canyon rim."

"Force-march double-time, hump seventy pound packs in bush, same, same," states dutiful Montoya.

Detective White changes the subject. "You've explained the assailant's injuries. Carson and Smith *together* lifted the rock-concrete weight from his head and chest. Falling back, his left leg stuck. Skull, ribs, cracked. One leg shattered. Still unconsciousness, the assailant's prognosis is that he'll survive, living a cripple's life. Employer G.S.S. disclaims all responsibility."

Detective White finishes for now and leaves. I drive Tom to Puck Place. Shoulder aching, Tom showers, insists on me taking him to Rep. Donaldson's office. Detective White's comments have left us thinking.

IV

Tom's attempt to avoid comment on his injury alerts Chief-of-Staff Megan Wright, who is in San Diego on "boss's orders." Tom insists his injury will not interfere with his duties. He doesn't convince Rep. Donaldson's Chief-of-Staff.

Megan Wright commands Tom, "The N.C.I.S. investigation permits no room for error on our part."

Tom gives her Detective White's report. It essentially summarizes Detective White's inquiries and responses from Tom, Father Davis, and Montoya in the church infirmary.

Tom tells us: "The security-firm Detective White noted may serve Albert's investigation. He's probing a border security firm linked to a cocaine cartel. The S.D.P.D. role ensures we're staying within the process."

Tom repeats the police report to Mother, who had remained at home in Puck Place. Tom's injury gives Mother the most important reason to be in San Diego.

Mother has met privately several times with Sarah Donaldson, perhaps having discussed Father's "Old Mexico" manuscript. After Tom's injury, Mother and I plan to remain at Puck Place indefinitely. The family is staying together.

Following Tom's injury in Marston Canyon, Tom meets Albert Jennings. Again, we've rigged Tom with the concealed com-device, as part of our satellite-drone surveillance.

I follow Tom's meeting with Albert through my PC. With it, I'm connected to Kara's computer in Cambridge, as is Mother now at Puck Place.

We've alerted Mother about our ongoing combined technology experiment. Mother's informal comments about our latest satellite-drone experiment could well reach Sarah Donaldson before our formal report does.

Albert picks up Tom at Sarah Donaldson's main district office in a gentrified part of Normal Heights. Among decades-old bungalows built after World War II are many refurbished rentals and condos.

The drone camera follows Albert driving to the 32nd St. Naval Base. Naval buildings compact into a maze dispersed over thousands of federal acres within downtown San Diego.

Mother and I know 32nd St. begins in neighborhoods with cafés and coffee shops. It ends amidst old houses, retail stores, and churches intermingled with the fenced 32nd St. Naval Base. Growing up, father lived at the poor end.

Puck Place, not many miles away, was quite a step up when Dad married mom, the daughter of the San Francisco Quinn Shipping family.

Meanwhile, Albert, driving towards the Naval Base, is recorded speaking: "Tom, use your family concerns to aide our investigation into a security breach of classified satellite-drone technology and stay focused on the two Navy private contractors we believe are responsible for the security breach. Keep your priorities straight. Detective White thinks your hiding something—we need her trust."

Mother and I hear Tom reply: "Detective White said my assailant's employer was a U.S.-Mexico border security firm. I assume, Albert, that *you* told her about my family's connection to Mexico. She's suspicious because she doesn't want surprises."

"I might've mentioned something I remembered from our college days about your family and Mexico, but nothing particular, I'm sure. We must work with Detective White," Albert insists.

Mother, Tom, and I, believe Albert is using us to get something. We've remembered that as Tom's college roommate, Albert often asked questions about the Berneray, Quinn, and Bermudez families. We revealed little.

Even so, whatever Albert knows about us in Mexico, he's surely told Detective White.

Albert drives up to the gate and shows his pass to the Marine Guard. Entering the Naval Base on Harbor Drive and 32nd St., Albert's use of an official pass means that Tom isn't subjected to a security scan that might've revealed the concealed listening device. Albert's pass enables our experiment to succeed again.

My confidence increases in our drone cameras and concealed listening device. "You know N.C.I.S. Head Quarters is here on the Base," Albert said.

Tom replied smoothly, "I did the N.C.I.S. budget analysis for my boss, Rep. Donaldson."

Tom continues to be heard loud and clear: "Detective White connects the Naval Base to civilian downtown San Diego."

Albert comes through just as well. "She knows the cocaine cartel market. The Base is near convention hotels, the tourist quarter, another marina, and an aircraft-carrier museum. Big-business container shippers dock close by Navy ships."

Tom presses Albert: "We will have difficult legal problems proving a technology security breach, as distinct from complex cocaine cartel issues. Proving connections between the two is even harder."

Albert targets their joint purpose. "You and I must determine whether two Navy private contractors causing the security breach also have cartel connections."

Our drone cameras follow Tom and Albert down narrow streets within the Naval Base to N.C.I.S. Headquarters. When they enter, we've lost them, visually.

We hear Tom's and Albert's voices greeting Detective White. She responds pointedly: "I've agreed to meet you at the Naval Base. Yours is a N.C.I.S. investigation. My superiors aren't clear on the S.D.P.D. role. Your preliminary evidence suggests room for cooperation."

Albert is prepared. "N.C.I.S. is investigating because federal audits reveal discrepancies in congressional committee budget expenditures for certain top-secret satellite-drone systems. The audits show two Navy private contractors with subcontractors among many civilian firms in San Diego."

Albert has numbers: "Contracts and subcontracts for the combined satellite-drone technology total about $2 billion. Budget discrepancies involve much smaller dollar amounts scattered among hundreds of contracts. No single discrepancy exceeds $100,000. But the total amounts to millions of dollars."

Albert identifies cross-border criminal conduct of the two primary Navy private contractors. "The satellite contractor receives large cash amounts from a Mexican security firm. The drone contractor pays cash to a Tijuana construction business. They all operate both sides of Border, with cocaine cartel connections."

We hear Detective White interrupt: "Probable money laundering signals the cocaine cartel at work."

"Exactly so," Albert responds. "Both private contractors conspire to use offshore shell companies to steal top-secret classified research. This research adapts satellite data-gathering to a new drone system. The classified data may be going to the cocaine cartel or border security firm—or both—using money laundering."

Detective White addresses cooperation: "Your preliminary findings are convincing, Albert. Your investigation should expose offshore financial evidence which can be used to prove the guilt of the two private contractors. If proven in court, the contractors will be guilty of criminally endangering U.S. national security and violating American drug laws. That raises issues of guilt under federal criminal laws."

Detective White concludes: "The border security firm raises complex legal issues, which include a cocaine cartel. These issues establish S.D.P.D. jurisdiction under California laws. I'll advise my superiors that we have reasonable evidence to support our joint investigations."

"I am pleased we are working together, Detective White," Albert's relief is palpable.

Detective White adds: "We'll need evidence proving guilt 'beyond a reasonable doubt.'"

Regarding that point, Detective White finally acknowledges Tom's presence. "Representative Donaldson authorizes you, Mr. Berneray, a lawyer, as a source for certain classified data. Defense counsel will attempt to taint your evidence. Beyond the recent assault, is there something in your background the defense might use?"

Tom replies, "My uncle, a Vietnam War veteran, is married to a Mexican citizen. Sometime ago, they disappeared from the family home in Santa Maria, Mexico. Their daughter and another family member were murdered. The daughter, Isabella, and I were engaged to be married."

To forestall further comment, Tom quickly adds, "Our families accept cousins marrying."

Detective White seems sincere. "I regret your family's loss. Along with your assault, it could compromise the worth of your evidence. Tell me more. We'll see."

Tom admits bare factual essentials. No family names identified beyond Isabella. Despite the investigator's routine, Detective White has asked for no names. This ensures that Tom's family will not be scrutinized as the investigations proceed.

We overhear no more from the three together. The drone cameras pick up Detective White's departure from 32nd St. Naval Base.

The drone follows Albert driving Tom to meet me at Shelter Island Marina. Albert drops off Tom and departs. I'm waiting on the Quinn Shipping family's private dock in the marina, a place we've been familiar with since childhood.

Tom and I walk around the Marina to the Fort Rosecrans gate guarded by a Marine. My brother concurs in my eavesdropping report of his meeting with Albert and Detective White. "Another combined-technology success," Tom grins.

Meanwhile, my job for the Donaldson intelligence committee includes a closed seminar on satellite-drone security. Our computers link us into a top-secret network.

Before the seminar, I have arranged for Tom to meet Professor James Sims at my assigned Fort Rosecrans room. He was my 'corporate organization' professor at Harvard Law School and is the keynote speaker on 'Satellite-Drone Technology, Security Issues, and Offshore Financial Centers.' It is General Donaldson's closed seminar for experts like me.

Sims is retirement age at the Law School. He's heavyset, balding. He wears tweeds and glasses. "Pleasure to meet Ann's brother. Ann's my best student. You're Harvard College class of '98 and U.C. Berkeley,

Boalt Law. You may know Chet Sims, who teaches offshore financial entities at Boalt. He's my son. "

"Representative Donaldson authorizes me to give you information off the record. I'm informed that her committee's security breach will be prosecuted in federal court. Forewarned, forearmed," Sims instructed.

Sims mixes known and secret data. "You're aware the previous administration privatized many security operations in Iraq and elsewhere. Private security firms have received top-secret classified satellite-drone technology. Sharing this technology with allies like Australia ceased."

Sims proceeds slowly, "Two San Diego private contractors have stolen secret American satellite-drone technology. This is the security breach being prosecuted. A global criminal security firm and cocaine cartel paid the two contractors for the technology theft. These criminals want to counter American or allied satellite-drone surveillance in such diverse places as the U.S.-Mexico border or North Australia."

Sims asserts: "A court trial will expose a new terrorist threat. A cocaine cartel and a security conglomerate are developing criminal drone technology that targets the U.S. and our allies, as well as cocaine cartel and security-firm competitors."

Sims explains, "A federal court trial will prosecute two private contractors for theft and sale of satellite-drone technology. Both private contractors held top-secret security clearances for this technology. Both contractors stole this same technology for cocaine cartel and security criminals who want to develop and use the technology to disrupt U.S. and allied antiterrorism-enforcement efforts.

Sims adds, "Rep. Donaldson believes a N.C.I.S. investigator will be selective in revealing the data that's being used in the prosecution. Where possible, within my own top-secret clearances, I'll provide data enabling Ann and Tom to check his data. Hopefully, you'll know if he omits anything." Sims later denied having told us any of this.

Sims returns to the seminar room. Tom and I follow separately. Nothing directly links the three of us. I sit with seminar participants. A few others are outside observers, like anonymous Tom. We keep satellite-drone technology secrets.

Seminar ended. Sims, participants, observers depart without further communication. Tom and I take away Sims' confidential information. A technology breach Megan Wright has discovered will soon be prosecuted in a big court case.

Tom and I agree. The impending federal court case delays transfer of U.S. satellite-drone technology to Australia. Rep. Donaldson and Chief G must learn how much the combined technology has been compromised by the security breach of the two private contractors.

The trial exposes the dangers of the cocaine cartel aligned with a global security conglomerate. Private contractors' theft of satellite-drone technology has potentially weakened powerful antiterrorist weaponry. The trial might also indicate remedies.

V

Tom and I don't say more until we reach Puck Place. I stop the car. Getting out, we encounter Corporal Montoya, Father Davis' "counselee."

We stand together in the empty cul-de-sac. "I'm glad they want you to report action in Marston Canyon, Corporal." My brother speaks sincerely.

Montoya is dutiful. "You handled the knifeman, sir. Good thing we got you to the church in time. Father Davis patched you up. You've work ahead to satisfy Detective White. She reports to higher-ups."

"I saw her today." Tom said. "Detective White basically ignored me. Except she suggested I have created problems for the separation of N.C.I.S. and S.D.P.D. investigations here in San Diego. She doesn't trust me."

"Like Marines in Iraq, sir." Montoya is sympathetic. "People don't like us even when we're attacked by their own kind. We get some things right, some wrong. We can't take it personally. Marines stick together. Just do the job."

Tom finally introduces me. "Pleasure to meet you, Ma'am," Montoya replies. "Father Davis mentioned you. Drone expert and all. Drones make the difference many times for Marines in Iraq. Doesn't matter who you are, if you know what I mean Ma'am. *Sempre Fidelis*."

"Yes Montoya, I know what you mean." Yes, I knew: Berneray, Quinn, Bermudez families. The warriors are Juan, Father, Alex, Tom, Esperanza, Diana. Gays are Kara and I. We're "Always Faithful," to each other as a family, as Tom said, "All of us together."

Montoya salutes us, disappearing into the shadows. Knowing it is 2009, Tom says, "Doing our duty is honorable, even if wars like Iraq or Vietnam are wrong."

At home, Tom and I meet Mother. We agree the prosecution of the two private contractors increases Albert Jennings' influence. The federal prosecutor needs Albert's offshore finance data. That serves the C.I.A. versus Rep. Donaldson and Chief G. Above all, the prosecution's use of Albert's data will benefit Albert himself.

Tom's mind is no longer with us in Puck Place. Surely, he's in Arnhem Land receiving Father's messages in light of Isabella's murder and the "Old Mexico" manuscript. All three of us wonder what the trial will mean for Tom's obligations.

FIVE

•————————————————————•

San Diego: Trial, Prosecution

Early morning nightmares engulf me. Malangi's bark painting shows Rainbow Serpent above the Arnhem Land cave, raising my wounded father. He flees evil Flying Fox.

I'm in a Baja storm. Albatross frees Father. Juan, Diana, Alex, Esperanza witness.

Beagle Island: I'm a child on the beach screaming, "Father! Mother! Come back!" From the thorn bramble, I carry Isabella to safety in my mother's arms.

Ann cries, "Danger, Tom!" I outrun the flashing knife in Marston Canyon. Montoya, patrolling, calls the priest.

Isabella materializes trapped in a blue car. Diaz Security agents' automatic weapons fire . . . thud, thud, thud . . . Isabella's gone. Hidden in desert bush, the Seri shaman woman sees the car explode in a fireball. On the ocean Isabella's parents, Quinn and Esperanza, escape Flying Fox and the black yacht.

I'm groggy, awake. Dream-light thickens into gloom. Puck Place. Same room, same bed since a boy. No Rainbow Serpent, no Father, no Albatross, no blue car fireball. No Isabella.

Morning light illuminates my nightmare, the bark painting, Father's "Old Mexico" family story. In Arnhem Land Father's attacker is Flying Fox. The same evil murders Isabella in Mexico, forces her parents' flight. In my mind's eye the Seri shaman woman witnesses Flying Fox become Diaz Security.

Dazed, I fumble my buzzing phone. Hurried, wide-awake, I hear Albert urge "We must talk soon about the court case, we need your help."

I confront "soon" after dawn.

I

Puck Place. Albert presses me to provide him evidence for the court trial. Albert wants me to be a source for evidence supporting prosecutions arising from the satellite-drone technology security breach.

Albert pleads persuasively. "You told Detective White that Isabella Quinn was murdered in Santa Maria. But you didn't reveal the killer—tell me who did it. I've learned a cocaine cartel is involved in the security breach Rep. Donaldson's Chief-of-Staff Megan Wright discovered. It also concerns our meeting this morning at Donaldson's office."

I don't say: "The killer named in Father's 'Old Mexico' manuscript and my nightmare is 'Diaz Security.'" I can't reveal Father's manuscript. I don't know about its origins or arrival at my home. Only my family and I can trust this unidentifiable source.

A legal due-process fact: lawyers seek to show the other side has used "tainted evidence." If proven to be "tainted," the evidence is not admissible in court. The court might even find certain "tainted evidence" to be grounds for throwing out a case.

The mystery of the making and delivery of Father's "Old Mexico" manuscript opens it to "tainted evidence" claims.

My nightmare is "spectral evidence." It is also inadmissible in court. Though under certain circumstances, a nightmare might *suggest* "emotional facts" which may be admissible as psychological evidence.

Instead I argue, "My fiancé's death is our family tragedy. I told Detective White about it in a cooperative spirit. You haven't given me one reason why I should delve more deeply into painful facts."

Albert sighs deeply. "Since you returned from Arnhem Land, your mother and an Episcopal priest have both told me they agree about your remarkable imagination. Through Detective White, I've learned the same thing from honest Montoya."

Albert stops. Quiet weighs on me. Finally, Albert says, "The prosecution must carefully identify sources of evidence targeting two private contractors responsible for the security breach. As you know well, a defense lawyer easily refutes problematic sources of evidence."

"I know, Albert, and I get to decide what to identify as a lawful source of evidence involving my own family's tragedy." Albert concedes, "Alright Tom, you win for now."

I bicycle to the office. I know basic facts. Rep. Donaldson's staff, led by Megan Wright, monitors classified satellite-drone technologies. Our classified evidence regarding these technologies, including my sister's drone surveillance, supports other evidence gathered by Albert and Detective White. This evidence furthers the prosecution's case.

The staff's role in the satellite-drone private contractors' case unfolds when we meet at our Normal Heights office. We've studied Rep. Donaldson's memorandum explaining our evidence given in criminal investigations and trials. The memorandum balances classified material, privacy considerations, and lawful access.

My colleagues and I defer to Megan Wright. She's white, petite, late-thirties, short dark hair, no makeup, tailored grey suit, black loafer shoes. She's all business.

Megan's blue-gold, crossed-oars tie shows she rowed for University of California at Los Angeles. She was one of the first female coxswains in U.C.L.A.'s eight-*man* rowing shells. This breakthrough for women in a man's sport impresses my mother and Sarah Donaldson. They rowed for U.C. Berkeley women's crew.

Megan Wright's father and sister, both U.C.L.A. alumni, hold local public office in greater Los Angeles. Her father knows General Donaldson. He introduced Megan to Rep. Donaldson. How long Megan works for our boss before running for office herself is unclear.

We sit around a conference table, Megan at the head. We reflect on downtown San Diego communities. Both incriminated private contractors work here in these communities.

Our Deputy Chief-of-Staff, Heather Roberts, lives in Little Italy. Her work for Donaldson's constituents, the downtown banks, reveals that the two contractors run small companies. The Navy pays both private contractors and their small firms to make satellite-drone component parts.

Jill Mangum lives in Mission Hills, near Rep. and General Donaldson. Jill's constituent work includes Historic Old Town, Balboa

Park, and the Marine Corps Recruit Depot. Her evidence shows the drone contractor's construction firm holds many Navy and City contracts. For *lawful* tax reasons, the drone contractor's firms operate offshore.

Sally Li lives in Point Loma. Her computer science expertise from Cal Tech serves banking constituents. She follows the satellite contractor's education and his major patents used by the Navy. His patents are vital to new classified satellite-drone technology.

Maurice Smalls lives in Lincoln Park. His father is a black minister. After Navy service, Maurice graduated from San Diego State University. Chip Roland resides in Hillcrest. He advises the annual Gay Pride Parade. Another San Diego State University graduate, Chip served in the Air Force.

Maurice and Chip's constituent work provides evidence showing each incriminated Navy private contractors' activities in the gay community.

Alejandro Valdez is also a San Diego State University graduate. His Mexican-American neighborhood is near the 32nd St Naval Base. He is a Lieutenant in the U.S. Marine Corps Reserves. Valdez's constituent work serves the Naval Base, Veteran Affairs, and Navy private contractors in engineering and construction, including the drone contractor.

Because of my family, Valdez has said, "Tom, you're a Marine and Mexican-American in feeling, *simpatico*." Valdez informs Rep. Donaldson's staff about the drone contractors' business affairs and employees in and around the 32nd St. Naval Base.

Albert and Detective White join us. They sit facing Megan Wright.

Megan begins, "Representative Donaldson's office provides evidence in cooperating N.C.I.S. and S.D.P.D. criminal investigations. There is a Navy private contractor, Steven Home, who allegedly transfers classified satellite technology. I'll refer to Mr. Home, as the 'satellite contractor.'"

"A second Navy private contractor, Ralph Jones, allegedly receives the satellite technology for use in a new drone system. Mr. Jones is the 'drone contractor,'" Megan Wright continues.

She stresses, "If proven, the exchanges between satellite contractor Home and drone contractor Jones breach U.S. security. The exchanges were part of a complex conspiracy to steal classified technology for a cocaine cartel and its security operator. Serious U.S. federal crimes, they're punishable by imprisonment and fines."

Megan adds that Rep. Donaldson chairs a military intelligence subcommittee in Congress. Its jurisdiction includes Navy private contractors working on satellite-drone technologies. For Donaldson's staff, Megan Wright monitors the technology contracts.

She continues, "Albert's investigation seeks evidence of criminal violations regarding particular patent-license contracts funded through offshore shell companies. Our office's constituents also provide evidence to N.C.I.S. and San Diego police regarding Mr. Home and Mr. Jones' cocaine use. This implicates a cocaine cartel and its security company in violation of Federal and Californian drug trafficking laws."

Megan Wright asks me, the legal counsel, to explain legal proof and evidence. "Our office provides evidence needed to prove criminal violations. A judge and jury require proving 'guilt beyond a reasonable doubt.' Our evidence is technical. It must be made understandable to all involved."

Megan notes that politics complicate our office's involvement in criminal investigations. "Two political parties fight to elect U.S. House Representatives for San Diego County. The opposition could claim our office ineffectively monitored Navy contracts vital to U.S. security."

She urges: "We must enable investigators, prosecutors, defense counsel, judges, and jurors to view evidence on our terms. Political distortions will then lack credibility."

Albert replies. "A separate security breach of classified satellite or drone technology is hard enough to prove. Here the security breaches are entwined."

Detective White adds drug trafficking issues. "Mr. Home's and Mr. Jones' cocaine issues concern our investigations and also implicate national-security matters. These present wide-ranging dangers from a cocaine cartel and its security firm."

Albert and Detective White agree: The prosecution demands evidence that addresses related issues of classified technology theft and cocaine trafficking in both investigations. Representative Donaldson's office provides vital evidence in these cases.

Detective White adds, "You know about the recent attack on Mr. Berneray. A connection may exist between this attack and our investigations. Staff members should exercise extreme caution."

Albert and Detective White depart. They'll interview everyone as soon as possible. Megan Wright personally reassures each Rep. Donaldson staff member.

Chief-of-Staff Megan Wright and I are alone. We've worked closely together for many years in Rep. Donaldson's office. We discuss my father's "Old Mexico" manuscript, my nightmare, and the early morning encounter with Albert.

Megan and I recall we've had reasons over the preceding months to distrust C.I.A. agent Albert Jennings. Donaldson has acknowledged that Albert's offshore finance expertise is vital to us. Yet his primary loyalty always is to the C.I.A.

Megan supports my refusal to give Albert evidence about my family tragedy, Isabella's murder, and my father's disappearance. We agree. Unverifiable, and thus "tainted," evidence characterize my father's "Old Mexico" manuscript. My nightmare of Isabella's death is clearly "spectral" evidence. Such problematic evidence justifies nondisclosure.

Megan warns me. Albert may force us to reconsider these points. I admit my anxiety that Albert is pushing me to identify "Diaz Security." I'm anxious about making that identification because it raises questions pointing to my unverifiable family sources.

Yet for Albert, risky legal technicalities about "Diaz Security" could expose new offshore data. It enhances Albert's C.I.A. agent expertise. The meeting ends.

Days pass. Investigations proceed, supporting the court case prosecuting the security breach. I hear nothing from Albert until one afternoon. Albert's message appears on my secure office line: "Back in U.S. tonight. Meet me at Julio's."

I bicycle to Café Cayman in streetlight darkness. Julio leads me through the empty café to Albert in a small office. As my college roommate, I'd seen Albert exhausted. He's exhausted now. Albert looks like he'd tried to sleep in his rumpled suit without success.

Gulping coffee, we chomp Julio's Cayman-style fish tacos. Albert's story engulfs me. Using a special writ from a U.S. court, Albert has accessed confidential offshore accounts in Cayman Islands. He's examined related accounts in Nevada.

Albert identifies two "Diaz brothers" associated with a global conglomerate. Its financial holding companies may control various security firms including Global Security Solutions, my knife-assailant's employer.

Albert explains, "The 'Diaz brothers' name recurs in various offshore company accounts I've found. The Diaz brothers seem to run a small family bank in Santa Maria. This small Diaz bank couldn't control a large, complex offshore conglomerate, so the Diaz brothers' name and bank are obviously a front for this obscure offshore security conglomerate."

Albert pleads: "Surely, Tom, you can help me understand who the Diaz brothers in Santa Maria are—your family has connections there, it's where your fiancé was murdered."

I'm evasive. "Albert, what I told you and Detective White about my family in Santa Maria should be enough for you. Given your C.I.A. and N.C.I.S. sources, you can trace the Diaz brothers. You don't need me."

Albert's next line surprises me. "Some IDs with the Diaz name appear in relation to 'business trips' in Arnhem Land. I attempted to check them out with Australian military intelligence Chief G, but the Australians refused to cooperate without Rep. Donaldson's authorization and she has refused my request."

I'd be persuaded if I didn't already know Albert's cleverness. Albert implores: "I'm the N.C.I.S. chief investigator in the prosecution of the Donaldson committee security breach. I'm the Donaldson committee's offshore finance expert, yet Donaldson backs up the Australians. None of them trust me."

Silence in the small room compels my thinking. It's now early 2009, just a few months after the President's January inauguration.

The new President has informed Rep. Donaldson that her military intelligence committee and the C.I.A. must cooperate. Her discretion governs this cooperation.

Rep. Donaldson and the C.I.A. have agreed to authorize Albert's investigation for the security-breach prosecution. The joint authorization triggers Albert's offshore-finance expertise.

Donaldson expects my cooperation to strike a balance. Albert's C.I.A. loyalty and offshore expertise support my role as investigator for the prosecution.

I finally reply, attempting to avoid tainted or spectral evidence. "Albert, Rep. Donaldson expects your N.C.I.S. investigation to be narrowly targeted. Pursue only evidence directly supporting prosecution of the two private contractors' security breach."

Albert gets emotional. It happens so rarely, Albert turns believable. "Listen, I've followed the 'Diaz' name from Mexico to Arnhem Land. I hit a wall, I'm not trusted. Everyone trusts you, Tom. Help me."

Donaldson permits me to contact her personally in extraordinary circumstances. Albert convinces me I must ask my boss whether to consider his appeal.

I tell Albert only that I'll make a call. Julio gives me privacy elsewhere in his café. On a secure line, Sarah Donaldson listens.

I recount the whole story involving Albert's identification of the Diaz name. It could reveal a complex offshore conglomerate. Exposure of global offshore financial manipulations furthers the prosecution of the two private contractors' security breach.

Donaldson already knows that Chief G in Canberra distrusts Albert and won't meaningfully cooperate with him. She asks me pointedly to explain our family connections concerning the Diaz name. I assume Donaldson wants to compare my evaluation with what she's talked about with my mother. She did that when she first sent me to Arnhem Land. I've already told them both that I've informed Detective White about Isabella's murder.

Finally, Donaldson authorizes my discretion. I decide how much to tell Albert about the "Diaz" connection, as long as it aids prosecution of both private contractors' security breach. I must avoid American military intelligence-sharing with Australia.

Albert's pleading thus results in Rep. Donaldson authorizing changed priorities. Donaldson's intelligence committee temporarily suspends transfer of U.S. satellite-drone technology to Chief G and Malangi in Australia.

Donaldson's staff now emphasizes evidence-gathering. Our evidence supports prosecuting two satellite-drone contractors' security breach.

Ceasing work with Chief G and Malangi in Arnhem Land means I suspend searching for my father. Donaldson insists I'll return to him later.

Mother states that my duty as Rep. Donaldson's staffer comes first. I'm certain my father would agree, if he knew. My sister acknowledges I'm correct about our parents.

I now prioritize gathering evidence enabling prosecution of the two private contractors on the U.S.-Mexico border.

Donaldson authorizes me. I decide how much to cooperate with Albert's N.C.I.S. investigation, including the "Diaz" connection. I choose in what ways my cooperation with Albert will confront Isabella's murder. Ultimately, I can expect only the unexpected.

Stated succinctly, my boss Rep. Donaldson authorizes me to aid Albert's N.C.I.S. investigation. It exposes an offshore conglomerate associated with the "Diaz" name. My focus is the U.S.-Mexico border. Nothing suggests Arnhem Land. I put it far away.

In the café quiet I conclude to Rep. Donaldson, "Albert must introduce into his N.C.I.S. investigator's database the keywords: 'Diaz Security.'" Saying no more, she signs off.

I give Albert the keywords, "Diaz Security." He quickly tests using the two words to access unknown data. He receives a revelation. The "Diaz Security" keywords expose numerous shadowy offshore shell firms within a hidden global security conglomerate.

Albert asks how I learned the keywords, "Diaz Security." I'm silent about father's "Old Mexico" manuscript. Instead, I admit, "Isabella told me in a nightmare."

Albert quickly grasps that my dream is spectral evidence, inadmissible in court. He immediately urges, "Let's just say that Tom Berneray takes responsibility as the source of 'Diaz security.'"

Outside Café Cayman Albert disappears into shadows. I bicycle under streetlights to Puck Place. Slowly, I evaluate what I've helped Albert Jennings bring about.

Rep. Donaldson has authorized shifting her staffs' work. We'll postpone transferring U.S. satellite-drone technology to Australia. Instead, we'll collect evidence supporting prosecution of the San Diego satellite-drone private contractors' security breach.

Albert's outsmarted me. I must postpone seeking my father in Arnhem Land. More directly than before, I'll face Isabella's murder in Mexico.

II

Albert asks me to monitor his use of "Diaz Security." Albert informs Detective White that Tom Berneray is the source of these keywords. They reveal extensive new evidence for incorporation in confidential databases.

Detective White learns Diaz Security is a global private-security conglomerate. Its numerous subsidiary companies like G.S.S. are central to our investigations. The two keywords unlock vital evidence enabling prosecution of the satellite-drone contractors.

Albert tells detective White that offshore criminal financial practices are covered by a treaty. This empowers U.S. courts to issue search warrants which Cayman Island officials recognize. Using the term, "Diaz Security," Albert accesses Cayman shell companies. The satellite-drone contractors, Home and Jones, have used these same shell companies.

Basically: Home and Jones deposit illegal cash in bank accounts in Mexico. The partners "launder" this cash, transferring it into numerous lawfully registered offshore firms. These firms are registered in the Cayman Islands, as well as Delaware or Nevada.

Detective White admits to Albert: "Berneray's identification of Diaz Security's links to Global Security Solutions shows we've underestimated our enemy. They're even more dangerous than we thought."

Indeed, our investigations turn deadly. Detective White reports drone-contractor Jones' murder.

Albert shares White's murder report with Megan Wright, General Donaldson, and me. Jones' murder leaves Home, the satellite contractor, alone to be prosecuted.

Jones had been free on bail staying at his condo complex located on South Bay Marina off Silver Strand Highway. The night security guard had called Jones at home requesting authorization for a visitor. Jones granted the admittance of a dirty-white van into the complex and his own condo garage.

An hour later, the night guard reported the van returned to the gate, without notice from Jones. The van driver said nothing, but licked his middle finger. The guard allowed the van to depart.

The next morning, the housekeeper discovered her dead employer fully clothed, floating in the pool. Coronado police determined the deceased was the subject in an ongoing Sand Diego Police Department investigation and contacted the case officer, Detective White.

Albert shares Detective White's murder report on Jones. Jones had consumed no alcohol or drugs. He had been bound with tape that had then been cut from wrists and ankles.

Blood from face wounds smeared the condo garage floor. A blood trail reached the swimming pool. Held face down, Jones had been drowned. His body floated below the surface.

No one lived near enough to the Jones condo to hear a struggle. No condo resident identified the van entering or departing the complex.

The housekeeper stated her employer's computer system was gone. Empty drawers and two desktops indicate it was a large system. Detective White noted Jones' computer is safe in his drone workplace at the 32nd St. Naval Base. But data-comparisons with Jones' condo computer are impossible.

When asked if he'd seen the same old, dented, dirty white van before, the night guard had said, "Possibly, not sure." He was unable to identify the van driver and saw no one else inside the darkness of the van. The guard added: "On the border, some men lick their middle finger to signal cocaine use, just as the van driver did."

The night guard recorded the van's Upper Baja license-plate number. American and Mexican border officials reported the number was bogus. Neither nation's border officials recorded sighting the van.

The night of Jones' murder, a Navy drone had flown patrol on the Silver Strand. The drone pilot noted various speeding vehicles, but no van.

The drone pilot recorded an eighteen-wheel truck driving up and down Silver Strand Highway. The truck slowed but didn't stop—*twice*. The Marine drone pilot didn't detect why the big truck reduced speed.

As Detective White reported, the murder confirmed that drone-contractor Jones led multiple lives. He was a private contractor working on the Navy's drone system.

Drone contractor Jones and satellite contractor Home stole classified technology for Diaz Security. Possible motive: technology would enhance Diaz Security's competitive advantage protecting a cocaine cartel. Drone contractor Jones was also a cocaine dealer. These lives destroyed each other.

Detective White tells Albert that Jones was a U.S. citizen living many years in San Diego. His mother was a Mexican national. Detective White's investigation confirms Jones' brother is a Mexican citizen, living in Tijuana. Jones' brother owns a business named Pedro Construction. Drone contractor Jones was a silent partner in his brother's firm.

Detective White confirms anonymous sources implicated Pedro Construction as a builder of hidden cross-border cocaine cartel tunnels.

Months earlier, a U.S.-Mexico Task Force exposed one of these tunnels. Prominent media reported it as a major law enforcement victory. Anonymous sources confirmed that the cocaine cartel operates more tunnels.

Above all, Detective White says, a cocaine cartel boss must maintain the criminal cocaine supply and sales network. The cartel boss's agent hired an expert defense lawyer for Jones when he was charged in the satellite-drone contractor case.

Jones faced national security and cocaine possession issues, demanding a doubly specialized lawyer. In such cases, the prosecution carries a heavy burden of proof. An expert defense lawyer increases that burden.

Given these considerations, Detective White concludes, the cocaine cartel boss probably didn't order Jones' murder. White's colleagues continue to investigate who is responsible for killing Jones.

Detective White now considers only how Jones' murder bears on the prosecution of satellite contractor Home. Detective White relies on Albert's database evidence incriminating Diaz Security and its subsidiary, G.S.S. Detective White discusses Diaz Security only if asked, leaving its revelations to Albert and me.

Jones' murder leaves the prosecution with the trial of satellite-contractor Steven Home. He, too, is free on bail. After his partner Jones' murder, Home was assaulted waiting in his car on Silver Strand. Navy drone-pilot surveillance dispatched military police to save Steven Home. But the attackers had time to escape.

Fearing for his life, Home seeks and receives police protective custody. The prosecutor makes a deal: Home provides evidence in cases in which he's charged. He pleads guilty to lesser charges in the cocaine case. Sentencing Home on the cocaine conviction awaits the outcome of the national security case against him.

Satellite contractor Steven Home is charged with theft of classified satellite-drone technology. The theft is a significant U.S. national security breach.

To the charges of classified technology theft and breached national security, defendant Steven Home pleads *not-guilty*.

The prosecution's argument against defendant Home depends on the following evidence: Albert's offshore database, Detective White's investigations, Rep. Donaldson's staff testimony, and expert witness testimony.

The skilled defense attorney will try to aggressively discredit the prosecution's testimony and evidence. The full defense case is presented in a separate chapter.

The federal judge presiding in Steven Home's trial is Norma Taylor. My grandmother in San Francisco knows Judge Taylor from an organization, Golden State Republican Women.

Judge Taylor is from La Jolla. She graduated from U.C.L.A. Law School in 1970. Her law firm served wealthy business clients. Republican President Reagan appointed her U.S. District Court Judge in 1987.

The federal prosecutor is Mori Friendly. A Massachusetts native, she went to law school in Boston. As a Navy Judge Advocate General (J.A.G.) lawyer in San Diego, Friendly won many criminal prosecutions.

After Friendly retired from the Navy, President Clinton appointed her U.S. Attorney in San Diego. Friendly has won numerous drug trafficking cases.

The defense lawyer is Ogden Neville Simpson. For decades he's represented moneyed clients in Orange County, California. These include celebrities in drug cases.

Simpson is counsel for the Home family, owners of Beach Front Properties. The firm's sales motto is: "You can trust our business. Our name is in every home we sell." The defendant is the family's only child, Steven Home.

Simpson's defense of Steven Home follows high-profile courtroom victories. Simpson defended property owners of the President's Western White House during the Watergate Crisis, when federal agents damaged private real estate. A state court upheld Simpson's defense of property rights.

During the Vietnam War, Simpson represented a U.S. Congressman in a drug-bribery case. The Congressman was charged with using marijuana to bribe private contractors at the Marine Corps Camp

Pendleton. The jury deadlocked on whether the evidence warranted conviction. Simpson won again.

The Steven Home trial takes place in downtown San Diego. Despite perennial sunshine, the reddish brown Federal Building's stark 1960s architecture reflects stern formality.

The U.S. courtroom is on the second floor. A polished hallway ends at a recessed window. Through the glass, seagulls float in air or strut on the ledge. The gulls' freedom contradicts the court's adversarial truths, relative justice, conflicted hopes.

From the sunlit hallway I enter the courtroom. No windows. The primary color is white. The judge's bench is white. Judge Taylor's high-back leather chair is brown, flanked by Stars-and-Stripes and state flag, California Bear Republic. The bench has a spread-winged eagle seal affirming *E Pluribus Unum*.

The courtroom seems small. Seats are behind long white tables. Across from Judge Taylor's bench are spaces for defense and prosecution. Lawyers sit or stand. Other spaces are for testifiers and jurors. There is room for court security, clerks, and some spectators observing the case unfold.

The trial channels words and silences. I watch defendant Steven Home. Behind thick glasses, Home blinks nervously. He's more used to a computer's light in darkness.

Home is balding with jowly face, baggy flesh. Grey suit, white shirt, dark tie hang loose about him. He looks older than "middle age."

Simpson, the defendant's counsel, wears a crisp black pinstripe suit and solid red tie. Short grey hair and wire-rim glasses suggest the Army captain he was during the Vietnam War. Despite his age, Simpson radiates youthful energy. He's tall, tan, only slightly plump. Always, his face is serious.

Simpson's polished appearance doesn't suggest he attended a night law school. After Vietnam, Simpson studied law part-time.

He made money running a large real estate firm in Orange County. Simpson's business customers often became law clients. Business practices provided evidence in law cases.

Friendly, the prosecutor, exudes calm sincerity. Slender, medium height, trim reddish hair, she looks like a youngish Protestant clergywoman. Her suit is Navy blue, with plain white blouse beneath her jacket. She wears a wedding ring, unlike Simpson. The prosecutor will be unemotional, cold, relentless in establishing guilt.

Black-robed Judge Taylor sits relaxed at the bench. Horned-rim glasses suggest a university president or a winning corporate attorney. Her easy confidence reminds Republican friends, like my grandmother, of her political work for a Republican President. Judge Taylor's short brownish hair is graying naturally.

Prosecution and defense lawyers choose jurors carefully. A jury represents the community. Juror selection occurs from a pool composed randomly from registered voters throughout San Diego County.

Each side can strike a limited-equal number of jurors from the pool. The lawyers question each prospective juror in order to best use the few strikes. Questions leave twelve jurors.

Prosecutor Friendly is confident about her chosen Hispanic, white senior-citizen, and black and Asian female and male jurors. They could have prejudice towards a wealthy white male cocaine addict.

Friendly uses the U.S. military service loyalty held by veterans or parents of veterans to dilute such prejudice among her selected jurors. Since overtly expressed prejudice is easiest to appeal, Friendly avoids it. Veteran military service is a surer standard uniting her chosen jurors.

Simpson's juror selection reflects local knowledge. In southern California, older Mexican descendants holding U.S. citizenship can be more conservative than younger immigrants. Older generation Mexican women and men often are small business employers of more recent immigrants.

Simpson knows Mexican-descended employers expect employees to overcome discrimination like the older generation did. Resisting drug use requires supportive, church-going family communities.

This older Mexican-American generation knows drug cartels destroyed their native Old Mexico. They also feel some loyalty towards wealthy whites who provide jobs for honest immigrants.

Friendly must prove Steven Home's guilt beyond a "reasonable doubt." The Prosecution's evidence must meet that high standard.

Simpson will present his client in a positive light, reframing witness testimony and undermining credibility of evidence.

Simpson's jury selection suggests he'll seek a divided jury. Failing that outcome, Simpson might hope that despite a guilty verdict, the judge could reasonably award a lighter sentence. These contingencies influence Steven Home's trial.

III

I will now summarize prosecution and defense opening arguments, witness testimony, and defense lawyer Simpson's maneuvers. I'll try to clarify complex technical evidence.

Friendly's opening argument. Expressing quiet conviction, the Prosecutor is at ease before Judge Taylor. Friendly reminds me of my Medieval History professor at Harvard. No dramatics while addressing arcane evidence. Steady, reasonable analysis of facts and motives persuade heart and head.

Friendly states the case against defendant, Steven Home. "With Ralph Jones (now deceased), Mr. Home conspired to steal top secret satellite-drone technology vital to U.S. national security."

Friendly affirms: "The co-conspirators contrived a complex plan to steal this technology for a global private security conglomerate. This foreign private agent would use the stolen technology to aid cocaine cartel trafficking. The private security firm and the cartel work across the U.S.-Mexico border, as well as elsewhere within the Pacific Rim."

Friendly holds without examining prosecution documents. The case is fixed in her mind. "Mr. Home's co-conspirator, Mr. Jones, was recently murdered. In protective custody—with his lawyer present—Mr. Home admitted to personal cocaine use supplied by his co-conspirator, Mr. Jones."

Friendly, extends the documents towards the jury. "His admission requires Mr. Home's conviction for personal cocaine use. The Judge will decide sentencing in due course. Detective White of the San Diego Police Department will testify regarding the pertinence of that case to prosecution of Mr. Home."

Looking directly at the jury, Friendly exclaims. "Admitted guilt on the cocaine charges leaves for trial Mr. Home's reckless endangerment of U.S. national security."

"The prosecution will prove foreign private security agents paid Mr. Home to steal classified American technology. Mr. Home stole from his employer, the U.S. Navy. The theft violated contractual promises. This theft repudiated Mr. Home's solemn oath to defend his country and uphold the Constitution."

Friendly finishes: "Mr. Home pursued a conspiracy. He knows the U.S. government designates private security forces serving a drug cartel, like the cartel itself, to be terrorist organizations. They endanger U.S. security and community life. For his crimes, Mr. Home must receive full penalty of law."

Facing Judge Taylor, defense attorney Simpson is grave. "The defendant Steven Home is a broken man. He admits cocaine addiction. Yet for decades he's served America as a trusted Navy private contractor. The Navy continues to use Mr. Home's patent technology to combat our nation's enemies."

Simpson brings the case pointedly to the community. "First, Mr. Home joined other private contractors in developing the Navy's top secret satellite-drone technology. The program makes San Diego's military-civilian partnership a leader in new combined weapons technology."

"Second," Simpson raises his left hand for emphasis, "The Navy authorizes public use of Mr. Home's patent technology for civilian purposes. These include better weather prediction, improved control of flooding, mudslides, and forest fires. Property values are protected."

Simpson pauses, a heavy silence. Muffled, fire and police sirens can be heard on the city streets.

The defense attorney's trim logic again fills the courtroom. "The U.S. government and the Navy repeatedly judged Mr. Home's service to be excellent. Employment reviews concluded his performance warranted renewing his high security clearances."

Simpson draws himself to attention. "Only recently did a government oversight monitor discover a security breach regarding Mr. Home's contractual duties. The prosecution must prove the defendant's role in the security breach beyond a reasonable doubt."

Simpson lets silence build again. Finally he says, "Proving this security breach is just the beginning. The prosecution claims there is a conspiracy. The defense will show that assigning Mr. Home leadership in such a conspiracy rests on flawed evidence. If a conspiracy exists, my client is its victim."

We hear prosecution testimony. Each witness must respond with hand on Bible: "You do solemnly swear that the evidence you shall give this court shall be the truth, the whole truth, and nothing but the truth.

So help you God." Each testifier says: "I do so swear."

Following opening arguments, Judge Taylor states the prosecution and defense agree that high security classifications limit testimony revealing secret weapons technology. Within these limitations expert witness, Professor James Sims, Harvard Law School, examines the issues.

Professor Sims' engineering and economics education was at M.I.T., followed by Harvard Law School (1968). From Vietnam to the Iraq-Afghan wars, Sims has served as a U.S. government security consultant monitoring Navy private contractors.

Sims is also an active business consultant. His special expertise includes satellite-drone technologies and offshore financial issues.

I wonder if the defense attorney Simpson knows I recently met Professor Sims in San Diego. Also, my sister has worked on classified projects with Sims since she was his student at Harvard. Sims periodically recommends my sister's security company for consultant opportunities.

Sims often presents complex classified data in testimony before congressional committees, and in court. He speaks forcefully. Like any good lecturer, he reshapes large data chunks into smaller, comprehensible bits.

He begins placing the technology issues within an understandable context. "People know that satellite technology is adaptable. Familiar civilian uses are weather reporting and GPS. In spy and war fiction, by contrast, satellites are used for surveillance and espionage."

Thoughtfully, Sims states: "Satellites also enable targeted missile or laser strikes from drones. We expect ever growing uses of this combined technology."

Professor Sims presents technical terms in more familiar images. "In Iraq and Afghanistan, U.S. armed forces and intelligence operators have adapted satellite-drone technology to combat and counterterrorism purposes."

He draws a new image: "The Navy's new combined satellite-drone computer network integrates classified surveillance, guidance and targeting capabilities inside a more efficient drone delivery system. Combined technology becomes a winged sniper."

Sims stops. We absorb technicalities bearing on Steven Home's theft. Sims begins again. "In the present case many classified patent licenses link satellite computer capabilities within a new drone operating system. The defendant unlawfully transferred certain classified patent licenses to his partner, Mr. Jones."

Sims pauses then proceeds solemnly. "This partner was a Navy private contractor for drone component parts of the new satellite-drone system. Nevertheless, this drone-contractor partner *did not* have security clearances for certain licensed technology he received from Mr. Home."

Defense attorney Simpson requests: "Professor, please be more exact about these classified patent licenses."

"Objection," Friendly exclaims. Judge Taylor's gavel pounds, followed by: "Objection sustained. The defense has agreed that any discussion of classified materials will be approved first in my chambers with defense and prosecution present. Open Court is not my chambers. I remind Counsel that protection of classified data from public disclosure is vital to national security. Professor Sims, continue."

Sims chooses words carefully. "The stolen patent licenses are embedded among various classified satellite-patent licenses within an individual drone's operating system. The stolen patent licenses triggered security codes in the network of computer satellite-drone interfaces housed inside the new drone operating system."

Sims explains, "Within this network, oversight monitor Ms. Megan Wright, Chief-of-Staff for United States Congressional Representative Sarah Donaldson, who is chairperson of the U.S. military intelligence committee, identifies suspicious uses of satellite-drone interface computer codes. She discovered the security breach. It constitutes misused interface codes transferred from the satellite contractor Mr. Home, to his drone-contractor partner, Mr. Jones."

Sims adds, "Other computer codes link the security breach to technical U.S. congressional budget appropriations."

Sims appeals to our mind's eye. "Imagine in the Vietnam War there are separate operational systems. The C.I.A. and Navy use *unmanned flight vehicles* for surveillance and intelligence purposes. *Conventional piloted aircraft* employ new weapons technology, such as lasers. In Vietnam we must identify: separate operational systems, one manned, and one unmanned."

He begs our close attention. "After the Vietnam War let's consider each development that evolves into *combined satellite-drone tech-*

nologies."

In the present case, Sims presents each technological advance constituting a combined system: "Computers and software; satellite communication antenna; GPS; real-time and delayed video stream; increasingly sophisticated cameras; digital communications; laser-guided weapons, including rockets."

Sims presents these technical advances "housed within a lightweight composite drone shell cruising over great or limited spaces. Pilots operate these technologies safe in a command station far from the drone's field of operation.

"Combined satellite-drone technology evolves through warfare and espionage. In the 1980s, the C.I.A. developed a combined system for surveillance purposes aiding the Contras over the Sandinistas in Nicaragua. During the 1990s Balkans air war, conventional piloted Stealth bombers operated along with unmanned drones. Drones became lethal weapons. The 9-11-01 Al-Qaeda attacks were a major stimulus. Drones flew search-and-kill missions pursuing terrorist leaders, including Osama bin Laden."

Sims describes recent advances in U.S. classified combined satellite-drone technology developed during the Iraq-Afghan Wars. Drone pilots had operated from secret bases in Europe. Now, secure bases in the U.S. itself give drone pilots intercontinental strike and surveillance control.

Sims urges those of us in the courtroom to remember: "By now, the Air Force has trained more pilots to operate unmanned vehicle systems, known as drones, than conventional piloted aircraft. Meanwhile, unclassified civilian combined technologies grow, although a drone's flight range is limited to a few hundred miles."

Sims includes costs arising from the security breach. "For research and development, the Navy, other U.S. military, and intelligence bodies spend billions of American tax dollars on private contractors like Mr. Home and his partner, Mr. Jones.

"Their conspiracy steals classified technology for use by a cocaine cartel and its security firm through offshore shell companies," Sims emphasizes. "The conspiracy turns U.S. government classified patents and patent licenses to criminal purposes."

Sims adds, "Congressional committees and their staffs, led by elected officials like Rep. Donaldson, fund and monitor these patent technology contracts. Her staffs' monitor, Ms. Megan Wright, identified Mr. Home's and Mr. Jones' classified contract violations. Investigators have identified further violations."

Defense attorney Simpson addresses the Judge. "The defendant's *civilian* patent-license contracts do not necessarily concern national security issues."

Judge Taylor agrees, granting Simpson's questions: "Are the civilian versus classified patent-license contracts Mr. Home transferred to his partner Mr. Jones distinct or somehow entwined? The expert witness does not address the issue. I ask him to do so."

The silent courtroom waits until Professor Sims speaks. "The Navy aids civilian development by releasing into public domain earlier *declassified* patent technology. Once declassified, this older technology is used for civil purposes such as better weather prediction or improved responses to natural disasters."

Sims explains: "The security breach originating with Mr. Home, which Ms. Wright discovered, included patent licenses used in the Navy's new classified combined technology. Mr. Home also transferred older declassified patent licenses. These declassified licenses present no national security breach."

Sims addresses both types of evidence. "In the defendant's personal computer, investigators uncovered *two classified* and several declassified licenses he'd transferred to his partner. Together, both patent license classifications could be used to build a satellite-drone system design from the 1990s."

Simpson asks: "The charge against Mr. Home results from *two classified licenses* transferred to his partner, Jones, correct? What percentage is this of all licenses constituting the older, stolen combined technology system? Did Mr. Home and his partner, Mr. Jones, actually build a version of this older system?"

Professor Sims answers exactly: "The national security breach arose from the defendant transferring *two classified* patent licenses to his partner. The defendant also transferred several declassified patent licenses."

Sims gives the results: "Both patent-license classifications hypothetically contribute to *designing* a modified 1990s-type satellite-drone system. *We have no evidence showing the defendants together or separately constructed this system.*"

Continuing, Professor Sims elaborates, "Within this design, the total percentage of licenses originating with Mr. Home is roughly 5% of about 100 patent licenses. The defense, prosecution, and the court agree that theft of *even one classified* license is a significant breach of U.S. security."

Prosecutor Friendly addresses Simpson's defense questions, "Expert witness evidence shows that, without question, Mr. Home transferred classified patent license technology to his partner Jones. Presence of *declassified* license technology does not put into question the unlawful *classified* license transfer."

Friendly presses: "The criminal act for which Mr. Home is prosecuted is an admitted *classified* technology transfer to his partner, Jones. Again, whether a percentage is large or small does not alter admitted proof that a classified combined technology has been stolen and transferred in violation of law, endangering U.S. security."

The next prosecution witness is N.C.I.S. chief investigator, Albert Jennings. His highly polished Oxfords, crisply pressed dark suit, and college tie mute his ghostly freckled face, hazel eyes, and cropped reddish hair. Hands folded. Body composed. Face earnest. His West Indian English accent is clear and smooth.

To those of us in the courtroom, Albert's oath to tell the whole truth is believable. He testifies that his N.C.I.S. investigation has discovered revealing evidence.

Albert persuasively affirms, "An urge to supply defendant Home's cocaine addiction triggered a complex conspiracy. Partners Home and Jones stole classified technology enabling construction of a satellite-drone system. An obscure private security company paid the partners for this theft."

Judge Taylor grants defense attorney Simpson leave to ask a question. "Agent Jennings, the defendant is on trial. Not an unnamed private security firm. You claim defendant Home conspired in the theft of satellite-drone technology for a security company you do not identify. Evidence, evidence, what is your evidence?"

Judge Taylor orders Agent Jennings to answer Simpson.

Albert's body tenses. "Investigators discovered a conspiracy centered on a hidden financial holding company conglomerate. Only recently we identified this conglomerate by the name 'Diaz Security.'

Inserted as keywords into confidential N.C.I.S. databases, 'Diaz Security' opens a factual maze."

Albert stares at the white wall. "We soon realized that Mr. Home and his partner Mr. Jones never learned the 'Diaz Security' name itself. They knew only that the border security firm Global Security Solutions (G.S.S.) was the subsidiary of what to them was an unnamed global holding company."

Albert guides us through this labyrinth in the courtroom. "Once Mr. Home and his partner discovered the unnamed private holding company, they manipulated it."

Albert emphasizes how criminals are manipulating criminals. "Home and Jones receive unlawful cocaine dollars, 'dirty cash,' from the holding company—through G.S.S.—to steal and build a classified satellite-drone system. One partner, Jones, deposited the cash payments in Mexican bank accounts of his brother's firm, Pedro Construction."

Albert speaks more slowly. "From these Mexican accounts, the partners transfer—launder—the cocaine cash. It's deposited in smaller lawful amounts throughout various legal offshore shell companies registered in the Cayman Islands or Nevada."

Albert's maze continues. "The lawful Cayman transfers lead to lawful bank accounts of various G.S.S. subsidiaries the partners own as offshore firms holding various lawful accounts in San Diego banks."

Albert stops. Silence prepares us for darker revelations.

His deep voice implores our belief. "The two contractors used some of this *laundered money* to pay G.S.S.—*the subsidiary of that same holding company that funds their combined technology theft*—to guard the cocaine cartel's border tunnels."

Albert reveals the partners' deeper conspiracy: "The laundered money also enabled Mr. Home to purchase—through his partner, Jones—cocaine from the same border cartel. When the conglomerate uncovered that it was the target of a scam, the partner, Jones, was murdered. Mr. Home's life is also threatened."

Judge Taylor interrupts. "Agent Jennings, the defense and prosecution accept that much of your critical evidence comes from confidential N.C.I.S. databases. It is admissible evidence, like expert witness testimony. Nevertheless, you must formally name the security company." Albert's answer, leads to me.

IV

Judge Taylor continues, "Agent Jennings, your warrant-search of offshore accounts relies on what the defendant, Mr. Home, apparently did not identify: the holding company's name, 'Diaz Security.' How did your investigation identify that name? The court must know that the evidence is truly admissible, for example, not 'tainted.'"

Albert answers Judge Taylor indirectly: "Certain facts led us to identify 'Diaz Security' by name. During the Iraq War, Home and his partner worked on C.I.A. intelligence operations using licensed patent technology. The C.I.A. contracted some of these same licenses with the previously named firm: Global Security Solutions. The C.I.A. did not examine the corporate financial structure controlling G.S.S."

"But Mr. Home *did partially trace* financial control of G.S.S.," Albert asserts. "Mr. Home earned fees from his own satellite patent licensed contracted to the C.I.A. The C.I.A. subcontracted this surveillance technology to G.S.S. to conduct clandestine operations."

Albert reveals: "Personal hacker skills enabled Home to monitor fees the C.I.A. paid for his technology and subcontracts to G.S.S. *But, G.S.S. added an unauthorized, therefore illegal, transfer. It surrendered operational control of the technology to the unidentifiable financial holding company that owns G.S.S.*"

Albert grips our attention. "Again, Mr. Home didn't *identify by name* the holding company he'd discovered. The cocaine boss confirmed for Home and his partner that G.S.S. guarded the cocaine cartel's cross-border tunnels. This boss now learned that the unnamed holding company controled G.S.S. as a subsidiary."

Albert exposes the partners' audacious plan. "They manipulate the unnamed holding company conglomerate's hidden control of G.S.S., a C.I.A. operative, and a security guard for the border cocaine cartel. With the cocaine boss as intermediary, the partners propose that G.S.S. leaders ask their parent holding company to fund theft of classified satellite-drone technology. *That is: pay Home and Jones to steal classified satellite-drone patent licenses in order to build cocaine cartel security's own drones.*"

Albert adds that Detective White's investigation found that the holding-company conglomerate accepted the partners' plan to improve the criminal security services G.S.S. offered the cocaine cartel by turning the drone to cocaine cartel-security purposes.

We in the courtroom gradually absorb the partners' extraordinary operation. Albert focuses on the conglomerate's subsidiary, G.S.S., as the source for naming "Diaz Security." Albert avoids mentioning me as that source.

Albert ends succinctly. "With the key words 'Diaz Security,' investigators traced the partners' Mexican and offshore accounts in N.C.I.S. databases. They exposed the money trail from the shadowy conglomerate to the partners, which enabled theft of the combined technology in an older drone operating system. This combined technology system would improve the conglomerate's criminal competitive advantage."

Defense attorney Simpson demands Albert's response. "Defense and prosecution accept evidence *originating* in N.C.I.S. databases, like expert witness testimony."

Simpson makes the point: "Agent Jennings, you haven't revealed where your initial 'Diaz Security' identification originates. Only *after* identification were the keywords, 'Diaz Security,' inserted into N.C.I.S. databases. How did investigators learn the 'Diaz Security' name in the first place?"

Albert finally answers Simpson: "Our source for the name 'Diaz Security' is Mr. Berneray. After learning about G.S.S. from Detective White, Mr. Berneray identified 'Diaz Security.' He speaks for himself."

Simpson's tanned face is expressionless, dark eyes empty. He draws the courtroom to me. Combating Simpson's questions feels like striking back at my knife attacker. Strength comes from hiding my father's manuscript, which protects my mother and sister from cocaine cartel retribution.

Simpson addresses me: "Mr. Berneray, you are Rep. Donaldson's staff attorney. Expert witness and Agent Jennings' testimony concerns national security or confidentiality. But your evidence unlocks much of this data, Mr. Berneray. How did you identify 'Diaz Security' by name?"

"The truth is," I insist, "Diaz Security came to me in a nightmare."

Incredulous, Simpson demands that Judge Taylor "remind the witness he is under oath to tell the whole truth." She does so, but grants Simpson's assertion: "Spectral evidence is not admissible."

I say: "Agent Jennings testified that Detective White told me that my knife attacker's employer is G.S.S. Her testimony will confirm that."

Simpson exclaims: "Mr. Berneray we want *your* testimony, *now*."

I look passed Simpson at three jurors he chose. I imagine speaking personally to each of these older Mexican-American women dressed conservatively in white and black. Each one wears a small silver crucifix. My aunt Esperanza Quinn often wears just such a cross.

"My mother's brother, Alex Quinn, married, Esperanza, the granddaughter of Mexican Revolutionary hero, Juan Bermudez," I say, truly. "The Bermudez family lived in Santa Maria, Sonora. When Juan Bermudez died, the President of Mexico delivered the eulogy there. I attended the funeral."

The three Mexican-American women jurors' faces are passive, bodies rigid. One of them fingers her crucifix.

I continue: "The Quinn's daughter, Isabella, and I were engaged to be married in Santa Maria. Since my sister and I were children, we visited the Bermudez family. We loved to be in the family of Juan Bermudez. When he died we felt anguish."

Simpson exclaims: "Answer the question, Mr. Berneray!"

Levelly, prosecutor Friendly reminds us, "Defense counsel started this line of questioning. 'Spectral evidence' is not admissible, of course. But it can lead to admissible evidence of certain 'psychological evidence.'"

Judge Taylor raps her gavel asserting: "Witness, continue." Simpson's face is blank.

The three Mexican-American women jurors stare at me as I speak. "After Juan Bermudez died a drug cartel took over Santa Maria. Miguel, Juan's grandson, condemned the Diaz bank. It financed cartel shipments of cocaine from Colombia into Santa Maria, then North, across the border."

I look straight at Simpson. "I was at law school. In Santa Maria Isabella visited Miguel and other family members. In the desert Isabella and Miguel were murdered. No one believed police claims that bandits murdered them. When I arrived the local priest told me that if I'd been with Isabella I'd have been murdered, too. After the murder, Isabella's parents disappeared from Santa Maria, fleeing on the Pacific."

The courtroom floats around me. I hear myself say: "I have never been back to Mexico. When this Navy private contractor case began, I joined Chief-of-Staff Megan Wright in assembling our staffs' trial affidavits. Then a man with a knife attacked me. Detective White identified this man's employer as G.S.S. Soon after Detective White named

G.S.S., I had the nightmare about Isabella's murder."

I answer Simpson's question with a true lie. "I often have that nightmare. This time, Isabella tells me that bank guards named 'Diaz Security,' murdered her. I'm a lawyer. I know that 'spectral evidence' is inadmissible. Yet psychological impressions may suggest or lead to facts that are admissible."

Courtroom silence invigorates the atmosphere. I feel the jurors, judge, Prosecutor Friendly, even Defense Attorney Simpson weigh my reasoning along with Albert's complex data.

Simpson's blank face betrays no feeling towards my "nightmare" evidence. He says, "We'll return to this line of questioning after the prosecution's testimony concludes."

The Mexican-American woman jurors watch me as I leave the witness stand. Once I'm seated they study the next witness. Still, I feel my nightmare rings as true with these women as Albert's data.

Next, Detective White presents her investigation results in conjunction with Agent Jennings. Detective White's reports are admitted evidence. I summarize the testimony and cross-examination of Detective White.

She is unemotional like an effective teacher chastising a good student for bad work. Detective White begins, "Agent Jennings' testimony clarifies how national security conspiracy issues arise from the defendant's cocaine use. It requires N.C.I.S.-S.D.P.D. cooperation."

Detective White's calm belies the drama she unfolds. "Defendant Home admits and awaits sentencing for receiving cocaine from his partner, Jones. The criminal exchange serves the two partners' wider conspiracy. They stole American classified technology for Diaz Security, through its subsidiary, G.S.S. This technology theft could promote Diaz Security-G.S.S. criminal capabilities to protect the cocaine cartel."

"But Mr. Home and his partner Mr. Jones are more audacious," Detective White says. "Their money laundering exploits the cash payments Diaz Security-G.S.S. makes to the partners for the theft and building of the satellite-drone operating system. Admittedly, no evidence shows actual construction of this system.

Detective White adds, "Mr. Home pays some of his ill-gotten cash in order to supply his cocaine addiction. Mr. Jones actually supplied the cocaine Mr. Home consumed."

We in the courtroom absorb Detective White's matter-of-factly stated evidence. "The partners transfer some of the cash received from Diaz Security to G.S.S. for guarding the cartel's border tunnels. The cocaine cartel boss *should* pay G.S.S. for guarding the cartel's tunnel operations."

Detective White hesitates. The impression is: her evidence is correct, even if incredible. "Because of the partners' money laundering scheme, the cocaine cartel boss *pays nothing* for G.S.S. services."

Detective White lets this sink in and then adds: "Diaz Security payments also go to Pedro Construction. The owners are Mr. Home's drone partner Jones and Jones' brother. These advantages could drive the partners' money laundering scheme."

Detective White knows the consequences: "Once Diaz Security leaders learn they are being exploited, they murder drone partner, Mr. Jones. They also go after Mr. Home. Criminals rob criminals. They pay the price."

Simpson's cross-examination of Detective White begins by professing "astonishment at the scheme the partners perpetrate against their criminal employer, Diaz Security."

He asks Detective White if "satisfaction of defendant's admitted cocaine addiction is sufficient explanation of the partners' remarkable money laundering scheme. It deceives Diaz Security into paying for both theft of the satellite-drone system and cocaine cartel's tunnels. Discovery means brutal death."

Responding to Simpson, Detective White declares: "You need to recall that Diaz Security uses satellite-drone technology in order to charge the cartel more for protection. Hidden from the C.I.A., Diaz Security leaders learned about Mr. Home's surveillance technology the C.I.A. licenses to G.S.S. Mr. Home and his drone-partner then approached Diaz Security with the business proposal to expand G.S.S. criminal services."

Detective White observes coldly, "Diaz Security bought into the partners' theft and construction of a combined technology system once used by the C.I.A. The criminal conglomerate wanted to possess powers like the C.I.A. There are mixed motives here: money-making advantages and pride of power."

Simpson asks, "What does Mr. Home and his partner, Jones, gain?"

White replies smoothly: "First, consider the consequences the partners face once Diaz Security accepts their proposal. Tough criminal penalties if it's exposed that the partners violated American security identified with their employment as Navy private contractors. Much worse, Diaz Security discovers it is the object of the partners' money laundering scheme. Each partner's life expectancy becomes very short."

Detective White then considers why Mr. Home accepted the risks. "We can't discount the influence of cocaine addiction. The defendant's personal computer files show the high physical and money costs of his addiction. It's truly expensive. For him, the addiction could be sufficient justification."

Detective White pauses. Courtroom anticipation grows. "Drone partner Jones's gains are more complex. As a cartel operative, the drone partner must pay for the cocaine he supplies to his partner, Mr. Home. Still, the cash Diaz Security pays for the theft and building of the illegal combined-technology system more than covers total cocaine costs to both partners. 'Profit margin' still favors partners individually and the cartel."

Detective White concludes. "The partners' money laundering shifts costs for guarding the cartel's tunnel operation from the cocaine cartel to Diaz Security-G.S.S.. The partners hide their deception in legal off-shore accounts. Diaz Security leaders somehow discover the deception and exact retribution."

Simpson insists, "The partners share the extraordinary risks. The money laundering scheme benefits drone partner Jones more than Mr. Home."

Friendly responds, "The scheme reaffirms defendant Home's willingness to violate lawful duties and solemn oaths as a Navy private contractor. Ms. Megan Wright's staff-affidavit testimony further confirms this."

Megan Wright's testimony summarizes affidavits from Rep. Donaldson's staff. After studying the affidavits, Friendly and Simpson allow Megan's summary testimony. She knows her staff and their evidence well. Prosecution and defense can call upon individual staff members for clarification purposes.

Megan is confident, wearing a plain brown pantsuit. Short dark hair frames a lean athlete's face without makeup. Trim, small, well-conditioned body. Loafers, not heals. "She looks like a 'hot babe' trying to look ordinary," I overhear a courtroom security guard tell his partner as he leaves.

Friendly asks Ms. Wright to categorize the defendant's classified work among Navy private contractors in San Diego. The Prosecutor states Megan's evidence will not reveal top-secret material.

Megan expresses faith in her staffs' reports. They show, she says, that "Mr. Home held high-security clearances for licensed-patent technology contracts. These contracts adapted classified satellite-surveillance computer technologies within advanced drone operating systems."

First, Megan turns to "Mr. Jones, the drone contractor, who joined engineers in constructing the drone's outer shell. He held a lower security clearance than Mr. Home."

Megan testifies that the satellite contractor and the drone contractor worked together in the same Navy project team. Only the Navy could authorize the drone contractor's possession of highly classified technology like Mr. Home's. Ms. Wright and others routinely monitor all such classified contract transfers.

"Without the Navy's authorization," Megan exclaims, "drone contractor Jones received two of Home's classified patent licenses. The transfer of Home's classified patent-license technology to the drone contractor triggered a security code showing unauthorized possession."

The trigger prompted Megan's closer systems analysis. She discovered the security breech. Unauthorized satellite technology transfers from Home to drone contractor Jones jeopardized the operation of classified weapon component parts.

Megan won't reveal classified weapons technology. But several staff reports Megan is authorized to share show Mr. Home works on a related *declassified* project.

Megan asks all of us in the courtroom to "imagine that the following *declassified* combined-technologies operation is *classified*. Imagine it. Exposing any classified component part threatens operation of the entire system. It constitutes a serious security breech."

"So imagine," Megan says, "a Marine patrol in mountainous Afghanistan accesses this satellite-drone technology. The Marine officer and the drone pilot cooperate to target a remote village. Within minutes, satellite-drone computer data reveals whether the village is friendly or should be destroyed. But if an enemy could intercept the combined system data that enemy would entrap the Marines."

Simpson insists: "No evidence shows that the classified technology Mr. Home gave his partner in fact has been used to construct an unlawful combined system."

Megan agrees: on that point Simpson is correct.

But prosecutor Friendly reminds us, "Evidence reveals the unlawful *transfer* from the defendant to his partner. It is the criminal act for which Mr. Home is being prosecuted and should be convicted."

Megan draws her staffs' summary testimony to a close. "In rare cases, San Diego Navy private contractors have been prosecuted for certain crimes, including drug violations. The present case, however, is unique. Criminal drug trafficking and national security issues are entwined."

Simpson demands: "Ms. Wright, your staff testimony includes accounts of Mr. Home's business besides work for the Navy. We should hear that evidence."

"Of course" Megan affirms, "Mr. Home and his partner pursue lawful private-contractor practices. Like other private contractors, they operated multiple lawful private enterprises for profit. Often, the U.S. tax code permits such enterprises to operate offshore, in the Cayman Islands, Nevada, Delaware, and elsewhere."

"Nevertheless," Prosecutor Friendly declares, "defendant Home and his partner Jones exploited lawful patent licenses and bank accounts, those summarized in Ms. Wright's staff testimony. Following previous N.C.I.S. and police testimony, we see Mr. Home and his partner turned certain lawful bank and offshore accounts to criminal money laundering purposes. The defense does not dispute this evidence."

Simpson's silence is louder than words. It suggests the prosecution's preceding evidence is too reasonable to challenge directly. Cross-examining Megan, Simpson pursues an indirect approach.

Asking Megan to explain certain facts in her staffs' affidavits, Simpson says: "Prosecutor Friendly and I agree that generally, Ms. Wright, your staff names Mr. Home and his partner together. Both names appear on most of their San Diego and offshore financial accounts. The same is true for each man's condo mortgage: one in Coronado, the other on Silver Strand. Why both men's repeated togetherness?"

Before answering Simpson's question, Megan looks down. Her action conveys a thoughtful response. "The appearance of both names is understandable for financial accounts and real estate shared by business partners."

"Business partners do business together," Friendly interjects. "Defense counsel and I agree also upon where either partner is doing business by himself. For example: Mr. Home owns companies using his own patent technology that operate under his name alone. Also, Mr. Jones, the drone contractor partner, owned a San Diego construction company. Jones operated it in his own name."

"We'll further explore this line of testimony after the prosecution closes," Simpson says. "The defense concludes cross-examination of Ms. Wright's staff testimony. We ask Ms. Wright to discuss Mr. Home's education and family background."

Megan's response is firm and sure. "Our staffs' affidavits show that Mr. Home was a brilliant undergraduate and graduate student. He won awards for patents integrating new computer and satellite technologies. He earned a Ph.D. The Navy hired him as an advanced-research private contractor. He helped pioneer adopting these new technologies to evolving satellite-drone operating systems."

Simpson presses Megan: "Your staffs' testimony also shows this brilliant student's dark side."

Megan pauses. She answers with sad conviction. "In graduate school Mr. Home knew a student who eventually became a tenured professor in the same university. Decades later, one of my staff was a student assistant for this professor. They maintained contact after my staffer graduated."

Megan notes: "All this evidence appears in staffer, Ms. Li's, affidavit. She interviewed her old professor about Mr. Home's student days. This professor agreed that Home was a brilliant student. He was also a loner, known to have a cocaine habit."

Simpson switches subjects. "Now tell us, Ms. Wright, about Mr. Home's community service, alone or with his partner."

Megan is earnest: "Mr. Home acted by himself when sponsoring science awards for 'deserving, at-risk students' participating in science fairs at several San Diego middle schools. He also assists his parents' Orange County real estate business in finding jobs for 'qualified'

Mexican immigrants." Megan explains that "qualified" means a local Catholic priest vouches for the immigrant's "trustworthiness."

Simpson presses Megan on the community service of Mr. Home and his partner, Jones. She answers: "Home's partner, Jones, pursued no community projects by himself. Together, the partners actively supported 'Gay Strong' community events. Also, immigrant labor the Home family provided often worked in several construction businesses Jones owned." Simpson's cross-examination ends.

Friendly concludes that prosecution evidence supports the defendant's guilt. Simpson's defense testimony, and prosecution cross-examination, begins next day. Judge Taylor adjourns the Court.

V

The black-robed Judge glides away. Shuffling feet empty the starkly white courtroom. Outside, the hallway ends at tall glass windows. I stand alone. Keeping truth and deception distinct pains me. Nothing distracts from the isolated city and bay lights in dusk. Even the gulls of the morning have abandoned me.

My trial testimony has been used as admissible evidence naming "Diaz Security." But I learned the name "Diaz Security" from an inadmissible, "tainted" source: my father's "Old Mexico" manuscript. Because Father named "Diaz Security," I trusted Isabella's naming it in my nightmare. That also is inadmissible evidence.

If the judge and defense knew I'd relied on father's manuscript, my testimony would've been rejected.

My deceptions reinforced Rep. Donaldson's decision that the trial requires suspending renewal of U.S. combined-technology transfer to Australia. The new Presidential Administration authorized renewed technology-sharing through transfer after the previous administration had destroyed it.

The renewed technology transfer was the reason Chief G and Malangi advocated my Arnhem Land mission. It also enabled the search for my father.

My deceptions reinforced the suspension of technology transfer and the search for Father in Arnhem Land. Australians supported my search because they wanted the transfer.

Isolation weighs on me. I'm a lawyer. Under oath I've told half-truths. Simpson would've easily undermined Father's "Old Mexico" manuscript as "tainted" evidence. I couldn't prove where it came from, or how it arrived at my home.

Legal ambiguities give me no absolution. I feel intractable obligations to my family, my boss, Representative Donaldson, and my friend, Malangi. My obligations are life and death facts, like Isabella's murder, that leave me alone.

My fingers and palms press the warm glass of the tall windows. Lights elude my grasp. Isabella and I are small children at the Bermudez home in Santa Maria. The game is to grab all marbles in one hand. With each try, one marble escapes through my fingers. She laughs. Relentless determination and failure are too much. I cry. Laughter stops. Her fingers wipe away my tears.

"Other things are important, *mi corazón*," Isabella says. I remember how she started learning English from Quinn, her father, the useable words she needed to live among Americans. The Spanish from her mother, Esperanza, was for what mattered most, like "my heart," the endearment Esperanza uses for Alex Quinn. Isabella used it for me. We were just children.

"Mr. Berneray." My name calls me back. Turning, I face Prosecutor Friendly. "Security alerted me that someone from my prosecution was lurking around the courtroom after hours. What are you doing here? Are you alright?"

My intuitive urge is to say: "I'm unfaithful to my oath to tell the whole truth." Instead, I find another truth. "I'm sorry. I was dreaming."

She studies me. "Not another dream from you, Mr. Berneray. Agent Jennings convinced me we could get by with you naming 'Diaz Security' from a dream. Let's leave it there."

"Jennings can be persuasive," I admit.

"Your sincerity was enough for Judge Taylor," she says. "Actually, I think it helped us with those older women jurors the defense picked. You told a powerful story. Sad about your fiancé, though. But no repeat performance, it'll cast doubt on all your testimony and that will hurt our side."

I apologize, again. She says, "Go home. Court starts early tomorrow. The defense is gunning for us." In wondering silence, she accompanies me down the elevator, past the security guards, outside the courthouse. Friendly leaves me on the sidewalk.

A taxi takes me to Puck Place. No Montoya patrols the darkness. Mother and Ann aren't home. I'm alone amidst memories of doing my duty owing to intractable obligations. I face Malangi's bark painting. Father still waits for me to find him.

SIX

━━━━━━━━━━━━━━━━━━━━━━━━━━━━━

San Diego: Trial Defense, Verdict

Café Cayman, the night before I testify in court. "Mrs. Berneray," Albert says to me, "Defense attorney Simpson wants you to support the Mexican Internal Security Force agent, Max Blanco. He'll testify that Home's partner, Jones, is the real criminal in this trial."

Albert asserts: "Simpson's defense argument is unusual. He will attack our prosecution testimony using an anti-Vietnam War incident Rep. Donaldson shared with you, her closest friend."

I don't understand how an antiwar mission Sarah Donaldson and I accomplished decades ago has any bearing on the prosecution of Steven Home. We never revealed any of our missions. Not even to our families. I don't see how Simpson discovered it.

Albert replies: "Simpson learned about your mission from Mexican I.S.F. Agent Blanco. It is Blanco's word versus yours, Mrs. Berneray. Simpson will build up Agent Blanco's testimony by targeting you and Rep. Donaldson."

Albert returns me to Puck Place. We pass the young Marine, Montoya, on patrol. I feel his aloneness. But my son, Tom, will be in court, trusting me.

Albert continues. "Mrs. Berneray, Simpson will exploit your relationship with Rep. Donaldson and her staff, especially Tom. Prosecutor Friendly didn't predict that Agent Blanco knew about your anti-Vietnam war mission. Friendly must address Simpson's reasoning."

Albert elaborates. "Simpson chose Mexican-American jurors. They're patriotic U.S. citizens. They also know the cocaine cartel destroyed their beloved 'Old Mexico.' Prosecution testimony shows Home and Jones pursuing a conspiracy together."

Albert slows down, like he's talking to a child, "Simpson's argument blames Jones for crimes against U.S. security. Simpson wants patriotic Mexican-American jurors to believe Jones dominated the conspiracy, using his partner Home's cocaine addiction."

Albert pauses and goes on. "Prosecution testimony shows two 'equal' partners conspired together. Simpson argues Home was a means to enable Jones to serve his cocaine cartel bosses—and make the Diaz Security conglomerate pay for it."

Albert concludes. "Simpson seeks to persuade the jury that Jones' dominance of Home mitigates Home's guilt in the conspiracy, and that Home was too weak to be an 'equal' conspirator with Jones. Simpson builds up Jones—he had a long history manipulating powers like the C.I.A. Coincidentally, one of Jones' successful manipulations surprisingly included the Donaldson-Berneray anti-Vietnam war mission."

I feel Albert doubts my ability to face Simpson and Blanco. I will battle them to understand why an obscure anti-Vietnam War mission aids the defense of Steven Home. Simpson's and Friendly's relentless questions and witnesses' answers will expose what Sarah Donaldson and I believed was buried. I write what follows as I experienced it.

I

In the morning courtroom: defendant Home and his lawyer, Simpson, his witnesses Blanco and Berneray, Judge Taylor, prosecutor Friendly, her witnesses Albert and Tom, certain spectators, the jury.

Simpson begins by agreeing that U.S. Navy top-secret classifications protect Home's licensed patent technology. It mustn't be disclosed to the jury. Public revelation of classified technology would aid U.S. enemies.

Instead, Simpson's defense begins with Blanco. He is a "Special Agent" in Mexico's Internal Security Force. He serves on the U.S.-Mexico Border Joint Task Force. Special Agent Blanco led Mexico's side in a Task Force operation against the cocaine cartel's border tunnels. He is a prosecution witness in other American criminal trials of cocaine dealers.

Special Agent Blanco sits at attention, hands on his knees. He is short, powerfully built like Seri horsemen I remember in Santa Maria. Black hair, immobile brown face, and dark eyes remind me of my sister-in-law, Esperanza's grandfather, Juan Bermudez. Incorruptible integrity personified. I easily trust Blanco's oath to tell the "whole truth." I know Prosecutor Friendly's cross-examination will test honest Blanco.

Blanco's education was in economics and history at universities in Mexico, British Columbia, and California. He trains Special Forces in border security. His bilingual fluency helps him communicate well to American, Canadian, and Mexican students. Age about 50, Blanco is an active field agent.

He wears a beige suit, white shirt, grey tie, yellow-white-black Argyle socks, and brown shoes. In Sonora his clothes embody middle-class respectability. He rejects the costly, flashy dress of a cocaine cartel boss.

Blanco's deputy agents are in the courtroom. Two former students of his, they blend in, informally dressed. They sit apart, presenting no single target. The young man is slender, medium height, shaved head, dark face disfigured by old scars. The small, Indian woman from Southern Mexico appears passive, too easily ignored. The three I.S.F. agents left their automatic pistols and knives with court-security.

Special Agent Blanco testifies about Jones' multiple lives leading up to his murder. Jones' hidden cocaine network supplied Home's addiction. A U.S. citizen by a Mexican mother, Jones also was a U.S. private contractor. He has worked for the C.I.A. or the Navy since the Vietnam War. He held a contract for fuselage parts in the Navy's drone system. Jones, the drone contractor, and Home, the satellite contractor, were partners.

Blanco admits: "Prosecution witnesses identified Cayman offshore money transfers requiring both Jones and Home's consent, together. The partners endorsed money laundering that manipulated Diaz Security into theft of combined technology and into *paying itself*—through G.S.S.—for cartel border tunnel operations."

But Simpson and Blanco argue that Home's role is passive. The special witness shows that Home gives Jones old satellite-drone technology. Home transfers old combined technology to protect U.S. security. Jones, not Home, uses G.S.S. to convince Diaz Security: possession of combined technology will beat competitors and enable the cocaine cartel and Diaz Security to counter the U.S.-Mexico Border Task Force.

Friendly challenges Blanco that Home was a "passive" coconspirator with Jones. Blanco admits that the expert witness, Professor Sims, confirms Home gave Jones at least two top-secret, combined-technology licenses. Defense attorney Simpson accepts that this threatens U.S. security. But the expert witness didn't explain why Home also transferred old combined-technology.

Simpson has Blanco answer: cocaine addiction could be, as the Prosecution admits, Home's motive for supporting money laundering schemes. Jones exploited Home's addiction. But addiction couldn't overcome Home's love of America. This is Home's patriotic motive in transferring old combined technology to Jones.

Home moans. Exhausted, he slumps back into silence at the defendant's table. Judge Taylor's gavel orders Simpson to preserve his client's dutiful form in court. Simpson exclaims: "Jones accepted old combined technology because his priority was to manipulate Diaz Security." Home remains quiet.

I wonder why Simpson's characterization of Jones and Home's motivations aroused defendant Home from silence. Home's tortuous pain made Simpson explain his statements about motives.

Blanco's testifies: "Jones benefited most from *leading* the money laundering manipulation of Diaz Security. Jones and his Mexican brother owned Pedro Construction. We have new evidence that shows Pedro Construction ran its own offshore firms to construct border tunnels. Agent Jennings' offshore Cayman data also exposes the fact that Jones and Home used Pedro Construction to manipulate Diaz Security."

Special Agent Blanco exposes Jones' deadly command. Through Blanco we feel Jones ordering cartel agents to lure unemployed Mexicans to border warehouses, promising work with Pedro Construction.

Jones orders cartel agents to kidnap the unsuspecting laborers. At Jones' command the Diaz Security subsidiary, G.S.S., provides guards to protect the cocaine cartel operators and control captives. Jones demands reports.

In the warehouses, cartel agents and guards halt escapes by guaranteeing death to captive workers' families.

Cartel agents organize captives into tunnel-digging crews. G.S.S. stations guards within and outside the warehouses. Inside, cartel agents supply captives with minimum food, water, and sleep. This supports around-the-clock digging.

Constructing a one-mile tunnel across the border takes about three months. Guards patrol the warehouse in Mexico and at the undercover building destination on the U.S. side of the border.

In completed tunnels cocaine cartel agents and guards kill and bury captive workers.

Blanco and his team learn how Jones supplies labor for the tunnels: from his parents' real estate business, Home sometimes provides his partner, Jones, immigrant workers for lawful construction firms in San Diego. Jones had cartel agents kidnap some of these workers to labor and die in tunnels. Jones' Pedro Construction offshore subsidiaries own the buildings where the tunnels begin and end.

Blanco shows that Jones rather than Home was best situated to manipulate Diaz Security. Jones held a low-security clearance for Navy drone fuselages. Partnering with Home, Jones learned about top-secret combined technology. Jones also led a cocaine network that built border tunnels for the cartel and Diaz Security-G.S.S. Cocaine addict Home depended on Jones.

Simpson uses Blanco to explain the cocaine market and security costs pushing Jones' leadership over Home: "Cocaine market costs shape Jones' operations. In Colombian jungles, producing *one* gram of cocaine costs $3.00. That same gram on American streets sells for $180. Mr. Home epitomizes Americans' insatiable cocaine demand. Addiction-driven demand makes suppliers like Jones dominant."

"Costs drive cocaine profits for everyone, including Jones," states Blanco. "Colombian and American military interdiction programs add to cocaine *production* costs. American local, state, and U.S. law enforcement increase cocaine *retail* costs. Transport into, across, and exiting Mexico influences *entry* costs. South Mexico's jungles increase— while isolated harbors like Santa Maria reduce—entry costs."

"Jones, not Home, maneuvered in Mexico's cocaine distribution network by exploiting failed government," Blanco asserts. "Mexico's government failures create a 'law and order' vacuum. For cocaine market-share, cartels fill this vacuum, *attacking each other and killing innocent people.* Cartel violence and corruption defy Mexico's federal and state armed forces and courts, despite American aid."

Blanco elaborates: "Some cocaine cartel bosses expect trusted operators like Jones to employ dependable security firms like G.S.S., hired at a price within cocaine cartel profit margins."

Another business factor is high-risk insurance: "Security firms like G.S.S. employ costly offshore risk insurance applicable to 'captive insurers.' They underwrite G.S.S., providing the cartel with well-armed and trained personnel. Jones has G.S.S. use a 'captive insurer' operated as a Pedro Construction subsidiary."

"In the U.S., a 'law and order' vacuum does not exist," Blanco knows. "The Home and Jones criminal prosecutions epitomize how American courts and police enforce the rule of law. American law enforcement bristles with firepower. Civilian and military armed forces use drones and other American technology like that deployed in foreign war zones. In certain places, the U.S. has built a border wall."

Blanco's voice turns sad. "However, harsh realities constrain American law enforcement. American gun-makers supply 90% of firearms used by Mexico's drug cartels. Commentators insist these weapons are stolen. Detective White reports that gun thefts in San Diego total, at most, a few hundred. Border cartels' firearms total *tens of thousands,* acquired from offshore gun dealers selling American weaponry to cartels."

Smoothly, Blanco adds: "U.S. rule of law, border walls, superior firepower and technology can't end the cocaine flow to consumers like Mr. Home. Jones' management of border tunnels insures that."

Simpson stops Blanco. His painful testimony is chilling. I feel evil swelling over the border into my family and my friend, Sarah Donaldson's, lives. Next, Simpson and Blanco will take aim at me.

Prosecutor Friendly demands—and Simpson submits to court and Friendly—documents showing Jones' connections to Pedro Construction's offshore subsidiaries and G.S.S.'s offshore "captive insurers."

Courtroom silence magnifies Friendly's quick study of the documents. She knows the Cayman-registered companies Home and Jones cosigned in their money laundering scheme. She compares Home-Jones Cayman cosigned firms to Jones' Pedro Construction subsidiaries and "captive insurers."

Friendly admits: "Jones ran a separate offshore operation so that Diaz Security-G.S.S., rather than the cartel itself, funded border tunnel construction. But the Cayman-cosigned scheme is the work of the Home-Jones partnership. Home's criminal transfer of combined technology within that partnership manipulated Diaz Security-G.S.S. into accepting the double money laundering scheme."

Friendly demands that Simpson explain how Blanco knows about Jones' Pedro Construction offshore subsidiaries and "captive insurers." Jones' condo computer was destroyed. Investigators found no such evidence in the Jones or Home computers at San Diego Naval Bases or private-contractor firms.

Simpson wears a blank face. He tells Blanco to answer Friendly "completely."

Without emotion, Blanco recounts his story. Months earlier, the media reported that the Border Joint Task Force had discovered and seized a cartel border tunnel. It was a major border law enforcement victory. Usually, cocaine cartel money and weapons keep the tunnels hidden. Detective White headed the Task Force team on the U.S. side of the border. Blanco led his team on the Mexico side.

For the first time, the Border Task Force licensed costly Navy satellite-drone technology. The drone pilot operated from a Marine Corps base on Silver Stand. The pilot reported to Blanco and White.

The Navy drone was equipped with new classified sound-detection computers and GPS to identify suspicious "noise sites." Combined technology sifts myriad sounds within hundreds of warehouses clustered along both sides of the border. This gives Task Force leaders Blanco and White a new advantage.

Blanco explains. In two border warehouses, the drone isolated recurring sound patterns: around-the-clock digging, and vehicles frequently entering and departing from each warehouse.

We in the courtroom assume the vehicles bring in supplies and haul away dirt. This Blanco confirms, "Task Force computers tapped a Mexican phone landline, and erratically, cellphone calls from one warehouse."

The technical information enabled "our Joint Task Force to conduct a 'Tunnel Operation.' We achieved surprise. Detective White's team entered an empty warehouse. She found paperwork identifying building-materials firms registered 'offshore,' in Nevada. That state registers many offshore firms."

"My team," says Blanco, "arrived in time to stop several security guards and cartel agents from killing all the captive laborers. In the struggle, each killer died. We rescued two badly wounded captives. They recovered and entered our protection program. They've given us much useful information."

Friendly comments coolly: "Sadly, no security guard or cartel agent survived for questioning."

Blanco scans the courtroom, finding his agents. Absolute loyalty unites the three. Blanco replies: "In hand-to-hand fighting, each killer's throat was slit. It happens, fighting cocaine cartels in Mexico."

The Mexican-American jurors express no emotion. Yet the implicit retribution against cocaine dealers and security companies that destroyed Old Mexico surely means these jurors agree with Blanco.

Arms across chest, Simpson listens as Blanco concludes: "The evidence in our tunnel operation became clear after Jones was murdered. His Mexican brother was then wounded in a drive-by shooting. He pleaded for our protection. In return, he exposed his brother's tunnel operations and Pedro Construction offshore subsidiaries—several of the same Nevada offshore firms Detective White found in our tunnel operation."

Blanco repeats the vital source of trial evidence: "Detective White left the Jones condo murder investigation to our Joint Task Force. We received the Mexican brother's evidence of Jones' cartel tunnel leadership and Pedro Construction subsidiaries after Prosecution witnesses testified."

Simpson adds that Blanco has already presented all this evidence.

Friendly admits: Blanco's new evidence reveals Jones used Pedro Construction offshore accounts to build cartel border tunnels. The separate scheme doesn't deny Home and Jones cosigned Cayman offshore accounts in order to steal combined technology. Home is being prosecuted for that theft.

Simpson will use me as a defense witness next. Simpson expects to maneuver "Mrs. Berneray" into building up the credibility of Blanco's testimony, focusing on Jones.

Judge Taylor grants Friendly's request to delay further examination of Blanco. Friendly will pursue that cross-examination in relation to me, Diana Berneray, as I testify for the defense.

II

My hands are cold. Simpson argues my testimony will expose an incident, also witnessed by Max Blanco, in which "Diana Quinn (née Berneray) and Mrs. Sarah Donaldson (now a United States Congresswoman) suppressed criminal conduct during the Vietnam War. Jones' criminal conduct is implicated in this Vietnam War incident and the trial of Mr. Home."

Friendly objects that Vietnam War evidence is too remote in time to be relevant to the defense. Friendly also demands documentation from Mexico's Internal Security Force (I.S.F.) proving Blanco can be a credible witness to events occurring decades earlier in Canada. Blanco would have been a young man.

Just before my testimony begins, Simpson submits Blanco's qualifications to the court. Blanco's grandfather fought in Sonora during Mexico's Revolution. Blanco's father was a Federal Army officer on the Mexico-U.S. border from the 1960s to the 1980s. In 1973-74 Blanco was a young undercover I.S.F. Agent representing Mexico in a joint operation with Canadian and American military intelligence in British Columbia.

Simpson has maneuvered Friendly into accepting Blanco's silent presence as I testify about the Vietnam War incident. The jury knows that Blanco is well qualified to later testify on the same incident.

In Blanco's shadow, I swear "to tell the whole truth." My oath fills the courtroom, but I speak to Tom. Seated behind him is Marine Corps General Donaldson who conveys his wife's, my dear friend Sarah's, presence.

The Donaldsons married during the Vietnam War. I was Sarah's maid-of-honor. My fiancé, Corporal Jim Berneray, was a groomsman for the-then *Major* Donaldson.

Simpson starts unexpectedly: "Mrs. Berneray, you are under oath." He hands me an old, familiar black and white newspaper photograph. National Guard bayonets face students quietly assembled in a vigil. Sarah Donaldson and I hold a banner exclaiming: VETERANS' COALITION AGAINST THE WAR.

"Identify the two women holding the banner, Mrs. Berneray," says Simpson.

Firmly I reply: "Sarah Donaldson, Coalition President, and I, Diana

Quinn, Vice President. Late in the Vietnam War, 1973, it was a pretty familiar photo in the papers, even on television in California. It was our only Veterans' Coalition Vigil, attended by other antiwar groups."

Judge Taylor exclaims impatiently to Simpson: "Your introduction of this photo is questionable evidence. Next to the Donaldson banner, I'm there as a student holding the placard 'U.C.L.A. Young Republicans Support Vietnam Veterans.' Show your proof through convincing evidence from Mrs. Berneray's testimony, or I end it."

Simpson is unfazed. "Identify three young women, Mrs. Berneray. Where are they and why? When is the photo taken?" He hands me an enlarged, glossy, black and white photograph.

I jolt forward. Both hands grip the photo. Words tumble. "With our passenger, Sarah and I are rowing across open water. Unexpectedly, a big motor yacht came down on us. The wake flooded our boat. We nearly drowned. The crew seized us, took us aboard the yacht. They surrounded the three of us on deck. We feared they'd rape us."

Coldly, Simpson demands: "Answer the questions, Mrs. Berneray."

Judge Taylor intervenes again: "Mr. Simpson, the witness's surprise undoubtedly is genuine. Your statement regarding the obvious need to answer the questions is unnecessary. Please continue Mrs. Berneray."

Judge Taylor's response to Simpson dissipates my shock. I answer: "The photo must have been taken in late 1973, right after our vigil imploring Congress to end American military forces in Vietnam. In this photo, which I've never seen before, we're on the yacht deck. The three of us are wet, cold, frightened, surrounded by strange men."

Simpson insists: "Identify the third woman. Where are the three of you, and why? You are under oath to tell the whole truth, Mrs. Berneray."

General Donaldson studies me. I reply unsteadily. "Most of the day we'd rowed in choppy, open water to reach Beagle Island which is off northern Vancouver Island, British Columbia. I can identify our passenger only as a veteran against the Vietnam War."

Incredulous murmur in the courtroom reinforces Simpson: "In a small boat through choppy, isolated sea you've rowed together for hours without knowing the identity of your passenger?"

The question hangs over me. Between Simpson's relentlessness and General Donaldson's stare, I'm speechless. Simpson's efforts to prove Jones' leadership so far seem to have no apparent link to events reflected in this photo. Blanco must know something I don't about the entire incident. Simpson is manipulating what Blanco knows but apparently I don't know.

Judge Taylor orders that I answer Simpson.

I feel Tom's trust and confidence in me. It inspires me to shape the "whole truth," saying least about Sarah Donaldson. See where that leads. It is Blanco's word against mine.

At this point no one is sure what I know. Or why it is different from what Blanco may know. What we have in common is the obscure antiwar incident off Beagle Island.

Silent, I quickly consider Simpson's defense logic. He wants Blanco and I to shift the jury's attention from Home to Jones. Our factual details should highlight Jones, thereby overshadowing Home. But I don't know what "facts" Blanco apparently knows.

I'm truthful: "Sarah Donaldson and I did not know our passenger's name because she came to us anonymously. Certain church peace groups supported our Veterans' Coalition. We worked with veterans discharged from and those still serving in the armed forces. The latter group included our passenger."

Simpson addresses me as if he's truly perplexed. "You are witness for the Defense. The court, jury, and I want to believe you, Mrs. Berneray. We hear you testify that you and Mrs. Donaldson transported 'those serving in the armed forces' from the U.S. You knew your passenger was a deserter?"

Friendly objects: "Defense question leads the witness." Judge Taylor overrules, accepting that Simpson seeks clarification of my testimony, as defense witness.

The exchange enables my next honest response to Simpson. "Actually, the truth is that this late in the war the military often designated people like our passenger as 'Absent Without Leave,' A.W.O.L. A.W.O.L. has much weaker punishments than desertion. We transported A.W.O.L. personnel, if they became antiwar protesters seeking asylum in a foreign country. In our passenger's case this country was Canada."

Amidst courtroom quiet we hear jet planes takeoff a mile away. I believed no one knew about our antiwar work with A.W.O.L. soldiers. Its revelation might distract Simpson from Sarah.

Simpson attacks. "Mrs. Berneray, you play with words. You admit the truth: in time of war, Mrs. Donaldson and you aided a member of the American military to abscond from obligated duty into a foreign country. You enabled the woman's flight, a crime against America. Identify this woman."

Simpson wants to frame our antiwar Veterans' Coalition as aiding deserters. He's appealing to jurors that Friendly has chosen who favor veterans' honorable service.

Judge Taylor orders me to answer Simpson. My words feel slippery as stones in tide pools.

I state historical facts. After Nixon's Watergate scandal, President Ford endorsed some peace groups' appeals. He granted amnesty to certain war resisters in U.S. armed forces. In principle, Ford's amnesty included military personnel designated as deserters and A.W.O.L. Principle and reality clashed.

Confidently, I say: "I'm not a lawyer. I can't address legal rules and intent defining 'amnesty.' I know very well the problems our antiwar veterans had in 'qualifying' for 'amnesty.' The third woman in that photo is a perfect case in point, exposing the perils amnesty seekers and their supporters faced."

"Evasions won't work, Mrs. Berneray." Simpson stands over me, voice frigid. "Your obscure history can't hide the fact that Mrs. Donaldson and you enabled American military personnel to abandon obligated service. You covered it up once. Your cover is blown. Answer the questions."

His words hit me. I mumble: "We didn't cover up our missions. No one asked us what we did, until now."

Pervading the courtroom, I feel palpable disbelief. It pains me. Our cause was right. Simpson's attack falsely maligns us and the veterans we aided. Anger chokes me. I'm hurting my friend's and my cause.

Simpson postures sincerity: "I ask you to speak the truth, Mrs. Berneray. You're being evasive."

Turning to Judge Taylor, Simpson pleads for understanding, palms upturned. "We don't doubt evasion is deception. Agent Blanco will speak to that deception." Simpson sits beside his client, Home.

My face burns. Hands tremble. Blanco, his two agents, the jury feed Simpson's entrapment. Silence gives consent. General Donaldson looks away. Tom is powerless, face contorted. Judge Taylor doubts me.

On Home's bowed head and slumped body, my words fall empty. They all believe I'm hiding something.

Friendly begins cross-examination. Her words flow smoothly, questioning. "Court and jury know the Prosecution did not choose this witness. We seek only the 'whole truth,' like the defense."

Friendly speaks calmly: "In an incident of witness's peace work for veterans in the Vietnam War, the defense counsel insinuates Mrs. Berneray is hiding something that somehow could be relevant to actions attributable to Mr. Jones. But we're left without evidence showing a connection to this witness's and her colleague's antiwar mission. Most importantly, we've heard nothing that bears on prosecution of Mr. Home."

Friendly faces the jury. She's as thoughtful as a junior officer standing at ease before a superior. "Consider Mrs. Berneray's testimony about a media image of 'Vigil for Veterans against the Vietnam War.' It shows diverse antiwar work. Three women seized from a flooded boat off British Columbia are part of the diversity we must understand."

Friendly ponders the photo's relevance to Vietnam War veterans. "Americans imagine many Vietnam veterans to be P.T.S.D. suffers or broken, homeless people. These images ignore that in a bad cause and defeat, nearly all veterans served honorably."

"Mrs. Berneray claims the women captured in this surprise photo reflects a Vietnam War veteran seeking Presidential amnesty. Insufficient evidence supports her claim. Defense counsel asserts deception on Mrs. Berneray's part. Defense counsel offers as evidence for his assertion only that Mrs. Berneray's testimony is incomplete."

"Who is right, Mrs. Berneray?"

For my answers, Friendly breaks down Simpson's surprise photo images into questions. Friendly's direct questions and my straightforward answers should show whether or not Jones' manipulations could have been present in Sarah's and my anti-Vietnam War mission. Indirectly, Friendly counters Simpson's focus on Jones over Home.

Q. How did the anonymous passenger come to be with you on an isolated sea, Mrs. Berneray?

A. We picked her up from a British Columbia coastal rendezvous. We knew the date, time, and place. Not how she got there. We were responsible for getting her to the rescue station on Beagle Island.

Q. Why the complex precautions involving the passenger pickup and transport, Mrs. Berneray?

A. Our Veterans' Coalition ran a system to circumvent capture by U.S. border surveillance and its erratic, covert collaboration with some Canadian police. Our system-model was the Underground Railroad during American slavery.

Q. Did your system require secrecy, as did the historic Underground Railroad, Mrs. Berneray?

A. Secrecy was our shield. Amnesty was controversial. To avoid publicity of court cases, U.S. agents harassed Veterans' Coalition work through phone taps and failed infiltration of our organization. Certain U.S. government agencies hired private contractors to attack us.

Q. Against such forces, did your system succeed, Mrs. Berneray?

A. Yes. Churches and colleges were vital. Before computers, they provided confidential networks linking peace groups like our Veterans' Coalition. Volunteers in a just cause, we willingly incurred risks.

Q. You knew your missions could result in lawful penalties, even imprisonment, Mrs. Berneray?

A. Yes. I'm not a lawyer. Yet coalition members received free—very expert—legal aid. We were advised to keep working parts within the network separate. It made discovery and legal proof difficult.

Q. Your passenger's anonymity at the time of pickup was part of the system, Mrs. Berneray?

A. Yes. To prevent discovery, or to limit legal proof if caught, each person in our network received minimal information. For example, at a church Coalition Vigil, an unknown someone slipped me the necessary information explaining and enabling pickup of the unnamed woman in the photograph.

Q. You didn't know from whom the information came, Mrs. Berneray?

A. No. We knew only our own role in the mission. Lawyers told us: admission under oath simply of the facts we knew would, when handled by a good lawyer, make conviction difficult.

Q. How did you pay for your mission, Mrs. Berneray?

A. We Veterans' Coalition members paid for our missions. My father established a life-trust for me. I was free to use it for our work. Also, since my childhood, my family and I have visited our house on Beagle Island. Travel costs to the Island are modest. It was my boat that we kept at the island for use in our missions.

Q. What sustained you and Mrs. Donaldson in a hard, ultimately dangerous, mission for a stranger?

A. For years Sara Donaldson and I rowed women's crew at the very competitive university level. We believe in each other absolutely. We were roommates for several years. We were each other's bridesmaids. My brother, my husband (then fiancé), and Sarah Donaldson's husband are Marine Corps Vietnam War veterans.

Q. What connects U.S. amnesty to your passenger's need to reach the Beagle Island rescue station?

A. Swearing before the rescue-station commander, she'd formally request and receive political-refugee asylum in Canada. An antiwar veteran holding this status was fairly sure to qualify for amnesty.

Q. Qualifying for Canadian political refugee asylum means the veteran loses U.S. citizenship?

A. Yes, usually. A few exceptions proved the rule.

Q. Why would an antiwar veteran receiving Canadian refugee asylum still seek amnesty?

A. After the U.S. veteran acquired Canadian refugee asylum, the F.B.I. or other agencies continued to harass the veteran's family. If the veteran acquired amnesty, harassment ended. The veteran could visit family in the U.S. and return to Canada in peace.

Q. Why would U.S. government agents harass anti-Vietnam War veterans, Mrs. Berneray?

A. Especially once U.S. defeat was apparent, some people spread blame to antiwar veterans. These veterans were criminalized and deprived of benefits. Some went A.W.O.L. and became deserters. Covert government harassment intended to limit such veterans seeking amnesty. That intent failed.

Q. Was amnesty granted automatically to those seeking it, Mrs. Berneray?

A. No. Amnesty seekers reported to designated U.S. military bases. Each claimant was offered a civilian counselor. The counselor compiled a case-report using the claimant's testimony and military record. The report could include external testimony supporting or condemning the claimant.

Q. Was the claimant's case-report used in an administrative hearing to grant or deny amnesty?

A. Yes. The hearing was before J.A.G. lawyers trained to handle amnesty proceedings within the Code of Military Justice. Claimants could appeal the hearing-outcome to special military judges. Military lawyers and judges were known to be fair, appeals rare. Outcomes usually favored claimants.

Q. You believed your passenger would receive amnesty after claiming Canadian refugee asylum?

A. Yes. In our other missions, individuals received justice in Canada and in amnesty proceedings.

Q. Mrs. Berneray, you were confident you'd reach the Canadian rescue station on Beagle Island?

A. Yes. I'd rowed those waters since childhood. I knew we were nearing Beagle Island.

Q. What happened?

A. Deadly shock.

Q. You feared for your lives?

A. Yes. From coastal haze, a motor yacht headed straight at us. Sarah exclaimed that we'd be captured. Strangely, to me the yacht's black hull seemed familiar. We pulled the oars in frenzy. The yacht passed by us, too close. The wake flooded, but didn't sink us. We started bailing. The yacht slowed, and came around again. Rifles aimed at us from the deck.

Q. Rifles?

A. Yes, rifles. A Spanish-speaking officer ordered us to transfer to their yacht. I replied in Spanish. We reached the deck, trembling. Rifles were still pointed at us. "Rescue! We rescue ladies!" yelled the officer in bad English. Suddenly, rifles shifted hand-to-hand, disappeared below deck. Empty-handed men surrounded us. We were all scared.

Q. What was going on?

A. Noise from the throbbing rotaries of a big helicopter engulfed us.

Q. That is when someone snapped the photo the Defense counsel uses to surprise you?

A. Apparently, yes. The photo can't convey the confusion caused by the rotary blades pounding the air, making the sea churn and the yacht rock. It was a huge Royal Canadian Navy helicopter hovering over us. Tentacle-like lines descended. Masked, armed dark figures scrambled over the deck. The seized yacht crewmen were dazed, now unarmed, handcuffed, and forced to their knees.

Q. What about you, Mrs. Donaldson, and your passenger?

A. A Canadian rescue station cutter arrived. Its officer ordered the "three women" to use the dinghy to get from the yacht to the cutter. Onboard no one said anything. The cutter pulled my boat. We soon reached Beagle Island.

Q. You learned what was happening?

A. Not really. The cutter officer and I acknowledged we were Beagle Island friends. The officer's subordinate took away our passenger. She eventually received asylum and amnesty. My officer friend commanded Sarah Donaldson and me not to reveal the incident. He ordered us to suppress it. We did that.

Q. After the attacks on the Veterans' Coalition, is it reasonable for you to have followed that command until now, revealing the incident only under oath?

A. Yes. At first, because we didn't want our missions to harm cooperative relations with Beagle Island Canadian officials. After Vietnam, Mrs. Donaldson entered politics in San Diego as a veteran and Navy advocate. She truly didn't know what the incident was about. Silence was our best policy. I must add: by the time Sarah Donaldson ran for election in the 1990s, very few individuals in San Diego publicly defended the Vietnam War. Also, the few people who remembered President Ford's Amnesty program could claim Mrs. Donaldson as an "amnesty" supporter. When Mrs. Donaldson first ran for office, her husband was a Marine Corps General on active duty in warzones. I know of no public questioning of his support for his wife, during or since the Vietnam War."

Friendly's cross-examination questioning of me regarding the yacht incident ends. Friendly says Simpson's introduction of my testimony as defense witness has no proven link to Jones. Blanco will address that point, responding to direct questions.

III

We in the courtroom assume Blanco truthfully answers Simpson's questions.

Q. Agent Blanco, the photograph that surprised Mrs. Berneray concerns your first I.S.F. mission?

A. Yes. My mission was to join a yacht crew. My cover was

photographer and English translator. The yacht's criminal cover was to prepare to transport a Mexican botanist to the rainforests on Vancouver Island.

Q. Agent Blanco, your mission was to penetrate the yacht's cover. What was the yacht hiding?

A. My mission was partly to discover how that yacht worked within Mexico's marijuana or cocaine networks. These networks had arisen since the 1960s to satisfy North America criminal drug markets.

Q. Why do you say: "partly," Agent Blanco?

A. I.S.F. wanted to prove its agents were trustworthy. Canadians needed Mexico's honest cooperation because the Vietnam War made the C.I.A.'s legal credibility problematic.

Q. You mean the C.I.A. conducts illegal operations?

A. American and Canadian military intelligence services share intelligence with I.S.F. Each military service checks the other. The C.I.A. hires private contractors. Their operations often were and are illegal.

Q. Agent Blanco, you knew the yacht was operating as a private contractor for the C.I.A.?

A. Canadian and U.S. military intelligence briefed me. I was assigned because the I.S.F. learned that a C.I.A. private contractor had used laundered money to operate the yacht in Mexican drug-trade networks.

Q. The present year is 2009. It is now public knowledge that U.S. agents worked with Mexican drug traffickers during the 1970s and 80S. Does this include the yacht incident in the early 1970s, Agent Blanco?

A. Yes. Canadian and U.S. military intelligence assumed an I.S.F. agent could best penetrate the yacht's secrets: a drug cartel operator and C.I.A. private contractor, masquerading as a botanist's yacht.

Q. Your cover was yacht photographer/translator. You snapped the photo that surprised Mrs. Berneray just as the Canadian Navy helicopter operation began? Did you know about this Canadian operation?

A. I took the photo as you say. I did not know beforehand about the Canadian Navy operation.

Q. Did you know why the yacht ran down the boat and the three women, Agent Blanco?

A. No. I overheard some crewmembers say that the yacht Captain must have ordered it.

Q. Could you identify any one of the three women in the swamped boat, Agent Blanco?

A. No.

Q. Did you believe the deck officer's claim that the yacht had "rescued" the women?

A. No. We all heard the helicopter. Rifles disappeared. Canadian Marines descended.

Q. What happened aboard the yacht after the Canadian cutter took the three women away?

A. Canadian Marines took the yacht to a Naval Base on Vancouver Island. The yacht captain demanded to be charged according to law, or released. A thorough investigation of the yacht and its crew revealed no incriminating evidence involving drug trafficking. I did the translating from Spanish to English.

Q. How did the Canadian investigation end?

A. Canadian military intelligence briefed the Canadian Naval Base authorities. Lack of evidence meant the yacht was released with what amounted to a warning never to reenter Canadian waters.

Q. Canadian Naval Base authorities, like the Beagle Island commander, suppressed the incident?

A. Yes, that was the case as far as I knew at the time.

Q. What happened to you after the suppressed incident? Did you learn more about it later?

A. The yacht captain never doubted my cover. In Victoria, he paid for my job. Canadian and U.S. military intelligence debriefed me. I completed my university history and economics studies. I remain an I.S.F. Agent. Over the years, I have received secret I.S.F. mission reports. The old incident has sometimes been mentioned.

Q. Why would I.S.F. occasionally refer to this decades-old mission in Canadian waters?

A. The incident wins I.S.F. credibility with Canadian and American military intelligence. During the Vietnam War, the Donaldson-Berneray yacht incident, and this present Steven Home drug cartel money laundering trail recurs in different forms. It can happen anytime, anywhere. In such cases, each nation's military intelligence understands I.S.F. is reliable.

Q. The yacht captain intended to capture and incriminate the women as drug traders?

A. That was the understanding I received from my operation debriefing in 1974.

Q. Drug cartel money laundering connects the Donaldson-Berneray yacht incident to the Home trial?

A. Yes. The C.I.A. private contractor used laundered money during the yacht incident, intending to attack and discredit the Veterans' Coalition. The same private contractor reappears in the Home trial.

Q. Who is this private contractor in both the Donaldson-Berneray incident and the Home trial?

A. A cocaine cartel leader and Mr. Home's "drone" partner, Ralph Jones.

Simpson submits into evidence I.S.F. documents. Friendly receives copies and lays them aside. Simpson resumes questioning and Blanco answers.

Q. Agent Blanco, what do the I.S.F. documents just submitted into evidence show?

A. Jones was a U.S. citizen. His brother is a Mexican citizen. Jones' San Diego engineering firm employs legal and illegal Mexican workers. During the war, in the early 1970s, Jones held contracts for C.I.A. projects in South Vietnam. Jones also ran a network selling illegal drugs to American military personnel in the U.S. and Vietnam.

Q. Do the I.S.F. documents show the C.I.A. knew about Jones' criminal drug network in Vietnam?

A. No. In Vietnam, Jones covered and kept separate his C.I.A. projects from his drug cartel work.

Q. How did Jones prevent discovery of the drug cartel network in Vietnam?

A. During the Vietnam War, Jones hid his drug cartel network using an offshore company. This company separately laundered payments received in the drug network and from the C.I.A.

Q. Did Jones use his offshore company for other illegal operations?

A. Yes. Jones' offshore company registered the yacht involved in the Donaldson-Berneray incident. Jones was a double agent: he served the cocaine cartel and the C.I.A.

Q. What is the name of Jones' offshore firm that registered the yacht? How was it discovered?

A. The name of Jones' offshore firm is simply: "Global Operations." The I.S.F. found all of this in the evidence Jones' brother gave us once he entered our protection program, after Jones was murdered.

Q. Is "Global Operations" related to G.S.S. and other offshore firms involved in the Home trial?

A. I asked Agent Jennings to address that question for I.S.F. We combined our offshore data with his. We answer: "yes," Global Operations is an offshore subsidiary of G.S.S., as well as Pedro Construction.

Simpson submits to the court documents that combine the I.S.F. and Albert Jennings' data. Copies go to Friendly. She accepts them without comment. Undoubtedly, she'll study them later.

Simpson and Blanco's welter of evidence impresses me. Blanco's testimony shows direct connection between the decades-old yacht incident and the Home trial. That connection is the cocaine cartel operator and C.I.A. or Navy private contractor, Jones.

Simpson's questions and Blanco's answers still claw at our minds in the courtroom.

Q. Agent Blanco, did Jones' C.I.A. private contracts extend over the decades from the Donaldson-Berneray yacht incident to Mr. Home's trial?

A. Not to the Home trial. As the "drone" private contractor, Jones worked for the Navy at the time, not the C.I.A.

Q. From the Donaldson-Berneray incident to the Home trial, Jones was a cocaine cartel leader. Did his deep experience enable money laundering manipulation of the Diaz Security company at issue in the Home trial?

A. Yes. Jones' decades of cocaine cartel leadership explain his money laundering manipulation of Diaz Security. Jones manipulated Diaz Security regarding both border tunneling and theft of combined satellite-drone technology.

Q. Agent Blanco, beyond Jones' clear involvement, are there other ways the Donaldson-Berneray yacht incident concerns the prosecution of Mr. Home?

A. Mrs. Donaldson and Mrs. Berneray depended upon Canadian officials' acceptance to accomplish their worthy antiwar missions during American hostilities in Vietnam.

Q. Isn't transport of fugitive U.S. military personnel to Canada in wartime illegal under U.S. law?

A. The yacht incident arose within Canadian court jurisdiction, burden of proof is on the U.S. Those who received political refugee status won. Legal culpability of Mrs. Donaldson and Mrs. Berneray in either nation's courts was never tested. Obedience to the Canadian officer's suppression order was, and remains, a strong defense.

Q. Again, beyond Jones' involvement, can you identify other connections between the yacht incident decades ago, and the present trial of Mr. Home?

A. Yes. I.S.F. evidence shows Rep. Donaldson continues to respect the Canadian officer's suppression order up to, and including, her staffs' testimony in the Home Trial.

Simpson again submits new I.S.F. documents into evidence. Friendly accepts copies without notice. Simpson's next questions and Blanco's answers perplex me.

Q. Agent Blanco, what does this new I.S.F. evidence reveal about Rep. Donaldson's present actions regarding the Vietnam-era yacht incident or Mr. Home's prosecution?

A. Mrs. Donaldson was first elected to Congress in San Diego about twenty years after the Vietnam War. Her constituents include the U.S. Navy and Marine Corps. She procures funding for science-and-technology development vital to U.S. security. She also defends the rights of military personnel charged in illegal drug cases.

Q. Does this electoral leadership have direct bearing on Rep. Donaldson staffs' testimony in the Home trial, including I.S.F. references to the yacht incident?

A. Yes. I.S.F. briefly cited the yacht incident. It supports I.S.F.'s request for a Border Task Force license of satellite-drone technology used in our cocaine tunnel operations. Rep. Donaldson's military intelligence committee approves I.S.F. and Task Force requests. Donaldson staff testimony includes all of these documents for use in the Home trial.

Q. Rep. Donaldson's staff testimony in the Home trial incorporates documentation from I.S.F., the Border Task Force, and Rep. Donaldson's military intelligence committee? All have references to the decades-old Berneray-Donaldson yacht incident?

A. Yes. In I.S.F., Border Task Force, and Rep. Donaldson intelligence committee documents, "Sarah Donaldson's" initials, "SD," reference the yacht incident. These few initialed references appear among hundreds of pages in her staffs' Home trial testimony. They were easily missed until I identified them as I.S.F. evidence.

Q. Does Rep. Donaldson add further comments beyond "initialed, 'SD'" references to the yacht incident?

A. No. And admittedly, she initials various other unrelated points throughout the documents.

Simpson pauses and then resumes his questions of Blanco. Blanco answers his questions by clarifying his I.S.F. documentary evidence for the courtroom. Blanco goes step-by-step to solidify evidence of Jones' leadership over Home in the present prosecution. Jones' manipulative expertise existed at least since the Vietnam War.

Q. Rep. Donaldson's initials recognize the yacht incident, her staff's testimony refers to the Jones-Home conspiracy, and Jones' leadership of multiple criminal cartels has been exposed: does all of this evidence confirm what Rep. Donaldson knew and knows?

A. Yes. I.S.F. evidence, including the "SD" initialed documents, shows that from the yacht incident to the Home trial, Jones exercised criminal dominance."

Judge Taylor grants Friendly's request for a brief adjournment. Quietly, I offer Tom new evidence, which he presents to Friendly. She uses it to examine the I.S.F. evidence in order to cross-examine Blanco.

During the adjournment, I wait outside the courtroom at the hall window. Sunlight illumines intermingling civilian-military life around San Diego Bay.

IV

Friendly, Simpson, and Blanco have aroused fears. The cocaine cartel and the shadowy Diaz Security conglomerate have targeted San Diego and America.

These dangers have narrowed into the trial of Steven Home. His broken appearance in court reinforces Simpson's defense promoting Jones as the leader. Home's earlier emotional outburst shows painful weakness. Blanco's evidence has touted Jones' cruel, domineering criminal leadership from the yacht incident to Steven Home's trial.

Simpson's defense has relied on Blanco's truth-teller image. That image surprisingly entangles Rep. Donaldson and me. Friendly must undermine that image.

Adjournment over, Prosecutor Friendly is back in the courtroom. Tom, Albert, and I take our seats. Friendly's cross-examination of

Blanco is about to begin.

The courtroom doors swing open. Friendly's assistants rush in. They give thick sets of paper to Albert and Tom. This transfer and the assistants' exit agitate the courtroom.

Quiet just barely returns. The Clerk of Court exclaims, "All rise," bringing Judge Taylor to the bench.

Frowning, Judge Taylor orders Friendly's cross-examination of Blanco to proceed. Friendly arranges the documents received from Tom and Albert. Both sit behind Friendly, at her command.

Blanco awaits the evidence Albert and Tom have passed to Friendly. Blanco understands Albert's access to offshore finance might lead to questions about his I.S.F. testimony.

Blanco also knows Tom Berneray is unpredictable. He's driven to defend his mother with his nightmare awareness of Diaz Security gained through guidance from his beloved Isabella's ghost.

Friendly's unrelenting calm matches Blanco's unquestioned honesty and rigid self-respect. Blanco's obvious integrity gives his words weight that Friendly handles with care. She must turn Blanco's his own answers to previous and new questions against him.

Friendly studies a document and says: "Agent Blanco, the I.S.F. identifies your family's courageous role in Sonora during the Revolution and your father's Federal Army command on the Border. These identifications neglect to state your birthplace. Why?"

Blanco replies steadily. "The I.S.F. hopes to protect its agents' families from abduction and death. In Sonora, place-of-birth can be used to trace a family name. Agents operate under assumed names. If an agent is publicly identified, family members may have to be given new identities, in another community."

Friendly presses: "Agent Blanco, you testify under oath. In Sonora, people commonly identify and associate family names with a certain community. This is so, particularly if the family is famous."

"Yes, it is true." Blanco states the simple truth sustained by the personal integrity shared with his two trusted agents. The Mexican-American jurors undoubtedly also know and respect this same truth.

Examining another paper, Friendly asks: "Agent Blanco, you identify family names with a place. Yet in your answer to defense counsel's questions you deny knowing the name of any of the women in Mrs. Berneray's swamped boat. So again, Agent Blanco, in the yacht incident, can you name one of three women?"

Friendly challenges the truth of a vital answer in Blanco's testimony. She strikes down Blanco's self-and-public image of incorruptible truth-speaker against criminal power.

The implication that Blanco committed falsehood visibly shocks his two deputy agents. Instinctively alert to defend Blanco's honor, they reach for holstered weapons. Both agents quickly realize they left knives and pistols with court security hours ago.

Mexican American jurors study Friendly in wide-eyed disbelief. The Prosecutor is questioning Blanco's intrinsic personal character, self-respect, and honor.

Judge Taylor gavels for order.

I think Simpson is caught unprepared. He doesn't question how Friendly learned that Blanco apparently testified untruthfully about the identification of a woman in my boat.

Simpson intended for Blanco and me to reveal what we both knew about the yacht incident. Simpson assumed Diana Berneray would be as honest regarding the incident as is the trusted Blanco. Neither Simpson nor Blanco himself are prepared for the test of Blanco's own trustworthiness.

"I can repeat the question, Agent Blanco." Friendly speaks directly into Blanco's blank stare.

Finally, Judge Taylor orders Blanco to answer Friendly.

Pain weighs heavy on Blanco replying: "Eventually, I identified one woman. The yacht officer ordered the three women aboard. As the Navy helicopter hovered, the very frightened yacht officer commanded me, 'English translator, shoot!' I snapped the photo of the three women surrounded on deck by the unarmed crew."

Self-consciously, Blanco strains each word. "Marines descended around us. The yacht officer panicked. He yelled in poor English at the three women, 'rescue ladies.' The officer's mind was going."

Blanco now recalls the unfolding drama: "Marines subdued the crew. The officer and I were left standing alone. He screamed at me in Spanish: 'Bermudez American woman escapes!' He was delirious."

Blanco's memory expands: Marines removed the officer. Now alone, Blanco easily identified the name, "Bermudez," the Revolution hero from Santa Maria. Blanco's grandfather fought beside Juan Bermudez.

Friendly interrupts Blanco: "Who is this 'Bermudez American woman' the yacht officer identifies?"

"That is the important question," Blanco concedes. "I received part of the answer from the young woman herself. I was impetuous young Blanco. At the yacht rail, I yelled 'Bermudez American woman' to the three women now aboard the Canadian rescue cutter. One face turned, fixed on me until the cutter was gone."

Friendly demands, "Agent Blanco, did you eventually learn that woman's name?"

"Oh yes, very soon," Blanco answers flatly. "At the Naval Base, Canadian military intelligence ensured that I was the translator. My cover held with the yacht captain, officer, and crew. I was only a student worker. The Canadian interrogator spoke fluent Spanish, but pretended to depend on me."

"Who was the woman gazing at you from the rescue cutter, Agent Blanco?" Friendly's icy calm.

Blanco speaks, more in control: "The Canadian interrogator questioned each crewman, separately. Marines searched the yacht foot-by-foot. Scuba divers scoured the hull. The interrogator kept the crew confused about who knew what. Afraid, far from Mexico, the yacht officer and each crewman repeated only 'we know nothing.'"

The yacht captain was a skillful deceiver, Blanco admits. In the captain's safe was the photo of the "Veterans Against the War Vigil." The captain also owned Spanish and English botany books about Vancouver Island rainforests. The books supported the captain's claim that he hired the yacht out for "a botanist's scientific tourism."

These assertions support the captain's story. In unfamiliar, foreign waters, he was too preoccupied to identify the two women in the "Veterans Vigil" photo. They were among the three women photographed on the deck before departing in the rescue cutter. The captain blamed "mysterious fate" for the "strange coincidence."

"Agent Blanco refuses to identify 'Bermudez American Woman,'" Friendly insists to the Judge.

Finally, Blanco makes the identification: "The Canadian interrogator's use of the 'Veterans Vigil' photo revealed the two names: 'Donaldson' and 'Quinn.' The woman named in the photo, who stared at me from the departing cutter, was Miss Quinn (now Berneray). She is the 'Bermudez American woman.'"

"Agent Blanco," Friendly demands, "what connects the 'Quinn' and 'Bermudez' family names?"

Blanco's memories flow. "In Sonora, my generation knows the one Bermudez granddaughter, Esperanza. She arouses feelings untranslatable. As a Pan American Games team member, her picture was everywhere. Men loved her, young Blanco included. A man tried to rape her. She killed him."

Blanco clearly remembers the unfathomable Esperanza. She married an American, only son of the San Francisco Quinn family. Magazine wedding pictures from Santa Maria named the Quinn family's one daughter as a bridesmaid. Blanco recalled knowing her simply as Esperanza's "American sister-in-law, Miss Quinn."

Blanco shrugs. "Associated with Esperanza Bermudez, the Quinn family name returned to me after I saw her in the 'Veterans Vigil' photo. The delirious yacht officer's 'Bermudez American woman' was Esperanza's 'American sister-in-law.' Miss Quinn 'escaping' in the cutter stared at me as I yelled the 'Bermudez' name."

Pushing Blanco to explain his painful lapse in truthful testimony, Friendly asks: "Agent Blanco, why did you deny knowing the Quinn (née Berneray) name?"

Blanco answers that his "statement was true before the yacht officer screamed the 'Bermudez' name." Blanco didn't recognize Miss Quinn at first. Also, Mrs. Berneray testified nothing about the matter. And, if pressed, Blanco would have testified that the captain and his officer claimed complete ignorance about it to Canadian interrogator. Since no one confirmed what Blanco saw, he says: "silence was reasonable."

Friendly's rigid detachment: "Agent Blanco, you and Mr. Simpson insist the Jones' criminal leadership is implicit in the yacht incident. Attention paid to young Miss Quinn in that incident requires evidence connecting her to Jones. Explain how your evidence might show that connection."

"A multi-part problem," Blanco confirms. "First, Mr. Tom Berneray testified to deep family ties his mother has in Santa Maria to her brother, Mr. Quinn, and sister-in-law Esperanza Bermudez Quinn. It is true we have no direct evidence linking Jones to Miss Diana Quinn, her brother, or the Bermudez family at that time."

"Second," says Blanco, "after the incident, the Canadian interrogator got the yacht captain to admit he worked for Jones. In the captain's cabin safe, searchers discovered papers showing Jones registered the yacht in Santa Maria for Diaz, a local merchant banker. Once he made the admission, the yacht captain swore—implausibly—that Jones hired the yacht to visit Vancouver Island to prepare for Diaz to tour the rainforests."

Blanco also testifies that the Canadian interrogator learned that Jones warned the yacht captain to look out for American drug smugglers. As a result, the captain seized the three women in the boat off Vancouver Island. The yacht officer ordered "me, the student photographer, to take pictures of the three women in preparation for turning them over to Canadian officials. This was the yacht captain's repeated confession."

"I simply reported the yacht captain's shifting story. At no time did I accept it," Blanco insists.

The yacht captain also professed amazement at being seized by Canadian Navy and Marines. The captain claimed he was merely pursuing lawful "scientific tourism" for the wealthy clients, Jones and Diaz.

Blanco repeats that he and the Canadian interrogator never believed the yacht captain's story. But once having confessed, the captain refused to budge from it, despite a vigorous interrogation. Finally, the yacht captain insisted upon being lawfully charged or released. Blanco had already testified to the latter.

Friendly pushes: "Agent Blanco, what more does your corrected testimony reveal about Jones?"

Blanco replies: "At my debriefing in 1974, U.S. military intelligence confirmed classified evidence from Canada and Mexico counterpart-services showing Jones conducted various undercover C.I.A. operations. Over the years, I.S.F. agents occasionally reencountered Jones. I.S.F. learned the C.I.A. protected Jones until he worked for the Navy, where he dominated and led Home in the present case, and was murdered."

With Blanco, Friendly finishes: "The Prosecution respects Agent Blanco's honest correction of his testimony. It indicates the problem of using indirect evidence from an old anti-Vietnam War incident to show Jones' criminal leadership over Home. Enough facts show Steven Home committed crimes against U.S. security that do not depend solely on Jones."

I perceive why Simpson's unusual defense argument pits Blanco against me, Diana Quinn Berneray. In narrow legal terms, Simpson's theory and evidence emphasizing Jones' leadership in the conspiracy could mitigate Home's guilt. Simpson's argument proves Jones to be the arch-criminal manipulator.

Realistically, Home wasn't a "coequal" conspirator. As he did with all the others, Jones manipulated his partner Home for his own ends. Jones' success led to overreach, resulting in his murder by Diaz Security.

I ask myself why Simpson uses Sarah's and my past to accentuate Jones' proven criminality. For lawyers, jury, and judge, the question is whether Simpson's defense highlighting Jones mitigates Home's guilt as coconspirator.

Judge Taylor announces lawyers' final arguments. My role completed, I study Friendly and Simpson as they address the jury.

Standing before the jury, Friendly resists Simpson's defense of Home, which employs the Vietnam War era Donaldson-Berneray yacht incident. Instead, Friendly emphasizes the testimony she and Simpson endorse: Home unlawfully transferred classified satellite-drone technology to his partner, Jones.

Friendly's target, admitted Home wrongdoing, is supported by Albert Jennings' Cayman offshore financial data. Home and Jones conspired to serve Diaz Security-G.S.S. in the theft of top-secret Navy satellite-drone technology. Friendly also uses Donaldson's staff testimony showing the partners Jones and Home engaged in a conspiracy.

But Friendly faces a difficulty. Albert Jennings' offshore data and Donaldson's staff testimony show the Home-Jones conspiracy achieved the U.S. security breach. Yet more than Home, murdered Jones has a long criminal record.

In order to win the maximum imprisonment and money penalty, Friendly must prove the individual guilt of Steven Home beyond a reasonable doubt. Proving only his coerced complicity with Jones limits imprisonment and monetary penalties for Home alone.

Simpson uses Blanco and Berneray testimony to exploit Friendly's difficulty. Simpson argues that the yacht incident illustrates Jones' ongoing criminal manipulation.

Since the Vietnam War, Jones successively manipulated the C.I.A. or the U.S. Navy, as well as his own partner, Home. Simpson seeks to shift the jury's assessment of guilt away from Home to his partner Jones. He is the proven, effective criminal leader.

Directly facing the jury, Simpson acknowledges that Home possessed Navy private-contractor status based on classified satellite-drone technology. Limited evidence proves Home betrayed his security classifications. Simpson wants to overshadow this limited evidence with abundant proof of Jones' criminal leadership.

Each juror listens intently. Friendly and Simpson again acknowledge to the jury: Home's combined-technology patents must remain secret. Publicly revealing just one or two top-secret technologies could harm American security.

Even so, Simpson argues that Home transferred to Jones old rather than new combined technology. Simpson insists older satellite-drone technology minimizes the terrorist threat to U.S. security from the cocaine cartel and Diaz.

Friendly refutes Simpson's contention, emphasizing that testimony doesn't show "why" Home transferred old combined technology to Jones. The proven facts are: Home transferred and stole top-secret satellite-drone technology. The transfer and theft of this combined technology threatens U.S. security.

Simpson and Friendly concede cocaine addiction could have motivated Home to conspire with Jones in theft of classified combined technology for Diaz Security.

Simpson argues that despite his cocaine addiction, Home consciously transferred older technology that was less threatening to U.S. security. Steven Home's love of America prevailed.

Friendly emphasizes that cocaine addiction didn't inhibit Home selecting old as well as new combined technology in the theft. The admitted choices of classified-technology theft show Home's willful intent. Home intentionally aided cocaine traffickers and other U.S. designated terrorist groups.

Focus on Home's mixed motivations reinforces Simpson's use of the yacht incident. It enables Simpson to assert that within their conspiracy, long experience easily furthered Jones' manipulation of Home.

Simpson wants the jury to think more about all that Jones' criminal leadership accomplished. From the yacht incident to the technology theft and border tunnel operations, Jones' criminal maneuvering dominated.

Jones' long-term dominance contrasted sharply with Home's broken appearance facing his present prosecution.

The lawyers' closing arguments are ending. I recall the importance of earlier jury selection. In various cases, Simpson has won a client's acquittal based on divided juries.

The prosecution of Steven Home raises profound national security threats. These threats pressure Friendly and Simpson to fight each other for jury unanimity.

Friendly's juror selections favor military veterans. Their patriotism demands protection of classified combined technology vital to U.S. security. Friendly's evidence has shown Home acting in a conspiracy with Jones that undermines U.S. security.

Simpson seeks to limit Home's admitted culpability by also appealing to pro-veteran jurors. Simpson argues: Notwithstanding Jones' exploitation of cocaine addiction, Home consciously transferred *older technology* to Jones.

Simpson's argument endeavors to convince the jury. Jones led in manipulating his own partner Home, the Navy, and the global criminal conglomerate, Diaz Security.

Friendly and Simpson know the Mexican-American jurors are proud to have earned U.S. citizenship. They share citizenship with American military veterans and their family members. Shared pride could be a basis for finding Home guilty.

Simpson has attempted to offset his basis for a guilty verdict with juror selections reflecting local knowledge. Steven Home had a priest's assurance that he was hiring only honest, hardworking immigrants. As a Navy private contractor, Home has aided Mexican immigrant middle school science students in San Diego.

Simpson has contrasted Home aiding honest Mexican immigrants with Blanco's evidence. It proves Jones constructed cocaine cartel border tunnels. Jones commanded G.S.S. and cartel agents to cruelly exploit and murder innocent Mexican immigrants who Home had helped.

Blanco's trustworthiness sustains Simpson's repeated argument. Jones gained most from theft of combined technology and building cartel border tunnels. Home received the cocaine Jones supplied.

Friendly dented Blanco's seemingly unquestioned integrity. Friendly's relentless cross-examination of Blanco perhaps has weakened

Simpson's defense highlighting Sarah Donaldson's and my evidence about the yacht incident.

Most importantly, Friendly exposes that Blanco's testimony under oath included an untruthful answer. By failing to question how Friendly discovered Blanco's error, Simpson accentuates it.

Friendly concludes. Steven Home knowingly sold and exposed U.S. security secrets that promoted cocaine cartel and security criminal terrorists. These exposed secrets could be turned against innocent Mexicans, like those captured and murdered in the border tunnels. Above all, Home's service to cocaine cartel and global-terrorist enemies has endangered all Americans.

Judge Taylor instructs the jury to decide the guilt or innocence of Steven Home on separate charges. Home conspired to transfer classified technology to his partner, Ralph Jones. Home's conspiracy enabled theft of this same classified technology. Home knowingly aided designated criminals, terrorist enemies of the United States. Home conspired with Jones in reckless criminal endangerment of American security.

V

The jury deliberated three days. Tom received and gave to me Sarah Donaldson's appreciation for my "truthful testimony."

Friendly also privately admitted to Tom that the revelation of Blanco's single untruth probably would influence the jury. Only Tom and Friendly knew what I'd advised Tom to tell Friendly: Blanco hadn't testified about the "Bermudez American woman."

During a brief trial adjournment, I'd told Tom that that name had been yelled from the yacht. Aboard the rescue cutter, I had had no idea who had screamed the family name. After hearing Blanco's testimony, I assumed it must have been Blanco.

Tom had enabled Friendly to exploit Blanco's silence. The papers Friendly's assistants rushed into the courtroom as the trial had resumed included photos of the Bermudez-Quinn wedding party in Santa Maria. Reproduced in old San Francisco Bay society pages, the photos were from digitalized online Bay Area press archives. Tom knew that, for a fee, he could access the archives naming the prominent Quinn family.

Tom had combined the old "Quinn-Bermudez" wedding photos with his close understanding of the role family names and locales played in Sonora. For Tom, the fiancé of Isabella, such facts are dear. These same facts gave Tom confidence that his I.S.F. background ensured Blanco knew the "Bermudez" name.

Using my yacht incident "recollections," Tom had constructed the questions Friendly had asked to cross-examine Blanco. Simpson had manipulated me in order to build up Blanco's testimony. Tom and Friendly had turned the test on Blanco.

I was waiting at Puck Place. Tom called me from outside the courtroom with the jury verdicts. On charges with lesser prison time and monetary penalties, Steven Home was found: Guilty.

On the charge that Home "recklessly endangered" U.S. security, the verdict was: Not guilty. Guilt on this charge could've put Home in prison for several decades, and forced him to pay very large multimillion dollar damages.

Thus, on this most dangerous charge, Simpson had convinced the jury. Directly or indirectly, Blanco's and my evidence proved Jones' criminal dominance. Jones had lead the criminal conspiracies behind the Donaldson-Berneray yacht incident, theft of satellite-drone technology, and the manipulation of Diaz Security in cocaine cartel tunneling.

Jones' dominant criminal leadership mitigated Home's guilt as a coconspirator in this trial. Home's admitted cocaine addiction confirmed his dependence on Jones.

Ironically, Friendly's arguments used Home's cocaine addiction to prove Home's guilt on other major charges. Despite Jones' dominance, Home consciously chose to steal and give to his partner older combined technology. This clearly threatened U.S. security, though not as much as new satellite-drone technology Home also controlled.

Responding to the verdicts in court, Home struggled to stand at attention. His trembling voice exclaimed: "Ralphy Jones loved me! Diaz made him do it! They killed him!" Home sobbed, collapsed, and was carried from the courtroom.

A few days later Judge Taylor sentenced Home to be imprisoned for no less than twelve years. He'd pay the U.S. government 30 million dollars. His prison term for cocaine possession would run concurrently.

Judge Taylor accepted the government's plan. Home would serve his prison time within the Navy's special custody. He'd be guarded from criminal attacks. Home's imprisonment would be under strict surveillance and restricted freedom of movement. He'd be treated for cocaine addiction. And he would continue classified satellite-drone technology research for the Navy as he had before the guilty verdicts.

Sarah Donaldson explained to the Berneray family: The trial had exposed past and continuing dangers the cocaine cartel and Diaz Security pose to the U.S. and Australia. Congresswoman Donaldson and Chief G represented, respectively, each nation's military intelligence. The trial's guilty verdict enables their transfer of satellite-drone technology to continue. Tom and Ann will aid the transfer. Tom can again search for his father.

SEVEN

━━━━━━━━━━━━━━━━━━━━━━━━━━━━

Final Battle Grounds

The trial's guilty verdict against Steven Home ended the security breach. The trial addressed stolen technology, which had endangered U.S. security. The trial also kept secret other classified satellite-drone technology, which now can be securely transferred from U.S. to Australia military intelligence.

Following the Steven Home trial verdict, Rep. Donaldson reappointed Tom as special investigator for her military intelligence committee. He resigned as her office's legal counsel. He'll work full time on transferring satellite-drone technology to the Australians.

Rep. Donaldson hires my consulting firm. I'm technical expert, Ann Berneray, narrating our technology-transfer. My partner, Kara Conrad, pilots drones, dubbed "winged snipers."

Tom and I face more conflicts. Tom's original Arnhem Land mission has acquired new meaning for finding our father. And C.I.A. agent Albert Jennings has gone missing.

My account records Rep. Donaldson ordering Tom and me on new operations in Arnhem Land and San Diego. The Berneray family and Rep. Donaldson confront what happens to Tom.

I

After the trial verdict, Rep. Donaldson pursues transfer of U.S.

combined technology to Australia military intelligence. Tom, my partner Kara, and I join Rep. Donaldson's agents. We cooperate with Australia military intelligence Chief G, and Arnhem Land Deputy Chief, Malangi.

Rep. Donaldson provides White House "plausible denial" for an undercover mission to Arnhem Land. The previous Administration's disrupted allied military intelligence-sharing received little media coverage. Our new operation to correct that failure isn't publicized at all.

C.I.A. agent Albert Jennings influenced early efforts seeking to reestablish shared military intelligence with the Australians. The transfer now begins. Yet Albert is conspicuously absent.

Donaldson's military intelligence committee has funded development of the Navy's classified satellite-drone technology. Her committee also funds our undercover operation.

Preparing for our technology transfer operation, I visit prisoner Steven Home. His prison sentence requires continued satellite-drone research for the Navy. Home is incarcerated in a special facility located in Fort Rosecrans, on Point Loma, San Diego.

The prison facility holding Steven Home carefully monitors his access to classified satellite-drone technology. Home works under strict supervision. He employs his own and other top-secret patent licenses.

Steven Home's unusual prison cell includes a sophisticated computer. The screen above a console table occupies most of one wall. Cameras keep Home under continuous surveillance.

The cell is about ten-by-twenty square feet, long and narrow. It has a toilet, sink, shower, and single bed. Food arrives, is consumed, and cleaned up daily. Marine guards remain on duty 24/7.

Barbed wire surrounds the cell facility. On a path within the wire, Home is allowed to walk two hours, daily. Far away, Home can see San Diego Bay. From there his cell is invisible.

Using the computer, Home applies patents to develop new satellite-drone technologies. Home's twelve-year prison sentence perpetuates his top-secret research for the Navy.

The Navy convinced the judge that the unusual prison sentence was warranted. Home's research coincides with treatment for cocaine addiction. He's protected from cocaine cartel agents. They seek retribution for the conspiracy that resulted in the guilty verdict against Home.

Now I visit prisoner Steven Home with a "technology problem" his trial didn't address. Australia military intelligence has made a discovery. An incriminated U.S. private contractor accessed classified computer codes previously shared by Australia and U.S. military intelligence.

Offshore financial data revealed the C.I.A. employed the U.S. private contractor, A.C.M.E. In the so-called Darwin Incident during early 2008, A.C.M.E. tried but failed to infiltrate an Arnhem Land weather station. Australians use the undercover station to expose cocaine traffickers.

A.C.M.E.'s bungled Darwin Incident ended Australia-U.S. military intelligence-sharing. Renewed intelligence-sharing required Rep. Donaldson convincing Chief G and Malangi that another Darwin Incident wouldn't occur. Donaldson ordered me to get reliable evidence.

This is the "technology problem" I'm asking prisoner Steven Home to address. When we meet he's stooped, but less emaciated than during the trial. He wears plain civilian clothes.

Silently, Home reads from my computer flash drive that states the "problem." His fingers then move rapidly over the computer keyboard. On the large screen, windows expand and contract, arranging data. Finally, the windows collapse into one showing a single report.

Prisoner Steven Home quickly has assembled a report revealing new offshore data. He's apparently hacked cocaine cartel offshore accounts.

This new data incorporates old trial evidence. Home has identified himself and partner Jones as private contractors. They've transferred stolen satellite-drone patent licenses to the offshore conglomerate, Diaz Security. All this was revealed in Home's trial.

Ingeniously, Home has combined the familiar trial evidence with new data. Home's new total evidence exposes other satellite-drone patent licenses Home and Jones stole for Diaz Security. This evidence remained hidden during Home's trial.

Home's total data shows:

1) Continuing U.S.-Australia military intelligence-sharing would have prevented the combined technology theft Jones and Home engineered for Diaz Security.

2) Effective shared U.S.-Australia military intelligence would have prevented the Darwin Incident and C.I.A. illegal deployment of private

contractor, A.C.M.E.

3) In Australia, global cocaine traffickers are developing offshore finance and technology into a criminal terrorist danger. This already prevails on the U.S.-Mexico border and was revealed in Steven Home's trial.

I deliver Steven Home's total data to Rep. Donaldson. She shares it with Chief G and Malangi in Canberra. Home's total data leads both sides to agree. The transfer of satellite-drone technology from U.S. to Australia now begins, dubbed: "Operation Arnhem Land."

From San Diego, a Navy jet transports the Donaldson committee's team to Australia. It includes Tom, my partner Kara Conrad, and me. We're transporting six state-of-the-art drones to Chief G and Malangi. Flying through a starry night, the Southern Cross appears.

Tom, Chief G, and Malangi understand each other. Multinational intelligence-sharing demands mutual trust, rather than unilateral self-centeredness. For that reason, Tom has told me, Malangi never trusted or agreed to meet Albert. Since Albert has vanished, the issue is moot.

We land in Canberra at an Australian Air Force base. We shuttle to a huge hanger. We meet Chief G, Malangi, his deputy Gwen Tone, and their support teams. Tom is happy. He and Malangi grip hands, two bodies slight and short, one face dark, the other white. Chief G orders: "Malangi and Berneray, transport the drones to Arnhem Land."

Chief G takes us to the Canberra Drone Operations Center. My adrenalin flows. Kara exclaims, "Just like the Balkans, whoever our drones target can be eliminated."

I'll start in the Drone Center aiding preparation of Chief G's Canberra team to operate our drone network over Arnhem Land. I'll leave Kara in charge of the drones being piloted from Canberra.

I'll then depart Canberra Drone Center and go to Arnhem Land. On the ground there, I'll provide continuous visual and verbal communications linking our drones in Arnhem Land to the pilots and co-pilots in Canberra. Piloted from Canberra Center, the drones will operate over Arnhem Land.

In Canberra Center, I listen to Chief G present reports from Malangi's field watchers. Local people have discovered cocaine traffickers. They've penetrated several hundred kilometers of open sea, rugged coastline, and isolated inland bush in Arnhem Land. The cocaine traffickers seem untraceable. Too few watchers cover too much territory.

Chief G summarizes Malangi's main finding: a watcher happened upon a cocaine-landing operation soon enough to alert local Aboriginal Homeland police. At night on a remote beach, the police found ragged captives. They were packing a battered, four-wheel drive van with cocaine worth many millions of dollars.

Malangi reported that the police learned nothing about the vans' origins, destination, or even who operated it. Van tracks to the beach from the bush eventually disappeared into rugged terrain. Lacerations and bruises covered the captives' trembling, naked bodies. Choked by terror, the captives expressed no understanding of where they've been landed. Any sea could wash that evil ashore.

A two-day walk from the van, police trackers have found two human bodies decimated by crows and flies. No IDs. On one body, police found a key to the chains binding the captives.

The tortured captives survived in a painful state of shock aggravated by the cruelty of the captors' repeated threats to attack families of any captive who didn't cooperate. The captives understood that wherever they'd landed was within striking distance of their families on remote home islands.

Malangi's expert interrogators assemble and report a common story. The tortured captives speak various dialects from isolated islands in the Torres Straits.

Skilled in the numerous regional dialects, Malangi's interrogators grasp the captives' repeated horror: at night, masked men appear from the sea, kidnap one or two young male island villagers, and disappear aboard "a strange ship."

Like pirates hiding among thousands of sea miles and islands, the kidnappers are impossible to identify and trace by separate, diverse national authorities across the vast region.

During months at sea, masked men continuously assaulted the captives. They learned their only hope for the life of their families was to land unnamed goods on an unknown shore. Illusory hope persisted till death.

In the Canberra Drone Center, after we've absorbed Malangi's tragic reports, Chief G states our mission. We connect the watcher's discovery of tortured captives, the cocaine van on the beach, and the drug trafficking "ship" to the establishment of a cocaine road through

Arnhem Land, backdoor to Australia's cities.

Chief G explains how the transfer of secret satellite-drone technology enables our operation. From the Arnhem Land Weather Station, Malangi deploys drones. Day and night, they patrol the isolated sea, coast, and bush where the cocaine landing occurred and others are reported.

Our six drones combine classified features of the *Global Hawk* and *Predator*: maximum altitude 45,000 feet, with typical mission-time averaging 24 hours. Maximum speed, 300 mph. Main uses: reconnaissance and laser attack.

Within twenty-four hours, a consolidated *Global Predator* can: depart base, search and map a territory the size of Iceland, engage in laser combat for four hours, and return to base.

Pilot and sensor operator (co-pilot) usually use satellite GPS to control a *Global Predator's* lasers, radar, computers, infrared cameras, radio transmission, and other communications.

Pilots and co-pilots fly *Global Predators* employing a "first-person" view. Kara instructs Australian pilots on the joystick that controls the drone's wings and propellers. I advise sensor operators on drone cameras, guidance system, and communications.

I instruct Australian pilots and co-pilots that this "first-person remote piloting" employs live images from onboard cameras with adjustable angles in a drone's nose cone. The system gives drone pilots and co-pilots precise flight data for surveillance locations and targeting lasers.

But satellite GPS is disrupted between Canberra Drone Center and Malangi's field operation in Arnhem Land. It is one of few global places with such satellite-GPS disruptions.

Radio communications work normally in Arnhem Land, except for camera-image transmission delays. I advise pilots and co-pilots on how to handle the delays, using one of the drone cameras for guidance. A drone's other camera maintains surveillance of sea and land surfaces.

My basic instruction: delayed transmissions slow *Global Predator's* surveillance images, images that can otherwise be used to map terrain or open sea, despite thick smoke, clouds, darkness, or bad storm conditions.

Delays also slow infrared camera detection of heat differences between objects. Still, a pilot can track people, gunfire, or vehicle motors under all weather conditions, day or night.

My point: be aware of structural delay in image transmissions. But don't allow a delay to prevent reading the drone's surveillance map or its laser targeting of people, places, and objects.

Finally, I insist, pay attention to when satellite-GPS is disrupted because drones are in Arnhem Land. In that unusual place, we depend more on delayed radio transmissions. Although GPS is erratic, the older technology remains. Outside Arnhem Land, GPS operates automatically.

II

Chief G orders Gwen Tone to transport me to join Malangi and Tom at the Arnhem Land Weather Station. In a mobile unit, I monitor drones, Malangi's team, Tom and a field operation.

Days and nights trickle by. My rotation system keeps several drones continuously fueled and airborne over targeted sea, coastline, and bush.

Canberra Drone Center and my mobile unit coordinate drone-flight patterns that cover every square yard of the surveillance zone in Arnhem Land.

A moonless, blustery, cloudy night: one drone picks up a slow-moving vessel on the sea. On a zigzag, crawling course the vessel eventually enters a remote inlet bounded by waves smashing black, high cliffs.

Two drones speed through the night, joining the third drone already over the inlet. Canberra drone pilots and I, the mobile monitor in Arnhem Land, easily can shift from surveillance to laser attack.

Malangi's ground watchers and police within the target zone race Land Rovers through the bush. Tone at the controls, a helicopter rises from the Weather Station, Malangi and Tom aboard.

Amidst whitecaps churning in, over, around jagged rocks, a twisting, narrow channel ends on a strip of white beach against a black cliff-wall. From that shore, lamplights blink.

Far above the windy, hissing sea, three silent drones circle as hungry ravens. Kara, her pilot-co-pilot team in Canberra, and I in Arnhem Land receive drone camera images of the dark vessel.

The inlet is fjord-like with jagged, wave-pounded cliffs. The inlet's center is relatively shallow water. Drone screens reveal the vessel is a large motor yacht, which anchors far up into the inlet.

From the yacht leaves a launch. It maneuvers to and through a deadly channel. Launch lights answer beach lights. Distant isolation instills confidence in cover of darkness. At anchor, the yacht waits.

Malangi's team converges on the inlet. Dreamtime spirits lead Malangi's Homeland watchers and police through the bush. I relay drone transmissions to guide the helicopter carrying Malangi, Tom, and Tone. Chief G orders Homeland Airborne Marines to depart Darwin in long-range gunships.

High overhead in the night sky, circling, quiet drones. Fuel used gradually. Drones track the launch's tortuous progress from yacht, through broken channel, to narrow beach.

Hours before dawn, the launch lands armed guards and several captives burdened with containers. On the beach, guards join a lone signalman. They force chained, loaded captives up a steep, winding path to the cliff top. Guards, hostages, and containers enter a van. It drives slowly into bush blackness.

Van and launch depart in opposite directions, each tracked by a drone. Led by another drone, Malangi's team uses PCs to gather undetected in the bush on cliffs overlooking yacht in the inlet.

Malangi splits his team in two, each covered by separate drone surveillance and laser screens. I message Malangi and Tom that the Marines are getting closer.

Malangi deploys one team on the cliffs above the unsuspecting yacht. It awaits the launch's return. I calculate the Marines' arrival time for Malangi and Chief G. Somehow, we'll have to delay the yacht.

Malangi dispatches the second team—two watchers and Tom in a Land Rover—after the van. The pursuit drone still tracks the van creeping through broken, remote bush land.

I transmit coordinates from the drone's infrared tracking to Tom's PC in the Land Rover. Drone silence and the watchers' faith in Rainbow Serpent carries the team through spirit country.

The van's occupants seem oblivious to our pursuit. My rotation system ensures that all drones remain fueled.

I know my brother. I assume he and Malangi's agents discuss van-pursuit as their Land Rover rolls into the night. Tom trusts our drone cameras, as well as the agents' faith in Rainbow Serpent spirits.

Embracing the mission without question, Tom also relates it to the search for our father.

Malangi, Chief G, and I study screens tracking each part of the operation. The Land Rover and its accompanying drone continue van-pursuit through bush darkness. Other drones circle high above Malangi's team on inlet-cliffs, following the yacht and launch. Marine gunships close on Malangi.

The launch reaches the yacht. In darkness far up inlet, the yacht's bow gradually turns around. The yacht heads back towards open sea.

My time calculations show the yacht should depart the inlet before the Marines' arrive. Malangi urges Chief G: "Order a drone on a yacht-intercept course." Chief G commands me: "calculate drone approach-time to target."

I begin countdown, aware the laser light will expose the drone to the yacht's radar and firepower. Automatically, I incorporate the "Arn-hem Land delay." It guides Kara Conrad in when to switch the drone to laser attack.

"Abort!" Chief G commands. Kara maintains surveillance mode, returns drone flight-path to tracking yacht. Drone remains cloaked in darkness.

"Report! Report!" Chief G commands as Malangi sees and drone screens show: from yacht into black-cliffs walls, machine-gun tracer fire streams.

Drone-screen images trigger our disbelief: the yacht lurches to-wards whitecaps rolling into black cliffs. As the yacht nears the cresting waves, the tracer-fire stream shortens.

"Malangi, what's happening on the vessel?" Chief G's question Malangi is unable to answer.

Sensing evasion, Chief G orders the drone again into yacht-inter-cept approach. Kara obeys, aiming lasers. Gunships now in place, ready to deploy Marines.

Chief G commands: "Engage interdiction!" Drone cameras see, record.

Kara aims a full-power laser, burning a ragged hole in the yacht bow. Water rushes into the hull, shifting the yacht weight forward. The rudder rises out of the water.

Gunships hover overhead. Marines descend lines onto the yacht. Cover fire spews from the gunships. Yacht tracer-fire ceases. Marines scramble over the deck, down hatches, in and out of cabins.

Someone on deck releases sporadic small-arms fire. It stops after two persons fall. The shooter collapses. Marines seize surrendering crewmen. Two bodies reported dead, one wounded.

Whitecaps mount, lift the yacht. Waves roll into cliffs. The yacht jolts, aground. Marines release the launch as winch and grappling hooks pull the yacht back into the inlet's center. The yacht floats as hulk.

Marines search the yacht. Our drone-screen images don't explain the tracer-fire into the cliffs from the yacht or its grounding separate from Kara's laser shot into the bow. Malangi intends to solve the mysteries. Shortly before dawn, Malangi is about to board the damaged yacht.

But Malangi receives Tom's message: "van halted." Malangi thinks fast, ascends a line into a refueled, hovering gunship. It speeds to co-ordinates Tom provides. A drone is already on course. Chief G and I receive camera images.

Out of sight in low cloud cover, the van-pursuit drone relays images. The Land Rover team remains hidden from the van through deep bush and shadows. Malangi's gunship closes in, his drone is faster.

Tom continues message to Chief G, Malangi, and me: for hours the Land Rover team has tracked the van. It has now stopped. We intercept garbled radio transmission from the van. Some guards leave the van during transmission. It ends, the guards return to the van. Nothing unloaded. The van resumes its creeping course.

Dawn is breaking. The drone finds the van halted again, now beside a narrow, twisting dirt road hidden in thick bush. The van engine idles, waiting. On the dirt road, an eighteen-wheel truck and trailer speeds around curves towards the van. The big truck slows, slows, slower, passes van.

Shifting into gear, the van follows at a crawling pace behind the truck's trailer. Out of the trailer's open doors rolls a ramp on small wheels. Ramp wheels strike the road, bounce, bounce, bounce then roll smoothly in tandem behind the truck trailer. The van drives onto, up the ramp, enters the trailer and the doors close.

Carrying evil cargo, truck and trailer regain speed. The big vehicle heads alone down the road snaking across broken bush-covered terrain. In the distance, Arnhem Land ends.

The pursuit-drone tracks every phase of the van's disappearance. We hardly believe our drone screens in Canberra, my mobile unit, Malangi's gunship, and the Land Rover.

We must stop truck and trailer before it leaves Arnhem Land, crossing onto Northern Territory Highway. There it will be hard to identify among hundreds of similar trailer trucks.

Using the pursuit drone's mapping, I answer Malangi's order to calculate the truck's arrival at the Arnhem Land border bridge. It spans a deep, miles-long canyon. "Truck reaches bridge in about thirty minutes."

Much sooner, the Land Rover team cuts cross-country, and converges on the bridge, along with Malangi's drone. It transmits images of this team immobilizing, shutting heavy iron gates at the bridge entrance and exit.

Two agents, Tom, and their Land Rover escape into the bush as the trailer truck reaches the bridge. I realize the bridge and its approach are just outside Arnhem Land's GPS disruption zone. The Land Rover team's drone joins Malangi's drone: Two circling drones' camera-eyes record every detail using real-time GPS.

Guards and driver dismount the trailer truck, wanting somehow to dismantle the sealed iron gates. Automatic weapon fire proves ineffectual. No explosives are available. Hard labor is useless.

Malangi's gunship is almost there. His words suddenly carry to all of us within hearing of the drone-transmissions. We don't comprehend; yet we feel his words are timeless, before time, in Dreamtime.

Marines in the gunship and agents in the Land Rover answer Malangi: challenge-response, challenge-response, challenge-response, challenge-response . . . .

"What's Malangi doing?"

Tone answers my question with strange words: "Malangi's Law Man persona is commanding his Homeland fighters to arouse Rainbow Serpent and her spirits. Call and response brings forth justice punishing wrongs wrought by Flying Fox."

I remember Tom using these same images to explain the bark painting that recorded our Father's disappearance in Arnhem Land. Hearing Malangi and his men through drone transmissions, we all take part in those images now.

Malangi's and his fighters' rhythmic words grow louder. From the

Land Rover Tom springs into a steady run. In and out of bush clearings and cover, his white face floats, an easy target.

"They'll kill my brother!" I shout, standing up in the Weather Station mobile unit before my drone screen, next to Tone.

She exclaims: "It's drone images, Berneray! Your brother follows Malangi!"

I understand: Drone cameras high above capture Tom in clear line of fire. Yet Tom runs through broken bush obstructed by gathering life. Malangi's and his Homeland fighters' words embrace Tom.

Near the bridge, gunmen aim at floating target Tom. He blurs in seething motion that spills over, around, above bush. Beside and before running Tom appear kangaroo, rabbits, and quivering clouds of flies. Swirling overhead gather crows, with shinning beaks, curled claws, piercing yellow eyes.

Targeting Tom, the gunmen are lost in the living, writhing mass. Behind it now, Tom runs, witnessing Malangi's answered call to Rainbow Serpent.

Gunmen's weapon fire is sucked into packed, shrieking crows. They strike. Claws, beaks, winged-weight swarm into the gunmen's faces, heads uncovered, weapons flaying, bodies, twisting, mouths screaming.

Gunmen's bodies crumple. Weapons are lost under living weight. Kangaroos lean back on their tails, hind feet hammering, crushing the gunmen's knees, ribs, backs. Rabbits crawl, crow claws and beaks drive deeper. Flies swarm.

The gunship lands behind the trailer truck. Malangi is first on the ground, Marines follow. Land Rover agents arrive. Both teams gather around the carnage. Marines post patrols. No surprises.

Last on scene, Tom drops to his knees, retches. Malangi reaches, raises Tom up. Answering Malangi's command, the animal life abandons the bloody ground. Some crows linger, circling like drones.

Marines enter the truck trailer, open the van, and lead hooded, chained captives into daylight. Hoods are removed to reveal cruelly battered heads, faces. Torn clothes: limbs and torsos mutilated. No one speaks.

On one dead gunman, Marines find keys to unlock the captives' chains. Liberation does not penetrate the captives' shock. Silent, they're evacuated by gunship to Darwin Naval Base for treatment.

Chief G, Malangi, and Marines organize ground transport across Arnhem Land to Darwin Naval Base: trailer truck, van, cocaine, bodies of gunmen. Gunships and drones escort.

Another drone stays behind at Malangi's command. Bush wind erases bloodied earth on the road ending at the bridge over Homeland border canyon. Bridge gates remain locked obstructions.

Last departing the battle site in Tone's helicopter are Malangi and Tom. I see them coming on my drone screen in the mobile unit at Arnhem Land Weather Station. We meet there.

Malangi, Tom and I now analyze and report on the drone transmissions during our Operation Arnhem Land. We combine these with evidence gained from interrogations and searches of the yacht, van, and trailer truck.

Malangi's linguist-interrogators examine the freed captives. While usually hooded and terrorized, the captives had learned their tormentors were security guards who only spoke Spanish. A Filipino yacht crewman knew enough Spanish to translate the security guards' cruel demands after kidnappings into the captives' various regional dialects. The Filipino gave the captives food.

Showing drone-transmission images, Malangi's interrogators persuade the yacht crewmen that confession will aid their defense in court. They'll be criminally prosecuted for terrorism, kidnapping, cocaine trafficking.

Malangi's interrogators compile the crews' testimony into our following narrative: Crewmen admit to being pirates hired clandestinely to operate the yacht in order to traffic cocaine. They swear their employment included neither kidnapping nor terrorizing of captives.

Crewmen tell interrogators that the yacht captain initially seemed normal. One night in Torres Straits, the yacht crew unloaded cocaine containers from an "odd ship," including security guards, their commander, and chained, hooded captives. The yacht captain watched the transfer without comment.

The Filipino crewman learned that the yacht captain, security-guard commander, and his men worked for a Mexico-U.S. border cocaine cartel. The men were friendly among themselves, often discussing their Mexican border homes.

The yacht captain shattered their cooperation. Among innumerable Arnhem Land islands, the yacht captain deviated off course, pursuing an elusive sailing schooner. It escaped unidentified.

On deck, surrounded by the crew, the enraged yacht captain blamed the security-guard commander's obstruction of personal orders received from the cocaine cartel boss.

The commander exclaimed that the yacht captain had jeopardized the cocaine boss's operation. The yacht meandered. Held at gunpoint, the captain took the yacht into the isolated inlet. He was then confined in his cabin.

In lantern light, watched by security guards, yacht crewmen loaded cocaine containers, other security guards, and captives into the yacht's launch. It returned hours later, empty.

Yacht crewmen secured the launch. The security-guard commander ordered the helmsman to navigate the yacht out of the inlet into open sea. Crewmen worked, witnessed.

The yacht captain burst from the cabin. With an automatic pistol he killed the security guards and fatally wounded their commander. The yacht crew abandoned the security guard commander to die.

At a mounted machine gun, the yacht captain commenced tracer-fire into the black cliffs. The crewmen felt the powerful impact of outside weapon fire. The ship's bow shifted forward. The helmsman abandoned his post.

The yacht lurched towards waves pounding the cliffs. The captain continued unleashing tracer-fire, heedless of his yacht rising on the swell. The ship jolted, grounded.

From inky blackness above the yacht, gunships and line-descending Marines materialized. The captain left the machine gun; randomly fired his automatic pistol, then stopped. The yacht captain pushed the pistol barrel into his mouth and pulled the trigger.

Crew narration ceased. Malangi's interrogators pressed the crewmen: explain the fight between the yacht captain and the security-guard commander, the captain's destructive behavior, his suicide.

Despite diverse languages, the crew's common response to the yacht captain's behavior is unfeigned shock. They want the commander to die. The interrogators agree that the commander is dying.

Chief G sees more. The commander can identify the yacht captain and his conspiracy. The yacht captain's self-destructive behavior and disruptions of the cocaine delivery expose the cocaine cartel's penetration of Arnhem Land. The commander must live long enough to name names.

III

Chief G orders Malangi, Tom, and me to support a special agent. She knows about our drone transmissions, captives and crew interrogations, evidence from the yacht, van, and trailer truck, the Home-trial data and his new report to me. She must persuade the commander with nothing to lose.

Malangi describes special agent Callahan Nunez: second-generation Australian, of Irish-Mexican descent. Her grandparents were on the losing side in Mexico's Revolution. Her parents migrated to Australia. Devout Catholics, the family is accepted in Sydney's Irish community under the old immigration policy: "White Australia."

Nunez is middle-aged, medium height, slight, fading reddish hair, hazel eyes, glasses, a plain dresser wearing sensible shoes. Recall her. She is quite forgettable, a blank. It is her useful cover.

You do remember Nunez's intensity, forceful reasoning, and black humor. Life isn't inevitably sad, but it's always hard. Australian hope, mixed with Mexican-Irish Catholic realism.

Grasp all this about Callahan Nunez, Malangi tells Tom, and me. We see why she is Chief G's best spy charged with outmaneuvering the security-guard commander who wants to die.

We're flown from Arnhem Land Weather Station to Darwin Naval Base. Malangi, Tom, and I meet Nunez at the military hospital holding the commander prisoner. Like him, we experience her interrogation strategy.

Carrying laptop computers, Nunez introduces herself in perfect English to Tom and me, who she calls "brother and sister Berneray."

Nunez acknowledges me and my "extraordinary skill in drone transfer and implementation." I'm present now as an expert witness evaluating our use of "combined technology" in a hard interrogation.

Briefly, carefully, Nunez conveys thorough knowledge of Tom's actions from the Home trial to his "brave run" at the Arnhem Land border bridge. He and Malangi "are a good team." She says nothing else concerning Tom.

Regarding Malangi, Nunez says only that she and he have discussed his command of laptop computers and combined technology in our time-sensitive interrogation.

"Our first problem is," Nunez explains, "the prisoner knows he failed to serve dangerous cocaine cartel employers. They've lost huge profits, big global operations costs, and a very large cocaine product affecting prices charged Colombian producers. Such losses mean the cartel or the security firm kills him anyway."

Nunez helps us understand further why the prisoner wants to die: "The prisoner's failure concerns loss of his men. They and their families depend on a successful commander to earn a living from a security firm. A good commander and his men also owe one another a sense of shared duty."

"The security company will kill a commander who fails on the magnitude of our prisoner," she observes. "The security company is less competitive for cartel business and reliable recruits. Such a commander also betrays the mutually dependent trust mercenaries require of each other."

Malangi adds: "The prisoner achieved 'commander' rank, at least partly because his men knew he fully shared their deadly dangers. Mutual risk and death are vital to the mercenary code. For a commander to be successful, money is a beginning. His men also must trust he has a crude kind of honor."

Nunez studies Tom and me, weighing her own capacity to persuade: "So, the prisoner seemingly has no reason to assist us."

Nunez says the imprisoned commander knows, too, that "Certain death means escape from failure affecting both the cocaine cartel and the security company. Also, escaping dishonor towards his men and families.

"Yet the prisoner is Mexican, a Catholic believer," Nunez states without doubt. "His sins ensure damnation, separation from God in Hell. Silence at least means he chooses his destiny. But this sin of self-will, self-determination may promote our interrogation.

"The prisoner's fatally wounded body retains its self-preservation instinct. It gives us time. Our medical people can't believe that even the prisoner's powerful body survived such killing weapons fire," Nunez continues.

Nunez adds, "Cocaine cartel and mercenary security bosses purchase all the loyalty money can buy. They might forget loyalties can be divided."

We enter a small infirmary room. A big man, bound and straight-jacketed, connected to wires and tubes, fills a large bed. Pitiless, dark eyes set back in broad, *mestizo* face. Hair buzz cut, head, skull-like.

An Aboriginal Homeland doctor and nurse examine the monitors. Two Marines with side arms stand by. Air conditioning barely counters body heat. Seen through the single widow, gunships await action.

Nunez identifies herself, Malangi, and me only by our technical ex-pertise serving Australia military intelligence. Otherwise, to the com-mander we're anonymous.

At the door stands Tom. About him, Nunez is silent. The prisoner can freely fasten upon Tom any meaning, association, or nothing.

Around the bed, upon mobile tables, Nunez places large laptop computers, screens open. The prisoner's vision can't avoid their collec-tive force when the images appear on the three screens.

Nunez begins. Into the infirmary room shuffle young men liber-ated from tortured, chained captivity aboard the yacht, then trans-ported by van and trailer truck. Speaking to each man in dialect, Malangi asks him to identify the prisoner. Each man approaches him. Into his face they shout words, spit blood.

Malangi translates each man's similar words from dialect into Eng-lish. Nunez translates English into Spanish. The prisoner personally tortured each captive, exclaiming: "'Obey orders, or worse happens to your family.'"

Inside the binding straps and straightjacket, the prisoner growls untranslatable profanity, coughs blood. His big body fights exhaustion, seeps strength. The nurse wipes blood from his face.

Again and again, in a voice flat, low, cold Nunez asks the prisoner to identify former captives. Finally, shaking with anger and weakness, as the nurse removes drying blood, the prisoner recalls a captive with too few teeth to eat food given him by the Filipino crewman.

"I bash captive's mouth. No teeth left. 'Collateral damage' like American drone killing civilians. Complaining ends." The prisoner's face remains expressionless, his cruel words are a factual statement.

Nunez states smoothly: "Former captives identify prisoner. Pris-oner makes positive identification of tortured former captive." A Ma-rine leads the young men from the infirmary room to the waiting medics' safe care.

Except for prisoner's labored breathing, the room is quiet. I watch Nunez calculate the prisoner's worsening condition. Hidden cameras record her success or failure. Like drones.

Nunez signals Malangi. Room lights lower. Three computer screens come alive with the same image: the prisoner's old passport photo. Although about ten years younger, his face was as fierce then as it is now.

Nunez reads the ID text. She articulates each word with hard sharpness, razor cutting flesh. "Pablo Martinez. Born, 1957; Jalisco, Mexico. Early experience: Mexico Border Defense Force, 1976-1984 (Retired Rank, Commander, for exceptional service to Federal Republic of Mexico)."

The screen image shifts: Martinez, badly wounded, aboard the yacht in Arnhem Land. Marines are taking him into custody. Nunez reads the ID text: "Martinez, Private Security Professional since 1984 (Rank, Commander): Nicaraguan Contras, 1986, subcontractor; Gulf War, A.C.M.E. Security, 1990, subcontractor."

The image shifts again: Martinez, bedridden, Darwin Naval Base Infirmary. Nunez reads ID text: "Continued Experience: U.S.-Mexico Border, Global Security Solutions (G.S.S.) 1992-2004, subcontractor; Iraq War, A.C.M.E. Security, 2004-2008, subcontractor; Private Client, Global Knight, Inc., 2008-2009, subcontractor."

I watch Martinez's gaze lock onto a screen: images slide from honored service in Mexico's armed forces to the botched mission and capture on the yacht in Arnhem Land, to his Darwin hospital deathbed.

Nunez's emotionless voice reads the ID texts identifying Martinez's mercenary service in global security firms associated with the U.S., including the C.I.A. and A.C.M.E. or G.S.S., serving the cocaine cartel.

New to me is Nunez's reference to Global Knight Inc. It shows what Chief G's team found when they combed the yacht and trailer truck for evidence. They combined it with data from the Donaldson Committee and Home trial. This aids our Arnhem Land operation and future criminal court prosecutions.

The computer screen image shifts once more: an eighteen-wheeler truck gearing down, slowing, ramp sliding onto dirt road, van following, ascending ramp, and then hidden behind closed trailer doors.

Prisoner Martinez gaze fixates on the next screen images: the trailer truck halts at the border bridge. Without ordinance, mercenary gunmen can't dislodge the barricade. Gunmen target the running man in the bush.

Malangi and the Marines' voices fill the infirmary room: challenge-response, challenge-response, repeated, repeated again . . . deafening force. The screen images are now in slow motion: gunmen, their gunfire now disrupted, absorbed in crows, kangaroos, rabbits, flies, all engulfing, swirling, slashing, spearing, clawing, tearing, and swarming.

Nunez signals Malangi. One screen image freezes: the gunmen mangled, bleeding to death, covered with squirming animal life. Prisoner Commander Martinez's face is immobile, blank towards the fixed image of his men.

"Before long," Nunez quietly tells Martinez, "these taped images will be introduced, with other evidence, to prosecute the yacht crew in criminal court for terrorism, kidnapping, and cocaine trafficking."

Nunez speaks low, intimately. Prisoner Martinez must hear each word: "Using this image," Nunez points to the frozen screen, "the defendants' lawyer will attempt to raise doubts, asking why the mercenaries lacked the ordinance to blow the bridge barricades. And where was their Commander Martinez when the danger was greatest?"

Nunez strategy: inadequate weaponry is Commander Martinez's fault. His competency is insulted. Worst of all, he was absent when his men encountered deadly combat, suggesting that their commander is a coward.

Martinez bucks, bellows. Restraints hold. Marines draw weapons. Doctor and nurse scramble away. Martinez shakes, coughs, and spurts blood. Within his restraints, Martinez collapses.

I think Nunez has miscalculated. Martinez gasps for death. Nunez speaks each word sharply: "Commander Martinez, we can ensure the court knows the truth about you and your men."

I hardly believe what I see, hear. Martinez's dissolving will strains to listen. Body trembles, blood somehow staunches. He gasps, "What do you want?"

Martinez's life fading, Nunez talks faster: "Australia will prosecute and convict the yacht crew members in one of the largest cocaine cartel busts in history, outside the U.S. and Mexico. Our evidence is overwhelming. Defense arguments attacking you mean simply, in a losing cause, your ugly face is an easy target."

Nunez signals Malangi. Computer screen images slide one-to-another: The yacht drifts, its captain and Commander Martinez clash among crew and security guards. The yacht captain shoots Commander Martinez and his guards on the deck. He fires tracers into the darkness, and then suddenly commits suicide. The yacht is aground.

"Identify this yacht captain. Blame him for the failure of the cocaine cartel's operation. Commander Martinez and his security guards attempted to save it. That should be easy for you to say after seeing our screen images," exclaims Nunez.

Confronted with a direct offer to betray the mercenary's purchased duty, obligations, and loyalty, Commander Martinez is deathly silent.

Nunez pushes: "The cocaine cartel and you, Commander Martinez, are guilty. That, our prosecution evidence easily proves. I'll save your mercenary reputation, in return for answers."

She turns to appeal, hands extended, palms up, "Commander Martinez, you have my promise, before God."

The commander's voice is barely above a whisper: "Yacht captain is son of Diaz brother, the lawyer who runs G.S.S. and Global Knight. This son, Manuel Diaz, is, was, hotshot, fearless, reckless, lucky, exceptionally competent, until anger controls him."

The commander's words are thin, raspy, haltingly: "Other Diaz brother runs business side of cartel. He organizes offshore finances of operation. 'Impossible to trace,' he said. His intelligence reports say bridge barricades never close. Obviously, he's wrong."

"The three Diaz family members trust each other absolutely. But lawyer Diaz holds blind hatred he passes to son Manuel Diaz." The commander's voice steadily weakens.

"Lawyer Diaz's hate is from his father, a banker in Santa Maria, Mexico, who died dishonored. Decades ago this banker's youngest son attempted to rape granddaughter of Revolution hero Bermudez. The woman wounded the Diaz son. He died, damned. Crows desecrated his body."

"Catholic father died brokenhearted. His son, the lawyer Diaz, blames Bermudez family. Lawyer Diaz passes on to his yacht captain son, Manuel Diaz, same hatred of Bermudez family members, even American in-laws." Commander Martinez's face, body look finished.

Nunez insists: "Diaz family matters don't explain the yacht captain's disruption of his own family's cocaine operation. Commander

Martinez, save your reputation. Seek mercy."

Commander struggles, gasps: "Believe me. Yacht captain Diaz claims he saw at sea a schooner sending a light-signal naming our Revolution hero, 'Bermudez.' Diaz pursued it. I didn't see signal. One crewman says he saw it. The van and truck rendezvous were pressing. I thought, I must save mission."

Commander Martinez's admissions jolt my reasoned speculation. Signaling the "Bermudez" name could've been a trap for Manuel Diaz. Could it have been Alex and Esperanza Quinn, aboard the schooner *Isabella,* who had illuminated the name onto the cliffs? Could my father be with them?

Nunez's emotionless words call me back. Confronting Commander Martinez's death yearning, Nunez presses him: "Explain Captain Diaz's machinegun fire into the darkness."

Martinez barely audible: "I truly don't know. What he saw in darkness caused madness. I want Catholic priest." Nunez's mixed appeals to Martinez's ego and residual faith is working.

Nunez won't stop: "Explain the stolen drone found disassembled aboard the yacht."

Commander Martinez whispers, angrily: "Diaz said he'd reconstruct and fly it, after cocaine delivery. He piloted drones for C.I.A., A.C.M.E. I want Catholic priest, now!"

This is the first I learn of the stolen drone aboard Captain Diaz's yacht. Ours are all accounted for. Malangi's searchers must have found this Diaz drone.

And Nunez was right. Martinez's dormant faith must have been aroused to hope for mercy from a priest administering last rites.

Commander Martinez's body disintegrates into dying gasps. Nunez relents. She'd arranged for the priest to wait in the hall. He enters the room. He's a complete stranger.

Before the priest speaks, Commander Martinez shocks us: "Name silent man."

Commander Martinez's sudden gasping order freezes us. Standing at the door, Tom is so surprised he speaks off guard, truthfully: "Berneray."

I don't believe Commander Martinez's dying words: "In San Diego trial you exposed Diaz Security. They'll kill you, Berneray. They murdered Bermudez American woman. Like me, Berneray, you will need priest."

The priest's duty to God for Martinez begins.

Malangi, Nunez, Tom and I leave the infirmary. Nunez thanks each of us and walks away. I'm afraid for Tom. He says nothing. I know Tom remembers another priest's assertion in Santa Maria: Tom's absence helped prevent his own death during Isabella's murder.

My conflicted thoughts trigger darker realizations. Martinez knew about a "Bermudez American woman." Surely Martinez meant Isabella. Tom had testified about her murder in Steven Home's trial. Martinez must also know that Tom's trial testimony exposed Diaz Security.

Martinez used Tom's two trial identifications to assert that Tom had become a target of Diaz Security.

Martinez also revealed that yacht Captain Diaz went "mad" following mysterious signals of the "Bermudez" name. The signals at sea and in the Arnhem Land inlet explained why the captain disrupted his cocaine mission. I think Alex and Esperanza Quinn and my father entrapped Diaz, exploiting his family's hatred of three families.

Finally, I remembered Agent Blanco's Home Trial testimony. The Diaz family had ordered cocaine boss Jones to pursue another "Bermudez American woman," Diana Quinn. She became my mother, after marrying Jim Berneray. He and the Diaz family were connected more than I imagined. And so am I. My whole family is endangered.

Back in the Canberra Drone Center, Chief G summarizes the effectiveness of our Operation Arnhem Land. We transferred satellite-drone technology from San Diego to Canberra. We deployed it supporting Malangi's Aboriginal Homeland agents and Marines in Arnhem Land. Our successful operation reestablishes U.S. military intelligence-sharing with Australia.

IV

Tom and I have returned to San Diego. Rep. Donaldson lauds my "skillful transfer of combined technology." My work in Arnhem Land was comparable to that of my mother, "Diana's brave service to anti-Vietnam War veterans. Like mother, like daughter."

Rep. Donaldson praises Tom's "courage and effective collaboration with Australian military intelligence. His local knowledge supported the successful antiterrorist, anti-cocaine cartel operation in Arnhem

Land."

Rep. Donaldson has ordered Tom and me to remain in San Diego. We'll continue to assist Chief G in Canberra and Malangi in Arnhem Land. Donaldson rehires my consulting firm to electronically connect computer centers in the three locations.

Tom and I operate from the Marine Corps antiterrorist drone center on Silver Stand, San Diego. Secure telecommunications link Tom and me directly to Chief G in Canberra and Malangi in Arnhem Land. A world apart, we communicate in real time.

We must explain the revelation Nunez pried from dying Commander Martinez. Aboard his yacht in Arnhem Land, Captain Diaz had a drone he'd intended to assemble and pilot.

In the Steven Home trial all parties accepted as "proven evidence" the opposite. Neither the cocaine cartel nor Diaz Security conglomerate subsidiaries possessed an operational drone. Rep. Donaldson, Chief G, and Malangi must understand this "opposing drone evidence."

Our cooperative investigation examines new evidence leading from Arnhem Land back to the U.S.-Mexico border. We've combined complex technology with traditional techniques.

Eyewitness testimony has proven Captain Diaz's personal guilt and suicide. Our new investigation must reveal wider criminality explaining the Diaz drone, disruption of his own family's cocaine delivery in Arnhem Land, and how the family uses Diaz Security subsidiaries: A.C.M.E., G.S.S., and Global Knight.

Pursuing Captain Diaz requires complex evidence. Diaz's gunshot deep into his mouth dissolved much of his skull, including the upper jaw. Diaz's lower jaw remained largely intact.

Chief G's experts and I located Diaz's lower jaw in global digital dental records. Years before, under his real name, Manuel Diaz was treated for serious lower jaw gum disease by a famous Miami dental surgeon.

Digital dental records next identified Diaz under the alias, "Pablo Tapas." Tapas charged A.C.M.E. for more lower jaw surgery, a "health benefit" included in C.I.A. employment contracts for security firms in the Iraq War.

Australian experts and I combined Diaz's false Tapas ID with the Steven Home Trial money-laundering data. This revealed A.C.M.E. payroll job classifications in Iraq for Tapas (Diaz). He held helicopter and small-plane pilot licenses, and captain's papers for yachts.

Our computer-integrated data showed Tapas (Diaz) transitioning professional skills. For the C.I.A., he learned expanded A.C.M.E. private-security operations requiring drone pilots.

This data exposed that in Iraq Tapas (Diaz) also used "A.C.M.E. drone pilot qualifications" as cover. He sold money-laundered cocaine for the Diaz family. His lawyer father headed Diaz Security subsidiaries, G.S.S. and Global Knight. His uncle has been business manager of a U.S.-Mexico border cocaine cartel.

Most significant, we discovered "Tapas (Diaz)" was the A.C.M.E. drone pilot in the C.I.A.'s failed Darwin incident.

Diaz piloted the drone from a Ro/Ro ship. The term means "Roll on, Roll off." It applies to a ship designed for heavy motorized vehicles to "roll on, roll off" at dock.

After the Darwin Incident, the alias "Tapas" no longer appears in A.C.M.E. payroll records. We again traced Captain Diaz under his own "Diaz family" name in our shared database.

To further examine Diaz, Malangi gave Aboriginal Homeland watchers photos of drones and Ro/Ro-ships. The watchers showed these memorable images among Arnhem Land traditional fishermen. They've traded in Darwin before, during, and since the Darwin Incident.

Photo images triggered the fishermen's memories: a "flying machine" (Diaz-piloted drone) and "strange" (Ro/Ro) ship entered an isolated Arnhem Land harbor. Off the ship a van rolled onto an old wharf, then into the bush.

Some fishermen identified the same van in Darwin, while the "flying machine" come and went. A few fishermen reported men from the van struggling with Aboriginal artists and "'their friend, Berneray.'"

Malangi, Tom, and I assume that Diaz witnessed the Darwin struggle (including my father) through the drone camera. A few fishermen recalled the "van men" failing in the Darwin struggle. The "flying machine," not the van, returned to the ship. It and the "flying machine" departed the isolated harbor.

Malangi's watchers next showed the fishermen photos of Captain Diaz's damaged yacht floating in the Arnhem Land inlet. One fisherman recalled seeing this same yacht, but in normal condition, meet a Ro/Ro ship somewhere in the Torres Straits.

This recollection is consistent with the yacht crew testimony. Cocaine, captive laborers, and Martinez security guards were transferred from a Ro/Ro ship to Captain Diaz's yacht.

Our computers compare this fisherman's memory with weather and oceanographic data. A rough match confirms that the fisherman's later "yacht" sighting followed months after the Darwin Incident. The yacht was the same one Diaz captained to his suicide amidst drone and Marine attack, without flying his own drone.

Malangi asks us to reconsider Diaz's self-destructive behavior: "Martinez said it began after sighting an elusive schooner accompanying 'light signals' naming Mexico-Revolution hero Bermudez. Martinez connected Bermudez to Tom and his fiancé, Isabella, 'the Bermudez American woman.'"

We decide: Diaz father and son's hatred of the Bermudez extended family undermined the cocaine delivery in Arnhem Land. Hateful rage caused Captain Diaz's "madness," firing tracers into the black cliffs at night as the yacht rose on a wave-swell, went aground, and was damaged under drone attack.

Within total drone camera images, Australian computer experts and I isolate Diaz's tracers and apparent target, a fixed light. Our analysis makes both visually distinct from the surrounding cliff blackness. We admit, possibly, that Diaz shot at a light aboard a vessel riding the swell.

Tom asks Malangi, "Could any vessel ride the swell just enough to avoid the waves crashing into the cliffs or running aground?"

Malangi replies that Aboriginal fishermen following Rainbow Serpent spirits might make that extraordinary maneuver. Yet even Malangi is doubtful.

Tom addresses Malangi, but thinks of Isabella. "Isabella's parents, Esperanza and Alex Quinn, fled Santa Maria into the Pacific after Diaz Security agents murdered my fiancé. Quinn Shipping trades in the Torres Straits, Darwin, and Arnhem Land. Serving the family firm, Quinn has surely learned hiding places."

My brother conceals rising emotion. "Alex Quinn surely remembers the yacht the Diaz family operated from the Santa Maria harbor. Conversely, Captain Diaz knows Alex Quinn's schooner."

Tom concedes that some years separate Quinn and Esperanza's disappearance in Santa Maria from Captain Diaz's cocaine delivery in

Arnhem Land. Passing time surely deepens Quinn's local knowledge. Also, Captain Diaz's rage undoubtedly increased once he discovered Alex Quinn, the hated Bermudez in-law, husband of Esperanza, and father of murdered Isabella.

Tom speculates: "Captain Diaz's destructive behavior is logical, assuming he and Alex Quinn seek revenge upon identifying each other's vessels in Arnhem Land waters. Quinn baits Diaz by signaling the 'Bermudez' name. Diaz bites, attempting pursuit until stopped by Commander Martinez. Undetected, Quinn pursues Diaz into the inlet. In cliff-darkness Quinn repeats the signal. Diaz responds madly. Facing drone and Marine attack, he commits suicide. Extraordinary seaman Alex Quinn, boat riding the swell, escapes unseen."

Tom's creative thinking prompts Malangi's own speculative evidence. One of his Homeland watchers met another Arnhem Land fisherman. This same fisherman was also among the Aboriginal artists who struggled with the van men in the Darwin incident.

We learn this fisherman-artist made his own bark painting of the Darwin struggle. His painting includes an "albino-man figure" becoming Flying Fox, escaping skyward to confront Rainbow Serpent.

This fisherman-artist witnessed "albino-figure" assisting the "flying machine" to depart and return to the Ro/Ro ship. The fisherman-artist then painted a blended image of "albino-figure" becoming Flying Fox.

Malangi wasn't in the Darwin struggle. Yet as a traditional Law Man, Malangi painted images Aboriginal artists remembered from the Incident. Malangi gave his bark painting to Tom. It hangs in our Puck Place home.

Malangi's bark painting of the Darwin struggle shows no "albino-male figure" becoming Flying Fox. Malangi's evil spirit faces Rainbow Serpent, unchanged.

On our computer screens in San Diego and Canberra, we compare reproductions of Malangi's and the fisherman-artist's different bark-painted versions of the Darwin struggle.

Tom and I identify the fisherman-artist's tall "albino-male figure." He is Albert Jennings.

I'm stunned. Albert's clearly-painted image suddenly appears as we trace Diaz from the Darwin struggle to the "Diaz drone" discovered in the damaged yacht during our earlier Operation Arnhem Land.

Malangi admits his intuitive "Law Man" suspicion of Albert's self-centered leadership arose during the Home trial. For that reason, they didn't meet when Albert came to Canberra. Albert knew of Malangi from Tom's first Arnhem Land mission report, which Tom had delivered to Albert.

This divided reception perhaps aroused Albert's suspicion that the Australians might discover his C.I.A. role in the Darwin Incident. Discovery would have jeopardized his cover in both a combined-technology transfer for Rep. Donaldson and in the Steven Home trial testimony. Feared exposure indicated why Albert suddenly vanished.

Yet, Albert's C.I.A. duplicity is revealed only after we have traced Captain Diaz's criminality. It explained Diaz's control of a stolen drone, contrary to Home trial evidence. Albert had given it to him.

In our separate locations of San Diego and Arnhem Land Tom, Malangi, and I conclude: Diaz was the C.I.A.-A.C.M.E. drone pilot in the Darwin incident. Months later, Diaz intended to assemble and test a new stolen drone after he delivered cocaine in Arnhem Land. The surprise encounter with the hated Bermudez family name led to the failed cocaine delivery, and Diaz's suicide. My reports thus have explained satellite-drone technology transfer culminating in Operation Arnhem Land.

Tom and I have continued watching our screens at the Marine Corps antiterrorist-drone center, San Diego. Rep. Donaldson and Chief G appear. They've followed my reports.

They now order Tom and me to cooperate with Agents Nunez and Blanco on the U.S.-Mexico border. Intelligence-sharing continues, with agents from the U.S., Australia, and Mexico.

At the Joint Task Force Center in Chula Vista (just outside San Diego), Tom and I meet Blanco. He and his two deputy agents appear unchanged since the Steven Home Trial.

Blanco explains: "Nunez is in Santa Maria. Her cover is insurance investigator for a Catholic Church charity. 'Women's Global Care,' is covertly funded by Australia military intelligence."

"Nunez interviews Catholic women in Santa Maria, the town dominated by the Diaz family. She is remarkable in persuading devout women to talk about Diaz family cocaine traffickers," Blanco assures Tom and me. We agree, knowing Nunez's interrogation of Martinez.

Nunez's cover includes having her computer connected to a

Church charity office. Diaz Security agents could break into it, but probably would not disrupt her direct communications with Church authorities. A secure military intelligence program on the same computer enables Nunez's updated reports to Blanco, Tom, and me.

Assisting Nunez is Blanco's secret agent, an elderly Bermudez cousin, Alicia. She connects Nunez with devout Catholic women in Santa Maria; married, widowed, and unmarried.

As housekeepers or clerical workers, these women have long been accepted as invisible as they serve at the Diaz family's desert compound and harbor warehouse-wharf offices. More intimate is the prostitutes' access. Each woman freely passes through fence gates, surveillance cameras, guards, and dogs.

For Nunez, these women observe that from the family compound the Diaz's youngest son, Rodrigo, pilots a drone. Rodrigo flies the drone to and from the Ro/Ro ship that docks at the harbor wharfs and warehouses. Several battered vans and aged eighteen-wheeler trucks also roll aboard the ship.

Nunez's informers hear cartel manager Diaz winning loud arguments with his lawyer brother. Global Knight is "cheaper" than G.S.S. to fund offshore finance of the "drone-Ro/Ro ship operation aimed at San Diego."

Our money laundering data shows Diaz Security owns Global Knight. This offshore subsidiary operates the same Ro/Ro ship docked in Santa Maria and used in the Arnhem Land failed cocaine delivery. Global Knight hired Commander Martinez's security force and funds Rodrigo Diaz's new San Diego operation.

Nunez alerts us at nightfall: Rodrigo Diaz, armed men, several vans and trucks have departed Santa Maria aboard the Ro/Ro ship. They're headed towards San Diego, tracked by our spy satellite.

At the San Diego Silver Strand drone center, Kara joins me. We study multiple drone-computer screens. Calculating the Ro/Ro ship arrival in San Diego Bay, we follow ground action, deploying drones.

Daily, Tom and Marine Captain Mark Mendocino run from the drone center across empty sand dunes and beaches bordering Silver Strand Highway. Chain-link fences, barbwire, and open spaces separate the runners from civilian commuters between Coronado and Imperial Beach.

Tom and Mendocino turn around at a Navy classified automated transmitter housed in an innocuous round cake-shaped building. Hidden amidst sand dunes and isolated beach on fenced Navy property, the facility secretly monitors satellite-drone transmissions along the international border.

The transmitter is unseen from Silver Stand Highway. Drone surveillance shows the transmitter is one mile in a direct line from the Jones condo. From there, Jones operated the money laundering theft of the combined technology resulting in the Steven Home trial. There, too, Diaz Security agents murdered Jones.

Tom and Mendocino decide the Diaz family might know about and target the transmitter. Mendocino places a Marine team on alert. Drone surveillance will trigger deployment of the Marines if the transmitter is threatened.

Blanco and the Border Task Force units await Rodrigo Diaz's Ro/Ro ship at dock in San Diego South Bay. The Border Task Force cooperates with San Diego City and County authorities. Mendocino coordinates units on Silver Strand Navy property, Coronado, North Island Naval Base. Our drones support them all.

In blazing sunset behind Point Loma, Diaz's ship enters San Diego Bay. Since leaving Santa Maria, the vessel has been under continuous satellite GPS observation. This now includes our drone surveillance.

During forty minutes: the vessel passes under Cabrillo Monument at the end of Point Loma, between Shelter Island and North Island, San Diego downtown and Coronado. It finally arrives at the Ro/Ro ship dock, city-side, South Bay.

Aboard ship, Captain Rodrigo Diaz meets a Border Joint Task Force team, U.S. Customs agents, and drug law enforcers, including dogs. In the background, Blanco and his deputies watch.

During the night and next two days, these teams scrutinize ship and crew. The flag of convenience is Panama. Papers and the ship's log show voyages between Santa Maria, Mexico, Brisbane, Australia, and San Diego. Diaz and his Mexican crew carry proper visas and passports.

The ship's main cargo is three eighteen-wheeler trucks. Registered in Queensland, Australia, they're being transported for licensing and final sale to a small trucking firm in Calexico, California. Captain Diaz presents the proper documents. The trucking firm's owner confirms the "older trucks" sold for a "very reasonable price, despite sea transport."

Aboard ship, investigators find no evidence of drug trafficking, armed men, or "several vans." Our satellite-drone surveillance shows no unloading prior to ship docking in San Diego.

Calexico trucking firm owner and Captain Diaz demand: Customs either show cause for detention, or release the three trucks and Ro/Ro ship. Border Task Force officials agree to release.

The eighteen-wheeler trucks roll off the ship. Absence of Nunez-reported vans and armed men leaves a mystery. Tom belatedly thinks to ask Blanco for Queensland vehicle registrations. Tom then sends the forms to Chief G's experts, requesting the trailers' spatial dimensions. Better late than never, Tom uses the Australians' reply.

Our satellite-drone surveillance tracks under cloudless, star-filled sky. The Diaz Ro/Ro ship departs San Diego Bay. Miles off Silver Strand in international waters, the ship stops.

Leaving San Diego City limits, the three eighteen-wheeler trailer trucks disperse on isolated county roads.

One truck orients east, towards Calexico. The narrow county road winds through rugged, hilly terrain. Our drone cameras record a memorable operation. From the truck trailer slides a multi-wheeled ramp. Down it drives small van. We'd witnessed the reverse operation in Arnhem Land.

The eighteen-wheeler crawls. The van falls behind, exits on the dirt road running to a small landing zone where a drone lands. Packages are unloaded from the van. The drone takes off. Our surveillance follows the unknown drone move from land to sea towards the waiting Ro/Ro ship. The van returns to the county road, catches the truck, disappears inside.

During the night this first eighteen-wheeler truck arrives in Calexico. It has been under continuous observation. Waiting at the trucking office are Blanco and a Border Task Force Team. They search the trailer, finding only boxed shoes. No van.

Blanco is ready with Tom's information. Queensland-registered trailers are seven feet longer than those registered in U.S.-border states. Blanco guides the team dismantling the cleverly-disguised partition inside the trailer front. Uncovered: the minivan carrying cocaine packs. Two hidden armed men surrender, outgunned.

Hours before dawn the second eighteen-wheeler truck sits in

"Travel Surprises," a private border trailer park in Chula Vista. The truck awaits engine repair. A service vehicle comes and goes.

Trailer park attendants keep strangers out. Border Task Force agents require a search warrant naming "Travel Surprises." The local court won't issue the warrant for twenty-four hours.

The third eighteen-wheeler truck reenters San Diego City limits driving fast towards Silver Strand Highway.

We alert Mendocino's Marine team. It is transported on the secure, Silver Strand Marine Corp Base beach trail. Left to continue on foot, the team deploys around the classified drone transmitter.

The Marines set the trap. Radio-satellite transmissions connect us to Mendocino's tech operator. A few miles away in the security compound Tom follows Mendocino's team on our drone cameras.

The darkest hour truly is before dawn. The third eighteen-wheeler drives in thin, pre-commuter traffic through Imperial Beach.

The truck enters Silver Strand Highway. On a long curve, the truck is unseen from rear or oncoming traffic. It slows. The ramp drops from the trailer. A small white van drives down the ramp and makes a U-turn across highway. The big truck regains speed driving towards Coronado.

On Silver Strand Highway, the van follows the chain-link, barbwire fence and stops at the security gate. A small ordinance explodes the gate. The van rolls onto Navy property around the sign: NO TRESPASSING.

The van crosses sand dunes, homing on the drone transmitter. Marines are poised. Our drone cameras and transmitter record. Tom follows on his computer. We hear Mendocino: "This is too easy."

The van slows. Armed men drop from its rear door and scatter over the sand. In the gloom, intruders and Marines target each other as shifting shadows.

Mendocino's tech person is shot, the communications unit shattered. Alarms trigger: two miles up the beach the Marine backup team speeds over the dunes. A gunship rises at North Island Air Station.

Minutes closer, Tom, with the replacement com-unit, runs over the dunes, legs lifting smoothly, top speed. Transmissions record Tom's steady breathing.

Orange-glow dawn shrinks the darkness. Along the sand dune crests, Tom's sharp profile is moving effortlessly.

On grey-shadow ground the intruder can't miss. Tom's body jerks, spins, falls. Mendocino sprints to him, grips the com, shouts coordinates for MEDEVAC.

Sobs choke me as I face my screen. Marines swarm. The gunship fires at will. Intruders are down. The van seized. Marines gather intruder bodies. No survivors.

V

At sea, the U.S. Coast Guard captures the Diaz Ro/Ro ship too late. Out of the rising sun, into the ocean wind, barely visible, soundless over the Silver Strand battleground, floats the intruder drone. Its laser fire destroys the Navy's drone transmitter. Marines' weapons fire finally shatters the intruder drone.

Mendocino messages us. Medics gather Tom into MEDEVAC. It flies directly across South Bay to Balboa Park Naval Hospital. My mother rushes to the hospital from Puck Place.

I'm racing to join her. On Silver Strand Highway, Military Police manage the temporary commuter traffic jam. Public news reports an accidental explosion fully under control on Navy property. Commuters can proceed safely.

I receive Blanco's report. The truck sitting in "Travel Surprises" is empty. No van or hidden compartment. Blanco thinks the "service repairmen" working on the truck were disguised Diaz Security operatives. They escaped in the service repair vehicle.

Mendocino again messages me. The third truck is found abandoned, empty and stripped on Silver Stand Highway.

I speed over the Coronado Bridge, I-5, highway 163. My mind's eye sees the boy Tom on Beagle Island: his special selflessness warns our family and rescues Isabella. Our drones have shown my brother, now a man with the same selflessness, doing his duty from San Diego to Arnhem Land.

Yet Commander Martinez's dying prediction has come true. The Diaz family revenge targeted Tom. The same revenge attacked our father, our mother, Alex and Esperanza, and murdered Isabella. Only I'm left unwounded, recording it. Like Malangi's watchers in Arnhem Land.

EIGHT

————————

Puck Place, October 2009

Mother and I face Tom's condition. During weeks in the hospital, Navy doctors agree: after Tom's killing wound, living is miraculous. But he needs reasons to continue to fight for life.

Mother and I know Tom's overwhelming loss is Isabella's murder. In the hospital he awoke delirious, screaming: "I wasn't there when she needed me." But we know his pain is caused by the Diaz family, inflamed by the Steven Home trial, and further aggravated by Albert Jennings' duplicity.

Tom blames himself for not finding our father. We plead. Pursuing Father ensured that Tom aided Rep. Donaldson, Chief G, and Malangi transferring satellite-drone technology from the U.S. to Australia.

"Tom, listen to me, it's Ann, your sister. Diaz agents murdered Isabella, targeted you. The Diaz brothers and sons attack the Bermudez, Quinn, and Berneray families because Esperanza defended herself from rape. All you accomplished for Donaldson and Malangi furthers the search for Father and memory of Isabella's life. We will still look for Father."

Tom's awareness comes and goes. Doctors, Mother, and I agree: Tom's critical condition is his tortured mind and heart, as much as his torn body.

Mother says, "move Tom home." Our family's past together in Puck Place nurtures Tom. In his room, photos mark happy family moments from childhood to the recent past. Tom and Isabella are conspicuous. Berneray, Quinn, Bermudez families together in photographs taken at Tom's Harvard graduation. Strangely, I remember that Tom's roommate, Albert, took that photo.

From Tom's Puck Place bedroom window, distant ocean haze is sometimes visible, as it was in his and my childhood. The nighttime canyon is blackness, starlight or moon shadows. That hasn't changed since we were children.

Tom, Mother, and I remember our Quinn and Bermudez grandparents. They visited San Diego years ago, brought by Alex, Esperanza, and Isabella Quinn in Alex's schooner.

Tom's bedridden body, labored breathing, and precarious hold on life engulf Mother and me. We're at his bedside day and night. We fight fear of death with faith in Tom's life.

Mother reveals more personal family pain. After the Steven Home trial ended, the longtime Quinn family friend, Judge Taylor, explained that the defense lawyer attacked Tom's credibility with jurors. The strategy was: hurt Tom's Mother, undermine Tom's testimony. Dredge up Diana Quinn's obscure anti-war work aiding veterans' escape from U.S. prosecution. Get jurors focused on cocaine dealer Jones. Not weak Steven Home. Not shadowy cocaine boss, Diaz.

As if in response, Tom awakens and mumbles bravely: "Steven Home's trial vindicated Albert's offshore data because I exposed Diaz Security. I didn't reveal my source to be Father's "Old Mexico" manuscript. I protected Mother and Ann."

Tom's whispered affirmation ends with unconsciousness. But Mother and I want to believe Tom's strength is growing.

Tom offers us another reason for hope. Tom again revives and recalls what he'd speculated to Malangi. At sea Alex, Esperanza, and our father had baited yacht Captain Diaz, signaling the "Bermudez" name. Diaz's vengeful rage wrecked the cocaine delivery and led to his suicide.

Weak but conscious, Tom confesses a secret. Before leaving on Operation Arnhem Land, Malangi's bark painting had inspired Tom to go to San Francisco's Chinatown. Tom ignored our mother's estrangement from her own mother, as revealed in father's "Old Mexico" manuscript.

Grandmother Quinn had eagerly aided her only grandson. She'd introduced Tom to her Quinn Shipping manager in Chinatown. But she'd warned Tom. His personal request strained bonds of strict confidentiality between the Chinatown manager and her firm, Quinn Shipping.

Despite his wounded body, Tom now draws strength from telling mother and I the secret he'd learned in Chinatown. Time pressing before he'd left on Operation Arnhem Land, Tom flew from San Diego to San Francisco. He'd been given an obscure address in Chinatown. He'd been given an obscure address in Chinatown.

Telling us, Tom's memory grows vivid. When he entered the door at the address he'd been given, a gleaming hatchet swirled above his head. The blade sank deep into wood. A warning, Tom knew. Chinatown hatchet men didn't miss.

Tom's voice gains force as he speaks to Mother and me. He'd entered a dimly lighted room. In shadows stood an older Chinese man in a black funeral undertaker suit. Not identifying himself, he'd simply said: "Your mother is the Quinn daughter, Diana, married to Jim Berneray."

Tom knew his grandmother Quinn had prepared her Quinn Shipping manager in Chinatown. Her manager had understood the grandson's single question: "Have you had any recent contact with Alexander Quinn?" The manager had replied only: "Perhaps."

Tom admits to us that he'd expected the Quinn Shipping Chinatown manager's answer to preserve plausible denial. Yet Tom understood the manager's reply to suggest right reasoning. Tom's search for Alex Quinn's whereabouts pointed to Isabella's murder and her parents hiding at sea. Our father's "Old Mexico" manuscript exposed Diaz agents as the murders and pursuers. Their vengeance targeted Quinn, Berneray, and Bermudez families.

Tom's efforts to speak to us become more painful. Trembling, Tom points to Malangi's bark painting: "I knew Alex's boat took wounded Father from the spirit cave. The Chinatown manager could've provided Quinn Shipping support so that Alex and Esperanza could escape Diaz in Arnhem Land. Alex and Esperanza also rescued Father after the Darwin Incident and disrupted Captain Diaz's cocaine drop."

Tom grips Mother's arm, voice fading. "Chinese traders employed by Quinn Shipping in Arnhem Land must've had doctors when you and Alex visited there as children with your parents. Nowadays, they'd be even more able to treat bad wounds like those Father suffered in the Darwin Incident."

Sinking again into unconsciousness, Tom gasps, "Mother, you could've told me about the Quinn Chinatown agents in Arnhem Land. It might've helped me find Father."

In Tom's room, creeping moonlight casts Mother in deepening shadows. Tom intimates that Mother knew something that could've led him to Father.

Mother sits beside Tom. Their bodies share stillness. Mother strokes Tom's face as when he was a boy. She remembers, "He reached me in the bramble on Beagle Island, never doubting." Her face is wet with tears.

I struggle to help her. "Mother, Tom knows we're a family of spies, each one a double agent. Nothing is unambiguous. Not even Isabella's murder and Father's disappearance."

I reach my arms around her. She answers me, "Ann, the drone master, always observing. But you've underestimated my duplicity." Mother lets me absorb her words.

Mother's tears cease. Her natural self-assertiveness returns. She admits, "I should've told Tom about Quinn Shipping's Chinese agents in Arnhem Land. My mistake, I didn't tell him. So Tom knew to ask *my mother*, who runs those Quinn Shipping Chinatown connections. She loves her grandson, Tom. She despises me, Diana, an only daughter who became Canadian. She abhors my denial of American patriotism. Mother says I'm the bewitched huntress Diana, cloaking all of her family in ambiguous moon shadows."

I tell Mother, "I don't understand. What are you talking about?"

She says nothing. Mother leaves Tom's room. She returns with what looks like a manuscript on printed out computer paper. She sits, handing me the manuscript.

"I've collected our Donaldson committee reports to share with father for his P.T.S.D. treatment," Mother says. "Just like we wrote to him after we rescued Isabella from the bramble on Beagle Island."

"Mother, I don't understand you." I can't bear repeating her admission of duplicity. Yet I'm seeing her mind work. She's exposing hiding places in her thinking.

I remember. She'd divulged Tom's special sensitivity retelling the "killer-whale experience" on Beagle Island. She'd beguiled C.I.A. agent Albert Jennings. I've already decided: she's working for Rep. Donaldson.

I tell myself, again and again, "To think like Tom, manipulate facts versus feelings." From Mother's stack of papers I extract Tom's first Arnhem Land report: "Mother, you knew something Tom didn't know."

Mother responds slowly: "Unlike Tom, I've known all along that your father was Malangi's agent. His work with Gunwinggu artists was authentic, yet it was also a cover. He was spying on the C.I.A.-A.C.M.E. operation against the Arnhem Land Weather Station. He'd discovered the cocaine cartel involvement. Jim learned of Albert's presence from the same fisherman whose bark painting you and Tom later compared to Malangi's."

Mother elaborates. "Tom's report about the Darwin Incident debacle essentially was correct, as was the seriousness of his father's wound. But Tom couldn't verify that Quinn Shipping's Chinatown traders had enabled medical treatment for Jim's wounds. There always had to be plausible denial."

"Malangi confided all this to me in Darwin after your father disappeared," Mother exclaims. "Again, Tom's report was right about the Aboriginal artists bringing Jim to Law Man, Malangi. Tom could speculate, but he had no direct evidence showing that his father and Malangi prepared the message stick calling Tom to Arnhem Land."

I'm incredulous. "Mother, you're saying: *our father worked with Malangi to bring Tom to Arnhem Land. It triggered Rep. Donaldson's transfer operations. And you knew about it.*"

Mother's smooth self-confidence returns. "Let's be clear, Ann. Father and Malangi knew the C.I.A. and Diaz cocaine agents were somehow connected in the Darwin debacle. The agents caused your father's wounds and disappearance. They're dangerous enemies to have."

Her coldly truthful self argues: "By 'recruiting' Tom, your father and Malangi mobilized Donaldson and Chief G's protective resources. Tom's search for his father and the American-Australian technology transfer joined forces against Diaz cocaine traffickers in Arnhem Land."

Addressing my astonishment, Mother insists: "Recall my trial testimony. In our antiwar operations, we knew only what our separate roles required for achieving our missions. Jim, Malangi and I applied that rule. Donaldson and Chief G thus began with message stick evidence delivered by Malangi in his Law Man persona. Rainbow Serpent images called Tom to Arnhem Land."

Mother appeals to me, "Everyone then continued with evidence revealed in Tom's investigations, Steven Home's trial, and your drone operations in Arnhem Land and San Diego."

Emotion seizes me and I assert, "Mother, the Rainbow Serpent spirit images have had bad consequences. Tom has suffered vicious Diaz cocaine cartel violence from Arnhem Land to the San Diego-Mexico border. And despite all you've admitted, Father hasn't returned."

Mother's trembling tendentious reply: "You, Tom, and I know how you're your father suffers from P.T.S.D. But, over the years, I've learned from his painful, erratic admissions what started it all. On a mountain road in the Vietnam jungle, his five-man Marine patrol discovered C.I.A. contractors smuggling Laotian heroin. A contractor fired an automatic pistol into writhing body bags thrown from jeeps."

Mother's voice goes flat: "Alone, shooting madly, father ran at the C.I.A. contractors. Exposed, seeking cover, the outnumbered Marines couldn't stop the contractors assaulting Jim. Then, from hiding, North Vietnamese soldiers swarmed, attacked, killed the contractors, and disappeared into jungle. The ambush intended for the Marines had shifted target to the C.I.A. contractors and drugs-sex traffickers."

Mother whispers: "Your father recovered, ashamed. Marines awaited MEDEVAC. Father held a sack the Vietnamese enemy troops left with him. He opened the sack and out fell bloody, severed left ears. The enemy soldiers had punished the American contractors for their evil. Your father's courage brought unusual justice."

"Judge me, Ann, but not your father," mother exclaims. "What your father and Malangi initiated by sending Tom the message stick made sense under dangerous circumstances."

Mother's mobile phone rings. Answering, listening, ending the call, she says: "At sea, using Quinn family codes, Alex has radioed the Chinatown manager. He says the *Isabella* should arrive tonight in San Diego. Alex wants us to meet at our Quinn Shipping dock on Shelter Island."

We stare at each other over unconscious Tom. Mother breaks the silence. "Alex radioed using Quinn codes to limit understanding in case someone picked up his signal."

I reason: "Malangi must've somehow notified Alex about Tom's injuries. Alex and Esperanza can sail from Arnhem Land to San Diego in about three weeks, the elapsed time since Tom was shot on Silver Strand."

Mother adds: "Alex relies on the Chinatown manager being relatively insulated from C.I.A. or cocaine cartel attention and interference. Alex and Esperanza should arrive tonight. Your father is surely with them."

We leave Tom with a nurse at Puck Place. In darkness, I drive with mother to Shelter Island. We wait dockside among amassed small craft floating within the Marina channels.

Around 2:00 a.m. Alex guides *Isabella* to dock. Esperanza is on deck, rope in one hand, her other hand waving madly. A third figure at the mast moves uneasily.

Esperanza secures the boat, runs, embraces us. Alex leaves the helm and joins us. Mother and I clamor towards Father. His handsome left profile pulls us. We embrace, grip each other, don't let go. He turns his full face to us. Mother sees, unmoved, exclaims, "I love you, Jim."

I'm speechless. The right side of my father's face is terribly disfigured, with discolored flesh and a closed eye socket. His cheek seems boneless, slack, scarred. The jaw twists down, visibly toothless, tongue slightly protruding.

Father's face expresses new contradictory beginnings. His voice broken, raspy, "I must explain to Tom."

We return to Puck Place. Tom's condition unites father, Mother, Esperanza, Alex, and me. We've overcome all the attacks, together.

Trembling, Father's fingers caress Tom's face. He stirs. Father comes into focus.

Father's constrained whisper: "We're here together now, Tom, my brave and courageous son. You did all we asked and more. You understood what I wrote at sea, wounded, in the "Old Mexico" narrative. We, the Quinn, Berneray, and Bermudez families, are united in resistance and hope. Isabella's death is not in vain. The struggles you, Ann, and Diana have experienced are helping me face my trauma. We will help you face yours."

In response to Father, Tom reveals his old self. "Father, I have just one question. Was it Callahan Nunez who delivered your "Old Mexico" manuscript to Puck Place?"

We all smile.

Father replies, "Yes. She's usually invisible in plain sight."

Leave us here. Awaiting the dawn, we tell family stories entangled in large conflicts. From each other we draw hope, courage, trust, and wisdom pitted against fear and fate. We endure. No surrender.

Visit us at *www.quidprobooks.com.*